McLeane took up his position behind the 7.7-mm machine gun he had swiped from the enemy.

"When do you want to open up?" Contardo asked.

"Let's see. The bend in the river is about a hundred yards off."

"A piece of cake."

"Yeah, but I want several pieces of cake. Let's let the boat get fully around the bend and then some. By the time her skipper figures out he's been had, her momentum and the current will have carried her within seventy-five yards. *Then* we'll open up. You take the wheelhouse. I'll take out any machine guns and then go for the waterline. After the wheelhouse, sweep the decks."

"You got it."

"With any luck, we'll drive them around on the east bank and have them at our mercy. I want the boat out of our lives once and for all."

The boat came around the bend and turned toward the bridge. "Ready," McLeane said, and he could hear Contardo pulling the bolt on the 20-mm. There was another sound—the river boat's transmission being shoved into reverse.

"They've figured it out! Open fire!"

MORE EXCITING READING!

McLEANE'S RANGERS

THE BOUGAINVILLE BREAKOUT

BY JOHN DARBY

ZEBRA BOOKS
KENSINGTON PUBLISHING CORP.

ZEBRA BOOKS

are published by

KENSINGTON PUBLISHING CORP.
475 Park Avenue South
New York, N.Y. 10016

One

The black, sulfurous smoke fuming from the summit of the Bagana volcano seemed strangely appropriate when combined with the dull gray of the misty predawn hours. The roar of the Grumman Helldiver seemed to pale in comparison with the threat of the horrible gray vastness of the rain forest that lay below, with only the stench of a seething volcano to give it the appearance of life.

"Nice place for a party," McLeane said into the intercom.

"Great idea, Major," the pilot replied from his front-seat position in the two-seat fighter-bomber. "You bring the pretzels and I'll bring the beer."

"You got a deal."

"Don't forget we've got a ten- to twelve-knot wind blowing from the southeast. Try not to parachute into that volcano."

"Spoken like a true lieutenant. There's nothing you'd like to see better than fried major, right?"

"Come on, Major; I was only kidding." The young pilot seemed a little nervous. No one wanted McLeane mad at him.

"So was I."

Relieved, the pilot said, "We're coming up on the drop zone now. I haven't picked up any Japs either in

5

the air or on the ground, but you still take care of yourself."

"I'm ready."

McLeane's deep, steady voice did not betray his own concern. There certainly would be *some* enemy patrols, even on such an obscure region of Bougainville, the largest of the Solomon Islands. And even if there weren't, there were the natives. No one was quite certain of the temperament of the dozens of squabbling tribes on Bougainville, but McLeane had read Conrad's short story "The Terrible Solomons," and hadn't failed to note that the foreigner who was the first to turn his back on them was apt to be the first to be *kai-kai'd* (eaten). Of course, some civilization had been introduced in the half-century since Conrad had made his observations, but still McLeane was intent on keeping his back to the wall and his finger on the trigger when dealing with the locals. He hoped not to have to deal with them at all, especially if—and nobody but they knew—they had allied themselves with the Japanese.

All McLeane knew were his orders, which had come straight down from Admiral Halsey's office in Comsopac:

"You will parachute into the Torokina region of Bougainville Island and scout enemy positions, if any, no earlier than Sept. 15, 1943. You will concentrate on the Numa-Numa Trail linking enemy bases on eastern and southern Bougainville with the region of Empress Augusta Bay, especially any such enemy positions as may exist in the vicinity of Cape Torokina. You will report by radio and then make your way south along the Empress Trail to Mutupina Point, where you will make contact with and be picked up by the submarine U.S.S. *Silverfish* on or about October 1, 1943 at 0700 hours."

So what if the mission included a belching volcano, cannibalistic natives, unknown numbers of Japanese soldiers, and, permeating it all were the dangers of the rain forest? William E. McLeane, Major, USMC, could have had a cushy office job at Henderson Field. At thirty-three, he was technically getting a little old for parachuting into situations on which the odds were ten to one against his survival. That sort of stuff was generally the province of hot-blooded twenty-three-year-olds eager to make a name for themselves and to collect a few more medals and ribbons to show off one day to their grandchildren. McLeane already had a shoe box full of medals and ribbons. But he had come to the South Pacific to fight, not push papers, and anyway he was better at fighting than any twenty-three-year-old marine he had yet encountered.

"We're over the Jaba River, Major. Twenty seconds to jump time."

"Right."

McLeane unbuckled his seat harness and slid back the rear section of the Helldiver's canopy.

"Good luck, Major."

"Thanks. And watch out for meatballs on your way home."

"Oh, I'll be sure to do that."

The red-orange symbol of the rising sun of Japan was commonly referred to by American pilots as "the angry red meatball." The symbol was routinely painted on the sides of Japanese fighter planes.

McLeane reached forward, patted the pilot on the shoulder, and hurled himself out into the predawn air. He fell for five or six seconds, which seemed like a week, before pulling the ripcord and opening his parachute. Yanked abruptly from free fall to a much slower pace, he listened as the Helldiver banked to port, climbed up into the clouds, and disappeared from sight and sound in the direction of its home base on Vella la Vella. Soon McLeane was alone with his thoughts and the rain forest, and absolute silence.

In the Solomons, the dry season went from May through October, and was accompanied by southeast winds. McLeane counted on those winds to carry him halfway up the slope of Bagana volcano to a spot about three miles north of the Numa-Numa Trail. The spot was reported by aerial reconnaissance to be relatively dry and, though still heavily forested, a safer spot to land than the snake-infested mangrove swamps which lined the trail.

As McLeane floated comfortably beneath his camouflage-colored chute, the ground approached with astounding speed. He looked for a clearing, but there was none, and the persistent southeast trade winds didn't give him much of a choice anyway. McLeane slipped into the gray of the ground fog and crashed through the upper branches of a large stand of meriwa trees. The conifers were small, about forty feet in height, and had soft needles.

The soft fabric of the parachute caught momentarily in the upper branches of a meriwa. McLeane dangled ten feet above the ground for a few seconds before dropping to the soft forest floor; it was as thick and soft as a goose-down mattress. McLeane picked up a handful of needles which, with an occasional small cone, formed the forest floor in the spot where he'd landed.

"I had to come halfway around the world to wind up in a bunch of pine trees," McLeane muttered.

His arrival was greeted by a chorus of warning chirps, squeals, and whistles from startled dabchicks, parrots, and hornbills.

McLeane quickly yanked his chute down from where it had come to rest in the lower branches of the conifers and buried it beneath the forest floor. Since that was a foot thick and made up almost entirely of fresh or decomposing pine needles, McLeane had no trouble

8

digging a hole with his hands and burying the evidence of his arrival behind the enemy lines. That done, he simply sat, leaned against the tree, and listened. Eventually the birds calmed down and went about their business. McLeane could hear a hornbill cracking a nut with its huge beak, but he didn't care about the birds. He was listening for the sounds made by men, especially men with machinery, jeeps, or trooping in formation. The sounds of natives bearing spears and other weapons were something McLeane knew he might never hear—until it was too late.

McLeane sat for fifteen or twenty minutes until he felt safe, alone. Then he stood, brushed the pine needles from his camouflage uniform, and checked his equipment. The radio was undamaged from the descent. His provision pack was likewise undamaged. Short of a grassy clearing, McLeane couldn't have asked for a better landing spot. It didn't take him long to realize he was a very lucky man to have found it. For as he started picking his way south down the slope leading away from Bagana volcano, McLeane learned more and more of the vastness, complexity, and, most of all, the virtual impenetrability of the rain forest. One by one, the wild plantains, areca palms, and alpinias joined the taller toa and opi-opi trees. Many were hung with lianas which could conceal snakes in wait for prey. These vines were joined to form a solid mass of vegetation through which not even a boar could fit.

McLeane picked up the foul stench of a mangrove swamp. He could not pass through it, even if he were able to get through the many plants that choked its edges. There was a bellow from a bull crocodile, and an answering bellow from another. McLeane turned east to skirt the swamp, using his old but well-kept and razor-sharp machete to hack a path. Even with the machete, skirting the swamp and traveling the two miles from where he had landed to the edge of the Numa-Numa Trail took the entire day. Crossing it was a native path. McLeane knew that the path was a native one by its height—barely five feet high, like the natives, who were shorter even than the Japanese. The path looked recently used. McLeane took this discovery, not without reason, as an ominous sign.

McLeane pulled his Browning-designed, Colt Al automatic pistol from its belt holster and screwed on the silencer. He slipped quietly onto the Numa-Numa Trail.

The trail was scarcely seven feet wide, less in spots, and useful only for foot patrols or horse-drawn small field artillery. Ruts in the soft mud showed that it, too, had been used, perhaps for both purposes, within recent days. He knelt and ran his fingers around a boot print that lay over a rut made by a narrow tire of the type used to carry artillery. The boot print was at least twenty-four hours old, and the tire track no newer than three days. Did that mean the enemy patrolled the Numa-Numa Trail only once a day? The possibility seemed likely. It also meant that they were about due.

McLeane, the automatic still in his hand, started down the trail, all the while looking this way and that, and listening to each and every sound.

From the aerial reconnaissance photos he knew the basic layout of the Empress Augusta Bay region, especially the small settlement at Cape Torokina. There was the cape itself, a thumb-shaped outcropping of land that consisted mainly of a coconut-palm forest and was no more than five hundred yards long and about half as wide. The cape stuck westward into the Solomon Sea, and was entirely surrounded by coral reef. West-north-west of the cape lay two islands, tiny Torokina and the somewhat larger Puruata, both surrounded entirely by coral reef. The beach areas near Cape Torokina were mainly covered by coconut groves, with an occasional mangrove swamp. North of the cape was the settlement, three buildings which made up the Buretoni Christian Mission. McLeane understood that the mission, founded in the late nineteenth century by British missionaries, served as a medical-aid center for the island's natives as well as a place for the locals to worship a different god from the ones to which they normally bowed their heads and, so it was said, sacrificed their victims. McLeane had no idea if the Japanese were using the mission buildings, but it seemed likely. There were no other roofs to put over one's head in the region, and the wet season was but a month and a half off.

The aerial photos showed that the Japanese had built a small dock in a cove not far south of the mission; to what end McLeane had no idea. It was far too small for a warship, even one as small as a PT boat. He also knew from Army Map Service topographical charts made before the outbreak of hostilities that there were a lot more rivers, coves, and trails than shown on the newer aerial photographs in which the prodigious vegetation covered a lot of places where a man could hide—or be ambushed.

A little over a mile from the beach the Numa-Numa Trail ceased to exist. It split in two, becoming the Piva Trail, which led directly south to the beach where it joined the coast-hugging Empress Trail, and the Mission Trail, which swung westward to the mission and Cape Torokina. McLeane reached the fork in the trail and took another close look at the boot and tire prints. Nearly all of them followed the wider Mission Trail. The few boot prints on the Piva Trail looked at least a week old. McLeane chose to follow the Piva Trail. It led, after all, in the direction of McLeane's planned escape route. Once he had checked out the beach and his escape route, he could find a safe place to sleep for the evening; dusk was fast closing in. In the morning, McLeane

11

would reconnoiter Cape Torokina and whatever Japanese garrison might be stationed there.

The Piva Trail was much narrower than either the Numa-Numa or Mission Trails, and much less used. McLeane was tired, and his alertness was waning. He felt safe. He had been behind enemy lines all day and had moved at will without being detected. Therefore, he nearly made a fatal error.

McLeane was just putting his .45 back in its holster when he heard the sharp snap of the Japanese command for "Freeze!"

He did as he was told.

Three Japanese soldiers had been manning a position at the junction of the Piva and Empress Trails. Beyond them, McLeane could see the coconut palms and the cool blue of the Solomon Sea. One of them approached him, pointing a 6.55mm Type "I" bayonet-fitted rifle at his gut.

"Damn," McLeane said to himself.

He knew a little Japanese. He had met the enemy before, usually under similar circumstances. "What are you doing here?" the man asked in his native tongue.

"Tourist," McLeane replied, also in Japanese, adding a grin to the insult.

"American dog," the soldier said, and poked him in the stomach with the point of his bayonet. That was a bigger mistake than McLeane had made in dropping his guard.

McLeane swept his left hand down and to the side, pushing the rifle and its owner to one side. There was a shout of frantic commands. One other enemy soldier ran close only to find that McLeane had spun his comrade around and into an arm lock. McLeane shoved the two together, impaling the second on his buddy's bayonet.

Instantly McLeane had his automatic out and its muzzle pressed against the back of the first Jap's skull.

"When are you replaced?" he growled.

"I'll die before I'll tell you," the man replied.

He did. McLeane's bullet made a neat hole in the back of his skull, but a big one in the front, and both enemy soldiers fell to the soil of the Piva Trail.

The third Japanese had been involved in making dinner when McLeane had stumbled into them. He was slow getting up, and before he had his rifle in his hands McLeane stood over him.

"When do your replacements come?" McLeane asked.

"Please . . ."

"Tell me."

"Twenty-four hours," the man said, shaking with fear.

"They really treat you great in this part of the empire, don't they?" McLeane asked.

The Japanese soldier, overcome with terror, bolted up the Mission Trail toward Cape Torokina. McLeane took careful aim and dispatched him with one shot.

It was too bad, McLeane thought; he would have liked to have gotten more information out of the man. Still, he now knew he would be safe for twenty-four hours. He could sleep during the night, then have twelve hours to reconnoiter Cape Torokina before making his escape to the south.

McLeane bent over the cooking fire the Japanese had built. Their provisions included rice, bean sprouts, bean curd, bamboo shoots, and rice wine. He opened one of the bottles of wine and took a swig.

"I hate rice," he said.

To the east of the Piva Trail lay one of the many mangrove swamps dotting Bougainville. McLeane heard the bellowing of crocodiles and decided to feed them instead of himself. He took the first of the three Jap soldiers by the back of his collar and began dragging the body toward the swamp.

Two

Despite his assumption that he was safe for twenty-four hours, McLeane decided not to trust to fate again, at least not for a while. After relieving the dead soldiers of their supply of sake, three bottles, he retreated several hundred yards down the Empress Trail—away from the suspected garrison at Cape Torokina. Past the mangrove swamp was another coconut grove. He made his way inland until he was far from sight from the trail. He found a thicket made up of the sinimi ferns the natives used to make their plaited armlets and of the spectacular white orchids whose flowers grew as much as three inches wide. McLeane hacked at the ferns with his machete, pausing now and then for a swig of sake, and by nightfall he had fashioned himself a bed of ferns and palm fronds. He finished the first of the three bottles of sake and fell soundly asleep with the sweet smell of orchids and a light sea breeze blowing over him.

He was awakened at dawn by a hornbill on a branch overhead. It was cracking nuts and dropping the shells on him. Scowling, McLeane picked up a stick and hurled it at the bird that, once disturbed, flew a dozen yards to a safer branch and resumed its breakfast.

McLeane grumbled, fell in and out of sleep for a half-hour or so, then yawned and sat up. After twenty minutes spent listening to assure himself of privacy, he ate his breakfast rations and abandoned his temporary bed. Picking his way through the coconut grove, he hid by the edge of the Empress Trail long enough to be certain the enemy wasn't around. Then he crossed the trail, traversed a narrow grove of palms, and stepped onto the beach. The Solomon Sea looked almost beatifically calm. He saw no ships at sea and no activity at all on Cape Torokina, the small thumb of land to the northwest. McLeane stripped off his clothes, ran across the narrow strip of sand, and plunged into the surf.

He stayed in the water just long enough to get clean and to be totally awakened for the day to come. It was certain to be a tough one. He dried himself and dressed beneath the palms, then headed up the Empress Trail in the direction of Cape Torokina. He was ready at any instant to leap into the palm forest to avoid an unexpected enemy patrol, and he kept his .45 in his hand. But there was no enemy patrol. There as, in fact, no man-made sound at all. For a moment, McLeane toyed with the notion that the Empress Augusta Bay region of Bougainville was relatively free of enemy emplacements. He was to be proven wrong.

No sooner had he reached the point where the Empress Trail skirted the base of the cape, than McLeane realized that a lot more was going on than had been revealed in the aerial reconnaissance photos. There was a network of Jap trails not shown on the photos, most of them connecting a gun emplacement on the northwest tip of Cape Torokina with an enemy camp located near the lagoon by the Buretoni Mission.

McLeane slipped through the unguarded southern coast of the cape, making notes and, when he could, snapping photos with his Leica. Moving quietly and swiftly, McLeane discovered a 75-mm artillery weapon solidly hidden beneath a pillbox made of logs and mud. Behind it there was a mound of supplies half-buried

15

beneath tarps. He hid for a time in the coconut grove as a lone sentry, yawning after a grueling twelve-hour watch, marched up to the pillbox, executed a sloppy about-face, and slumped back toward mainland Bougainville.

From the cape, McLeane could see a thirty-foot launch tied alongside the small, newly built dock that the aerial photos had managed to pick out in the small Buretoni Cove. McLeane drew maps and took photos of everything. The small launch, which could hold no more than two dozen soldiers, meant that the two offshore islands, Torokina and Puruata, were lightly defended, probably with no more than machine-gun nests. Certainly the launch wasn't capable of carrying any weapon as substantial as a 75-mm field piece. McLeane could also see a tiny city of sixty Japanese huts near the Buretoni Mission. With six or seven men to a hut, that would make for a garrison of between two hundred-forty and three hundred men; sparse coverage for such a long and vulnerable stretch of coastline. With daily replacements—the three men he had sent to greet their ancestors were replaced daily—that meant sparse coverage probably bored half to death and not on its toes. All the necessary ingredients for a successful surprise attack were there. The 75-mm gun could be a problem, but thankfully it was not his problem. His job was to see what was in Empress Augusta Bay and to get out, having aroused as little commotion as possible. After finishing one roll of Panachromic film, McLeane retired to the relative safety of the coconut forest inland of the cape.

He reloaded his camera, stashing the spent film cartridge in a watertight container and pushing it deep into a pocket of his pack.

The enemy camp was beginning to show the stirring of life. The customary crouches, groanings, and hangovers of a military dawn needed no translation. Pausing whenever an animal made a noise and blending into his surroundings as he knew so well how to do, McLeane moved silently through the forest. He skirted the enemy camp to the inland side, and headed for the largest of the three buildings in the mission. It was there that the commanding officer's headquarters was certain to be found, and McLeane wanted to have a look at it.

The forest came right up to the back of the mission, and so did McLeane. An immense congregation of fruit bats, flying home to their daylight nests, made enough of a racket with all their squealing and beating of wings to cover McLeane's movement through the underbrush. He approached unnoticed by the Japanese sentry who patrolled laconically in front of the building.

McLeane peeked in a back window, and immediately ducked down. There were figures inside—and voices. One voice in particular stood out as commanding. McLeane thought he heard the tinkling of teacups. There were footsteps, and the window opened slightly.

"Damned foul jungle air," the commanding voice said in Japanese. He was the CO, no doubt about it.

McLeane hunkered down to listen, praying that the Japs' breakfast conversation would include something more significant than the smell of the air.

"Rotten boredom," a different voice said.

McLeane heard the clicking of chopsticks. Rice, he thought, always rice. Rice for breakfast, rice for lunch, rice for dinner, rice for brunch. No wonder the yellow bastards were so mean. He wondered if he couldn't talk MacArthur into shipping the S.O.B.'s some burgers and fries in the hope that they would ease their apparently insatiable appetite for lands to conquer.

"That shipment of 75-mm ..." —McLeane didn't understand the word that followed, but felt certain it was *ammunition*—"... is already three days overdue."

17

As the conversation grew more complex, McLeane understood fewer words.

"No use for it. What do we do? We ... at ... Who needs to make holes in paper ... ?"

McLeane thought the next words were "We shoot only at targets. Who needs to make holes in paper targets?"

The CO said, "Americans too ... to land here."

McLeane wondered: too *smart* or too *stupid?*

The other man laughed. "I bet they land at Mutupina Point, were the ... guns are."

Where the *what* guns are? McLeane asked himself. There weren't supposed to be guns at Mutupina Point. There weren't supposed to be Japs at all. That spot was, in fact, considered by the marines as being safe enough for him to make contact with the American sub that would pick him up.

The CO said, rather wistfully, "I would not mind ... six or seven 155-mm guns. But the geniuses in Rabaul say the Americans will land south of Mutupina Point. I bet the Americans forget Bougainville entirely. I hope they land at Rabaul. The geniuses at Rabaul ... it."

"*Deserve* it," McLeane interpreted.

"I bet we ... the rest of our lives in this miserable place."

There was the cracking of a twig, and McLeane spun toward the sound. The Japanese sentry had sneaked out back to take a leak, only to find himself staring at an American commando.

The sentry yelled "Freeze" and went for his sidearm, but McLeane was faster. He hit the sentry with a slug to the chest, sending the hapless man flying backward into the underbrush.

The window was rammed wide open. The CO stuck his head out and, in an instant, proved the wisdom of his final words. McLeane's bullet hit him right in the middle of the forehead, blowing the back of his head off and dropping him to the floor of his headquarters. The man to whom the CO had been talking wore the uniform of a captain. McLeane got him with another head shot as he was turning to run from the room.

Seconds later a warning siren sounded.

"Oh, shit," McLeane swore as he tore through the underbrush to the Empress Trail. He ran northwest up the trail—in exactly the opposite direction of his carefully planned escape route. It was just as well, since Mutupina Point was now known to be heavily fortified, not deserted as previously thought.

Behind him were shouts, confusion, and the start of footfalls.

He came to a small lagoon which widened into a mangrove swamp, infested, no doubt, with crocodiles. At its narrowest point it was crossed by a small and flimsy wooden footbridge. McLeane hurriedly wedged a couple of grenades between two gapped boards and pulled their pins. He ran up the trail, readied his .30-caliber Winchester with the fifteen-round magazine so often used by marines in the South Pacific, pulled the pin on another grenade, and crouched to wait.

A half-dozen Jap soldiers came running up to the footbridge just as it disintegrated in a hail of splinters and flame. Three fell, and the others stumbled around, stunned by the surprise and the concussion. The footbridge was no more. McLeane got to his feet and hurled the grenade amongst them, and soon, they, too, were motionless on the ground.

He retreated up the trail and hid behind an especially wide banyan tree. Another squad of enemy soldiers emerged—cautiously—from the direction of the mission. McLeane gave them the time to get out among their fallen comrades before opening up with his semiautomatic Winchester. He dropped four and injured a fifth before the Japanese apparently decided that they were facing an entire Allied squadron, not a solitary USMC major with, as he had once been described, "more balls than a Christmas tree." The enemy retreated back to their camp to figure out whether to brave the crocodiles and wade across the lagoon, to take all day to circumvent the lagoon and its surrounding swamp, or to forget the whole thing.

McLeane knew it would take them half an hour to make up their minds, and in that time he could be miles away. He slung the Winchester over his shoulder and began to jog up the Empress Trail.

It was close to noon before he reached his temporary destination—halfway up the slope leading to the Bagana volcano, but on the opposite side from that on which he had landed. He had gotten there by taking an inland offshoot of the Empress Trail; it ran parallel to the southern bank of the Laruma River. He was now three or four miles from Cape Torokina, but those miles were nearly impenetrable forest. After resting a while, he wrote out the message that he would radio to head-quarters at Guadalcanal, and he translated it into the code of the day:

"Empress Augusta Bay protected by no more than three hundred enemy troops, poorly pro-visioned. 75-mm gun SW corner of Cape Torokina. Probable machine-gun batteries on offshore islands. Supplies running up to three days late, probably more. Consider bay area good landing site. Enemy expects landing south of Mutupina Point, where it has 155-mm guns. Repeat, 155-mm guns, at least six of them. Enemy garrison at Cape Torokina tired, poor morale likely. Cannot for obvious reasons contact U.S.S. *Silverfish* at Mutupina Point on 1 October as ordered. Suggest same date at Cape Moltke."

He thought a moment, then added:

"Personal message from Wm. McLeane to Brigadier General Thompson: I want that Ranger outfit I've been asking for. I'm tired of nearly getting my ass shot off on these solo ventures.
                          With all due respect, Mack."

McLeane made radio contact with the nearest marine listening station, on Vella la Vella, and tapped out the coded message.
After receiving the acknowledgement, he leaned against a lontar palm and fell fast asleep.

Three

For a week and a half, McLeane stayed in the interior of Bougainville, eventually making his way halfway to the summit of the Bagana volcano, where he had a clear view out to sea. He saw no shipping, other than the dugout canoes of coast-dwelling native fishermen. There were patrols twice daily by Japanese reconnaissance aircraft flying back and forth from Bonis Airfield at the northwestern tip of the island to Kara or Kahili Airfields, on southeast Bougainville. But the patrols flew high, sometimes above the clouds, clearly looking for an invasion fleet, not for anything so miniscule as a solitary scout.

One time an enemy flying boat landed at Cape Torokina and stayed a few hours before roaring off to the southeast. The new base commander making his arrival, no doubt, McLeane thought. His suspicions were confirmed within hours when the 75-mm cannon mounted on the cape began firing twice as many practice shots as before. There was no doubt that the enemy was now considering Cape Torokina and Empress Augusta Bay as a potential Allied landing site. It was far down the list, though, or else a lot more activity would have been seen. McLeane took notes and made photographs of the terrain and, when he got the chance shot a wild boar.

The boar kept McLeane in cooked meat for the duration of his stay on the island. Building a campfire presented no problem. There was plenty of wood on the slopes of Bagana. And he wasn't worried about the smoke from his fire being detected by the Japanese. Bagana itself produced enough smoke to mask the output of a small industrial complex.

McLeane occasionally saw a native hunting boar or gathering fruit. The native always ran off upon sighting the foreigner. McLeane took to using a trick he had learned from a regular marine on Guadalcanal—wrapping candy bars and other treats in small American flags and leaving them on the native trails. He did this eight or nine times, and each one of the treats was gone the next day. McLeane hoped the natives would remember the kindness—and the flag—when the time came to return to Bougainville.

Three days before he was due to be picked up by submarine off Cape Moltke, thirty miles to the northwest, McLeane abandoned his slope-side camp and set out for the rendezvous. His scouting expeditions had given him a passable knowledge of the uncharted trails, and he had no trouble making his way along the south bank of the Laruma River to the point where it crossed the Empress Trail and flowed into the Solomon Sea.

McLeane hid in the bushes and listened for ten minutes before stepping out onto the Empress Trail. Even then he stopped to inspect the ground, as he had done so many times before. There were boot prints, many more than he had seen on the Empress Trail south of Cape Torokina. So the Japs had stepped up their foot patrols of the coastline. But there were no tire treads, and the most recent boot prints looked at least a day old. That last indication could be either very good or very bad. It could mean the Japs weren't coming back for a while, or that they were due anytime.

He had no choice. After risking twenty minutes to freshen up in the placid waters of the Solomon Sea, the first bath he had had in ten days, McLeane dressed and headed northwest, following the trail along the coast. He was delayed for more than a day when the Empress Trail simply evaporated; a large lagoon, not shown on any charts or aerial photographs—it was almost entirely enclosed by high palm fronds—in the Pukuito region of west Bougainville ended the trail. Beyond it lay a native trail, but hacking his way around the hangar-sized lagoon took McLeane all day. At least the lagoon discouraged the enemy, since the Japanese boot prints stopped when the Empress Trail did.

Once around the lagoon, McLeane ventured a few hundred yards into a dense coconut and lontar-palm grove where he made a bed for himself for what was to be his last night on Bougainville. Exhausted, he fell into a deep sleep, dreaming of life back in Nebraska. He recalled vividly the barrels of nails, the stacks of roofing material, and the walls mounted with hammers, nails, screwdrivers—all the things one needed to make a good life for oneself in Nebraska. There was the ringing of the old brass cash register, and his father's patience when an old townsman couldn't pay the bill for the stuff he needed to fix the holes ripped in a roof by a summer tornado. In the Solomons they didn't call them tornadoes. They called them monsoons. The effect was much the same.

McLeane was awakened at dawn by the light touch of a hand on his shoulder. He opened his eyes to see a native bushman, smiling nervously, looking down at him.

"Jesus fucking Christ," McLeane said.

The native quickly displayed one of the tiny American flags McLeane had left wrapped around the petty gifts left on the trails, then he poked a finger against the identical flag stitched to the right shoulder of McLeane's shirt. McLeane raised himself up onto his elbows.

Urgently, the native pointed down the slope toward the shoreline and ran a finger across his throat, as if to signal imminent death.

"Japs?" McLeane asked.

The diminutive, coal-black man looked puzzled.

Frustrated, McLeane got to his feet and said "Hirohito! *Banzai, banzai!*" He pointed down the slope.

The native smiled broadly again and bobbed his head up and down. McLeane reached into his pack, withdrew a solid steel hunting knife, and pressed it into the man's palm as a gift. Bobbing his head up and down, McLeane quickly gathered up his pack and headed off to the northwest.

As the native stood, slightly amazed, proudly admiring the gift that was of incalculable value in the Solomons, McLeane disappeared into the underbrush.

He followed a small native trail, bending low and running in a near-squat, until he could pick up the larger trail which his scouting had shown to lead northwest toward Cape Moltke. If there was a Jap patrol after him, or even in the seldom-patrolled area, it was an ominous sign.

Stopping now and then to look and listen, McLeane made his way to the Empress Trail about a mile and a half south of Cape Moltke. There were no recent marks, from either boot or wheel, in the mud of the Empress Trail. That fact especially unnerved McLeane. If the native's warning was correct, that meant that the enemy's arrival was imminent.

At least McLeane knew they would be coming from the southwest, as the enemy bases in northern Bougainville were much too far away for foot patrol. The Japs, who were looking for him, had to be coming from Cape Torokina. And if the urgency shown by the native was any indication, they weren't too far away.

Working quickly, McLeane lashed a grenade to the base of a bamboo stem at the edge of the trail, then he tied a bit of liana to the pin and ran it across the trail. He tied the other end of the strong, thin vine to the base of another bamboo. The line was barely two inches off the ground, and nearly invisible. It would give the enemy patrol something to think about, and would warn McLeane as well.

He headed northwest, toward Cape Moltke, which was four or five miles away. The rendezvous with the American submarine was a good twelve hours off. If the trail held up, McLeane would have no problem making the rendezvous. But the Japanese might have other ideas. He decided he had no choice but to plunge ahead.

McLeane began jogging up the trail, his .45 in his hand, the silencer screwed in place. Let the Japs and his hand-rigged booby trap make the noise. The latter did, before he was five minutes gone.

The explosion, a half-mile behind him, was accompanied by several screams of pain.

Knowing that the Japanese squad—typically twelve men—had probably been reduced by at least four and was certain to be more careful about what they stepped on or tripped over, McLeane picked up his pace, pausing once more to build another identical booby trap. Then he broke into a moderate run and continued on up the trail. When, after an hour, he hadn't heard another explosion, McLeane knew that the Japanese were treading more carefully, and moving more slowly.

It took him eight hours, considering the meanderings of the Empress Trail, to make it to Cape Moltke.

The cape was rounded, barely a cape at all, but more like a bulge in the western coastline of Bougainville. The beach was smooth, sandy, and fringed by an especially dense palm forest with the usual hack-your-way-through-it underbrush. The Tauri River swept down from the southern slope of the Tiour Balbi volcano to form a good-sized lagoon almost entirely hidden beneath a canopy of palms. The volcano belched sulfurous smoke even more actively than did Bagana. McLeane got a glimpse of the lagoon through a dense covering of sinimi, orchids, and lianas, but saw nothing. He wasn't much interested in the lagoon anyway. It was the submarine he cared about, and her arrival was still four hours off.

McLeane quickly found a defensive position on the southeast edge of the lagoon from which he could barely see the first ten feet of it. Behind three coconut palms that were growing so closely together they formed a triangle, he was protected on three sides yet given just enough space to shoot through the cracks between the trees. And he did not doubt that he would need the protection. The rendezvous with the sub was four hours off; the Japs were about three hours behind, assuming they were still chasing him, and McLeane felt sure that they were.

He sat in his hideaway between the palms and allowed himself the luxury of sitting and resting. He knew he couldn't fall asleep; that could be fatal. But he could rest his weary bones on the soft tropical turf and close his eyes and daydream of better times or, failing that, of making contact with the U.S.S. *Silverfish* as scheduled.

The three hours passed almost in a flash. McLeane had, in fact, fallen asleep, and it was only the late-afternoon clamor of a large congregation of fruit bats that woke him. He checked his watch and swore when he saw what time it was. The Japs could be upon him at any time. He got to his knees and, his .45 out and ready, looked around. He seemed still to be alone. Wiping the

27

sleep from his eyes, he looked out to sea. The view was far from perfect, but when he saw nothing he was convinced there was nothing there—on the surface anyway.

There was a possibility, a remote one, that the *Silverfish* was waiting for him, her radio antenna poked above the surface of the Solomon Sea in the rapidly waning sunlight. McLeane hooked up his radio and hoisted the antenna. Expecting to hear nothing in response, he spoke into the microphone: "Tonto, this is Lone Ranger, do you copy?"

There was some static on the line, as if someone were fumbling with a microphone.

McLeane repeated himself. "Tonto, this is Lone Ranger, do you copy?"

Indeed, someone had copied. "Would you stop that bloody row?" an Australian-accented voice replied.

"What?" McLeane replied in astonishment. The Aussie voice was very near.

"Lone Ranger, this is Tonto," the voice said, somewhat tiredly this time. "You're almost on top of me. Turn down the gain would you? My tired old circuits can't take the strain."

McLeane turned down the gain on his transmitter, as told.

"Who are you?" he asked.

"James Corrigan, Captain, the Royal Australian Air Corps, and I suspect you and I are about a hundred feet apart."

"Where the hell are you?" McLeane asked.

"In the bloody lagoon, where I've been swatting mosquitoes and waiting for you to show up for nearly two days now. That fancy submarine of yours was needed elsewhere, so Comsopac asked dear old Captain Corrigan to go hunting for you. It appears I've succeeded. Come on aboard and let's get the hell out of here."

"Where the hell are you?" McLeane asked.

"In the lagoon, where do you think?"

"You have a submarine in a lagoon that may be ten feet deep."

"No, I have a Catalina with the best camouflage job you've ever seen. Now, are you coming aboard or not?"

McLeane was amazed.

"O.K., I'll come aboard."

"You won't need your radio anymore. I'll stick my head out the nacelle window and holler. You have ears in addition to a noisy radio, do you not?"

Damned Aussies, McLeane thought.

"Yeah, I have ears," he said, shutting off and packing up his radio.

McLeane hacked his way to the edge of the lagoon, and there she floated, as big as a giant swan and ten times as glorious. The amphibious aircraft had two engines, could land on sea or land, and was one of the most versatile vehicles ever designed. She was a DC-3, and this one, at least, was painted to blend into the grays, dusky blues, and greens of the rain forest.

The rain forest was a hangar for her massive wings. Painted the way she was, the Catalina was virtually undetectable. McLeane vowed to give some thought to Catalinas in the near future. For the moment, his main objective was to get off Bougainville alive.

The plane was tied bow and stern to the palm trees that lined the lagoon. The Catalina had a huge central nacelle with two blister canopies in the stern which allowed entrance and exit while at sea. The stern was only a short hop from the shoreline. McLeane watched as Corrigan unlocked and slid the canopy open. He was ruddy-faced, fifty-ish, and looked as if he had been through a few beer bottles in his life. He retained a certain barroom toughness that McLeane remembered well from growing up in Nebraska.

"Let's hurry it up, mate," Corrigan said. "I'd like to get back to civilization before my beer goes flat."

McLeane tossed Corrigan his pack. "What do you call 'civilization'?"

"Will Guadalcanal do, or would you have me fly you all the way to Hawaii so you can do the hula with some native girl?"

"Guadalcanal will do."

"Then will you cast off the stern lines and toss them to me? I'll get the bow."

McLeane untied the stern lines and tossed them to Corrigan, who then disappeared into the fuselage, only to reappear a minute later clambering out of a bow hatch. The big man tossed the bowline into the bushes on both sides of the plane.

"I save old rope for times like this," Corrigan shouted. "It saves me having to walk all around the blasted lagoon."

"Shut up!" McLeane shouted back, bringing his Winchester to the ready and cocking an ear inland. No novice, Corrigan disappeared into the bow hatch and shut it. Soon, he reappeared in the stern port.

"What is it?" he asked, a lot quieter this time.

"The birds."

"What about the bloody birds?"

"They've stopped making a racket."

Both men suddenly were quieter even than the birds, which *had* shut up for the first time in quite a while. Off to the south, McLeane, then Corrigan, began to hear the faint sound of Japanese voices cursing the roughness of the trail and life in general so far from home. "I'll get my Browning," Corrigan said.

"No. Just crank this thing up and get ready to go."

"Are you mad? The noise of the engines will draw them like flies."

"Flies can be swatted. Do as I told you."

"You got one minute, starting from the time I turn over the engines, no more. If you're not in the back door by then, I'm leaving without you."

"It's a deal," McLeane said, heading back up the trail he had hacked through the bushes.

McLeane ran back to his triangle of palm trees, braced himself, and sighted across the palm grove toward the spot where the Empress Trail emerged from the rain forest. The voices were growing louder, and then they were drowned out by the roar of the Catalina's twin engines.

All of a sudden, eight Japanese soldiers burst out of the trail and into the palm grove. McLeane cut one nearly in half with his first round and winged a second in the shoulder. The six remaining soldiers fanned out, taking refuge behind the nearest trees. They were good, this bunch, and madder than hornets for twice having been bushwacked by McLeane. While McLeane put their wounded comrade out of his misery, they switched trees, fanning out wider and closer.

Corrigan gunned the engines to give McLeane a reminder that time was running short.

McLeane saw motion to his left and peeked out for a look. The look nearly cost him his life. A chunk of bark the size of a baseball was torn out of the tree by a Japanese slug. "Goddamn it," McLeane swore, spinning to his right to get a bead on his attacker from the other side of his fortress. As he turned he found himself not twenty yards from another Jap who had managed to sneak up on him from behind. There was an instant when both men stared into each other's eyes before firing. The Jap brought his rifle to his shoulder; McLeane fired from the hip and emptied half the bullets still in his magazine into the man's body.

There was another shot and another chunk of bark flew from McLeane's palm tree.

Corrigan gunned the engines again. "You ain't kiddin'," McLeane said, and ran like mad for the plane while bullets kicked up turf all around him.

The Catalina had started to move away from shore. McLeane leaped onto the tail section, pausing only to toss a grenade into the trail he had cut between the palm grove and the lagoon before diving into an aft entry port. There was an explosion and another scream. McLeane slammed shut the blister canopy and went forward, shedding his Winchester and ammo belt along the way.

The Australian was in the portside pilot's seat and gestured for McLeane to take the copilot's position. The Catalina moved slowly out of the lagoon until the wing tips were free of any chance of getting caught in the bushes. Then Corrigan turned the plane southeast, into the wind, and pushed the throttles full ahead. The massive plane shook and roared, and spray flew all around. Two enemy soldiers could be seen on the beach, taking futile pot shots at the aircraft.

"The bastards never give up, do they?" Corrigan asked. "How many did you get?"

"Three or four," McLeane replied, leaning back in the seat and breathing a sigh of safety. For the first time in two weeks, he had nothing to worry about, other than a chance encounter with a Zero, but the odds were against it.

"How many did you get the whole time you were on this charmin' little rock?"

"I ran out of fingers. I don't know, Corrigan. I don't like to count bodies."

"You don't seem to be too bad at makin' piles of 'em."

The Catalina lifted out of the water and banked away from shore. Soon it was five thousand feet above the Solomon Sea and the coastline of Bougainville was merely a gray slit on the horizon.

"You wouldn't happen to have a keg of beer around here someplace, would you?" McLeane asked.

"Sorry, mate. I never drink when I fly. I'll tell you this, though, I'm gonna have me a few pints when we get back to Guadalcanal."

"I'm buying. Thanks for hauling my ass off that rock."

"Anytime, anytime. Just try to avoid these hasty exits if we ever do it again."

"There's lots of things I'm gonna do different from now on."

"Such as?"

"Such as getting a few men behind me so I don't have to be on the alert twenty-four hours a day. Such as finding a better way of getting to these islands than a parachute. I lucked out this time. But I'm sick and tired of all the other times when I wound up on top of a hundred-foot-high tree."

"You ought to get yourself one of these little numbers," Corrigan said, slapping the wheel proudly.

"I was just thinking along those lines, now that I've seen what she can do. You mean you sat in that lagoon two days without being spotted by Jap air patrols?"

"I am living proof."

"Mind if I fly her for a while?" McLeane asked.

"Be my guest," Corrigan replied, taking his hands off the wheel.

McLeane took over, flying from the copilot's position. He put the Catalina through a few basic maneuvers before returning the controls to Corrigan.

McLeane smiled. "Only an Aussie would be crazy enough to let a man take the controls of his plane without first bothering to ask if the fellow knows how to fly."

Corrigan was unfazed. "Only a Yank would be crazy

enough to take his first flying lesson on a PBY in the middle of a war. I figured that if you asked to fly her, you already knew how.''

McLeane shut his eyes and yawned. ''I think I'm gonna buy me one of these babies when we get back to Guadalcanal.''

Four

Brig. Gen. Archie Thompson had been scrutinizing McLeane's photographs, drawings, and typewritten report for several hours when McLeane arrived at his office.

The general, a gray-haired man in his early fifties who had never lost his air of marine leather or his ability to get along with both upper and lower echelons, was McLeane's longtime friend and supporter. He had backed McLeane on numerous occasions when the major's unorthodoxy came to the attention of the stiff-necks at Comsopac. He smiled and stood at the sight of McLeane.

"Mack! So you lived through another one. And did a goddamned good job, too. I won't compare your drawings to Rembrandt's, but they contained all the information we needed."

"Thank you, sir."

"Damn it, I wish you could learn to call me by my Christian name. Haven't we known each other long enough?"

"I've tried, sir, but I'm always afraid that General MacArthur will walk in just as I'm saying something like 'Hey, Archie, how about you and me goin' out and grabbin' a few beers.' "

Thompson laughed. "That *would* get his back up.

35

Well, call me what you like. And I can get you a cold beer if you like."

McLeane consulted his watch. It was eleven in the morning, and he had been back at Henderson Field on Guadalcanal for two days. "It's a little early for me."

"It's up to you. Coffee?"

"Sure thing ... Archie."

The general smiled and pressed a button on his desk. When an aide appeared, he ordered two regular coffees, which were produced within minutes.

Sipping coffee and going over the maps and photos, Thompson said, "So the gist of your report is that the Empress Augusta Bay is poorly defended and supplied."

"That's about the size of it. Though the Japs may be having second thoughts ..."

Thompson finished his sentence for him. "... Now that you've killed their CO and his chief of staff and wiped out half the enlisted men."

"I didn't get *that* many, sir," McLeane said, embarrassed. "Maybe ten or twelve in all."

"Only ten or twelve? By God, I wish I were twenty years younger. I'd be out there with you."

"You're welcome now. You can hold your own."

"I'm grateful for your confidence, but I'm afraid the mere hint of the idea would make MacArthur shit his pants. Pompous buzzard. 'I shall return.' "

It was McLeane's turn to laugh.

"What was most useful in your report was learning that Mutupina Point is heavily fortified. Our recon photos don't show anything like it. The Japs must be really dug in deep."

"They have a 75-mm dug in pretty deep on Cape Torokina. But it has a limited horizontal field of fire."

"A 75-mm we can handle. I imagine you've guessed that Empress Augusta is a prime candidate for D-Day on Bougainville."

"The thought has occurred to me."

"There's a big confab in a few weeks where we're all supposed to pick the spot. I think your information will prove instrumental in making a case for Empress Augusta Bay. My God, how can they defend an outpost supplied by donkey trail?"

"Don't sell the bastards short. They're clever and there seems to be no end of 'em. You kill one and two more take his place."

"That will end eventually. So ... what can we have you do now? You want a few weeks off?"

McLeane thought a moment, then said, "Maybe one or two."

"Done."

"However ..."

"Go on."

"I have an idea which I'd like to lay out for you. It won't take me five minutes."

The general nodded.

"I would like to form a Ranger unit—four guys and myself. I need a marksman, a demolitions man, someone who can speak Japanese and as many of the Melanesian dialects as possible, and—I don't know—an all-around backup man."

"O.K.," Thompson said.

"I'll need an HQ. It only has to be a shack over at Carney Field or, preferably, along Tango Lagoon."

"Tango Lagoon? Why do you want to be there? It has no airstrip."

McLeane lowered his voice. "I'll also need a PBY."

"Anything *else?*" the general asked, incredulously.

"Yes, sir. I want that Aussie pilot who picked me up, and I'll need a secretary. You know how I am with paperwork."

Thompson drummed his fingertips on his desk.

"Come on, General, I nearly got my ass shot off on

Bougainville, and I've grown attached to the thing over the years. I need men to back me up and an amphibious plane to deliver us to our targets. One argument you can make for the formation of the unit is that we can be multiservice—available to whoever needs us in an emergency. In a moment's notice, you know, that sort of thing."

"I can hear Comsopac now," Thompson said.

"Tell them that if MacArthur really wants to 'return' to the Philippines in grand style he ought to try parachuting alone into a rain forest."

"I think I'll ignore that last advice if you don't mind. Mack . . . do you really think we can sell this idea?"

"Yes, sir. I think we can. Let me form the unit and then you pick a target. If we make out O.K., I get to keep the unit."

There was more drumming of fingers on desk.

The general mused. "Four men . . . a PBY with that Aussie pilot. Corrigan, isn't that his name?"

McLeane said that it was.

"A shack on Tango Lagoon, and a secretary. Of the female persuasion, I suspect."

"I'll settle for no less than Betty Grable."

"What will you call your Ranger unit? You remember that time we had to shoot down letting Greg Boyington call the 214th VMF 'Boyington's Bastards'? Wouldn't look good in the press, so he settled for 'The Black Sheep'. What do you have in mind, 'McLeane's Motherfuckers'?"

McLeane smiled. "It's up to you," he said.

"Well then, you write me up a formal request, outlining your needs for the unit, and I'll put through a request for the formation of 'McLeane's Rangers'. How does that sound?"

"It sounds fine to me, sir."

Thompson finished his coffee and leaned back in his

chair. Out the window, a flight of P-38's was taking off for a raid on one of the two airstrips on south Bougainville.

Thompson said, "What's on your agenda for the rest of the day?"

"I owe Corrigan a few pints. Aside from that, I have no plans. You want to go fishing or something?"

The general shook his head sadly. "The pressure of command, Mack. I have three or four appointments this afternoon, not to mention a business lunch in half an hour."

"Jesus, your life sounds worse than mine."

"Never accept promotion," Thompson said. "If they ever try to make you a colonel or, God forbid, a general, tell 'em where to stick it."

"I never thought of making general, sir," McLeane said. "In fact, I never expected to live long enough for the possibility to be raised."

"Well, if you get your Ranger unit, you just may live long enough to see a few stars put on your hat," Thompson said.

"I won't hold my breath," McLeane replied.

"The Zoo" was the name affectionately given to the unofficial hangout of those soldiers, sailors, air corps men, and marines who were quartered between Henderson Field and Lunga Point. A rundown fighter-plane hangar, it had been converted by volunteer labor—and a lot of free beer—into a passable imitation of a cocktail lounge, complete with a bar, a dance floor, a radio which got both ball games and Benny Goodman, and a dozen square tables accompanied by mismatched chairs. There were also the usual decorations—fish netting on the walls, sea shells for ashtrays, yellowing photographs of various platoons, the occasional broken wood propeller or souvenir of the Imperial Japanese Army driven off

Guadalcanal the year before, and, now and then, nurses from the big army hospital near Henderson. McLeane preferred the Zoo to the officer's club, where he was looked down upon, or secretly envied, for doing Ranger work when he could be parading about Guadalcanal, dressed as and acting like an officer and a gentleman. McLeane was welcome at the enlisted men's club, where he was admired for being one of the few officers to put his butt on the line on a regular basis, but enlisted men tended to feel ill-at-ease when an officer was hanging around. So McLeane went to the Zoo, where nobody seemed to give a shit about name, rank, serial number, or anything else.

It was midday when he walked in to the strains of Tommy Dorsey coming over the radio. The place was pretty full, and about half the men who noticed McLeane's arrival and his rank—he was in his regular uniform, just having come from the meeting with General Thompson—jumped to attention and saluted. McLeane waved them back into their seats. He looked around the smoke-filled, noisy room for the Australian. The long bar was fully occupied, but no one stood out except for a wiry American who looked Italian and, who was proclaiming loudly that the St. Louis Cardinals had no chance of beating the New York Yankees in the World Series but that the Brooklyn Dodgers, had they not suffered a succession of conspiracies on the part of National League umpires, would be in the series with the Yanks and would be hot to avenge their outrageous defeat in 1941, which also had been the fault of bad calls. McLeane moved on, and within a minute heard a familiar voice call out, "Over here, mate."

Corrigan had commandeered one of the small tables and was leaning back in his chair, his feet on the table. A bottle of beer was in his hand. Another stood waiting for McLeane.

"First one's my treat. All the rest are yours," Corrigan said.

"It's a bargain."

McLeane sat down and took a swig, then leaned back and put his feet on the opposite corner of the table.

"How'd it go with the big brass?" Corrigan asked.

"The same as always. Thompson and I get along pretty well."

"I don't get along with generals. Not that I spend that much time with 'em."

"What are you doing in the Solomons anyway? How old are you, Corrigan?"

"Over fifty, but not old enough to be your father."

"What's a fifty-year-old man doing on the front lines?"

"My participation in this little conflict was not entirely of my own choosing," Corrigan said.

"You were drafted."

"You're a bleedin' genius, McLeane, like all Yanks."

"They can't draft a man your age. Not even in Australia."

"Let's just say they made an appeal to my conscience which I was unable to refuse."

"They paid you off."

"Well, there was a slight monetary consideration involved, but not of sufficient magnitude to get me eager to be shot at."

"So I ask you again—what are you doing here?"

"I flew the cargo routes all the way from Guadalcanal to Manila before hostilities broke out. I know every bleedin' island in this part of the world. They gave me my old commission back, a little bit of loose change, and the chance to do something more interesting than hauling freight back and forth from Sydney to Aukland."

"So that's it," McLeane said, "You're the expert on

the local geography."

The Australian nodded.

"Congratulations, Captain. You've just become the first member of McLeane's Rangers."

"What's that?" Corrigan asked suspiciously.

"The elite Ranger unit I'm putting together. You just become the pilot."

"Now, wait a minute ..."

McLeane didn't let him finish his sentence. "Of course, the formation of the unit is still pending approval from above, but I don't expect to be turned down."

"McLeane ..."

"I'll help you out with the flying whenever I can—now that you know I can do it."

"It may not have occurred to you, but I already have a CO who tells me what to do: Derek Paul, Colonel, RAAC. He may have an opinion."

"I'm sure the reconciliation of his opinion with that of General Thompson will prove to be an interesting event," McLeane said.

Corrigan shook his head sadly, drained his beer bottle, and slammed it down on the table.

"Shangaied again." There was a tone of inevitability in his voice.

McLeane suspected he wasn't really angry, but was in fact intrigued. He simply couldn't admit to liking an idea instigated by a Yank. Anyway, there was a diversion, a commotion at the bar. McLeane drained his bottle, collected Corrigan's, and went to the bar to investigate the commotion and to get new beers.

The commotion came from that part of the bar where the Italian from Brooklyn had been carrying on about baseball. He had squared off with a gigantic Cleve-lander, an army man, who felt that *his* town's team was better than any other. The argument had moved rapidly from baseball to the differences between Brooklyn and Cleveland, and they were legion. By the time McLeane arrived on the scene, the fight had begun.

The Clevelander was easily twice the size of the lance corporal from Brooklyn, but the fight was one-sided and short. Ducking, parrying, getting in a few low blows and some quick judo moves that McLeane had never seen before, the Brooklynite soon had left his opponent lying sideways on the floor, vomiting beer and bile.

McLeane stepped up to the scene. The victor, sensing another opponent, spun and squared off for another fight. It was then that he noticed McLeane's rank and snapped to attention.

"At ease, Corporal," McLeane said.

"Sir ... Major ... I ... unh ..."

"Where'd you learn to fight like that, Corporal?"

"Brooklyn, New York, sir."

"What part of Brooklyn?"

The corporal's eyes widened. "Flatbush Avenue and King's Highway, sir."

McLeane mused, "I didn't know that was that tough a neighborhood."

"It wasn't when I was a little kid, sir, but the past couple of years ... I'd say five to ten ..."

"How old are you?"

"Twenty-two, sir. Begging your pardon, sir, but are you *the* Major McLeane?"

"I'm the only one I know of," McLeane replied, a giant in comparison with the diminutive Italian, who was no more than five-eight.

The corporal stuck his hand out to be shook, and was appropriately rewarded. "I've read a lot about you in *Stars & Stripes* and even saw you mentioned in *Life* one time. But I never thought I'd meet you in person. I'm really sorry about having to have busted up that bum, but he was gettin' on my nerves about the Dodgers, and

I guess you know how much a man can take before he does something."

McLeane said that he knew, even as the corporal's victim was recovering, struggling for consciousness. At least he had stopped throwing up.

McLeane said, "Corporal, I think you'd better haul your ass outta here before the MPs arrive."

"Sure thing, Major McLeane."

"First . . . your name?"

"Vincent Contardo, sir. Sir . . . are you planning on putting me on report?"

"Not exactly," McLeane said, smiling enigmatically.

"Sir?"

"Get the hell outta here," McLeane said, and the corporal quickly obliged.

Corrigan sidled up, two full bottles of beer in his hands.

McLeane looked at the fresh beers.

"I put 'em on your tab," Corrigan said.

"Thanks a lot."

"*Volunteer* number two for McLeane's Rangers?" Corrigan asked.

"Could be, Captain, could be," McLeane said.

They went back to their seats, McLeane dislodging with a glance the two PFCs who had taken their places.

"And what's this one's job going to be—staff greaseball?"

"All-around backup man. For this unit I'm forming, I need a pilot, a backup man, a demolitions expert, a crack marksman, and a linguist. I think I have the first two."

"I know what *I* can do. What do you know about *him* other than he can beat up a drunken Yank? There are hairdressers in Sydney who can do that."

"I'll find out what he can do. I'll put him through his paces. I'll look up his service record . . ."

". . . And find out he's a contract killer for Murder,

44

Inc. or whatever it is you call that band of dagos who have been laying waste your pretty countryside."

"*That* is exactly the kind of man I'm looking for."

"To stand *behind* you? You'd turn your back on him?"

"Only when he knows that I'm his only way home"— McLeane laughed—"and Brooklyn is a long way from Bougainville."

"Oh, so that's where we're going again."

"I can't say for certain, but I wouldn't be surprised."

The two men drank their beer in silence for a while, watching the commotion caused by the arrival of four WAC privates. One, a tall woman with auburn hair and a touchingly soft face, reminded him of the girls he knew back home in Nebraska. She captured McLeane's attention.

"Who are the new arrivals?" McLeane asked.

"Never set eyes on 'em before, mate. Which one takes your fancy?"

"The tall one."

"Oh, the red-haired bird."

"Yeah, redbird. Good name for a girl."

"She's got a nice set of jugs, too. But I don't know her. You're the one who's the bloody hero. Go up to her and say hello."

"I just may do that," McLeane said, only to have his mind changed when a buck sergeant tried it and was greeted with a sharp "Get lost" that brought a chorus of jeering from the other men in the room.

"Maybe tomorrow," McLeane said, putting his feet back on the chair.

"Some hero," Corrigan said.

"Business first. We're gonna need some tail guns for your Catalina. That hand-held Browning you keep lying in the bilge just isn't good enough."

"Some 20-mm guns can be mounted in there, one on

each side. You come up with 'em, and I'll mount 'em."

"I'll come up with them. Assuming this whole plan is approved."

"She's a good plane, Major ..."

McLeane interrupted. "My rank is major. My name is Mack."

"As you wish. Anyway, she'll give us over three hundred kilometers per hour ..."

"A little over two hundred miles an hour ..."

"And has a range of around five thousand kilometers ..."

"... Three thousand miles ..."

"... Cruising at ... I'll put it in your language ... one hundred-thirty miles an hour at ten thousand feet."

McLeane pondered, then said, "That'll be about right. We may have to tack on some wing tanks for longer flights on occasion, though."

"It's been done," Corrigan said with a shrug.

"What's the wingspan?"

"A smidgeon over a hundred feet. Small enough for most of the lagoons we'll be parkin' her in."

"And you know all of them."

"Every bleedin' one."

McLeane took a swig of beer and stared once again at the auburn-haired girl at the bar. "I wonder where she's from," he mused.

Five

Two weeks went by, while McLeane, with nothing else to do, swam, dived for exotic shells, and tossed footballs around on the field next to Henderson. He had been the second-string quarterback on the Columbia team that had come from nowhere to beat Stanford in the Rose Bowl in 1934, stunning the football world. McLeane had never gotten to play in that Rose Bowl game, which had ended in a 7–0 shutout, but his arm was still good and he was able to toss the pigskin sixty yards without thinking twice. He had long been the nemesis of opposing army, navy and air corps teams when impromptu games erupted near Henderson, and had spent his two weeks off indulging himself in that glory. At last he got the call to come to General Thompson's office.

McLeane arrived dressed to the hilt, clean-shaven and looking fit after some good, honest exercise and a time in the sun, not the rain forest. General Thompson greeted him with a smile.

"Congratulations, Mack, you've got your chance."

"Chance, sir?"

"I had to give them *something*."

"What was it?"

"You get one shot. One mission. If you pull that off, you can keep your unit—McLeane's Rangers is now the

47

official name."

"And the personnel and equipment?"

"I managed to *persuade* the Aussies to let you have Captain Corrigan for a while, and his Catalina as well. It will also be armed with two 20-mm Brownings in the stern blister canopies. I'm working on a spot for you at Tango Lagoon, but you may have to sleep in tents for a while."

"That's fine with me, sir."

"There's an office for you down the hall which you can use to go through the personnel records and look for men. As for a secretary, we just got a new bunch of WACs in. They're down in Room 3C now, being taught the ropes. I trust you'll pick one with all the necessary credentials."

"Oh, you can count on that," McLeane said with a smile. "What's the mission we get our one chance on?"

Thompson spread a map of Bougainville across his desk. "Here's the enemy airstrip at Kara, on the southern part of the island. On the southern perimeter of the airfield is a munitions dump that's been protected by a concrete bunker that seems immune to our air attacks. That munitions dump is being used by the Japanese to supply the garrison at Empress Augusta Bay. I guess you can imagine the strategic importance of its being taken out."

"Especially if we're going to land troops at Empress Augusta Bay," McLeane said.

"You didn't hear that from me."

"And I won't tell it to anyone."

"I'll leave it to you to plan your own attack. All reconnaissance photos will be made available to you. As always, you have the run of the building, and the files. Just take it easy on the new WACs, would you? They're neophytes in this man's war, not accustomed to Ivy League officers like yourself."

"You give me too much credit."

"Bullshit. You could charm the teeth out of a crocodile."

McLeane smiled, pumped the general's hand, headed toward the door, then stopped. "That one with the auburn hair . . . ?"

"Margot Thomas." Thompson sighed. "PFC. This is her first assignment outside the States. Damn it, Mack, I'm geting to know your taste."

"I'll keep you abreast of what happens," McLeane said. "Within the bounds of propriety, of course."

McLeane found his office more than adequate. It had two desks—both with phones—two filing cabinets, and a single window that looked out over the airfield. McLeane opened the window to let in a breeze, and watched a formation of P-38's taking off, probably for another of the softening-up raids on enemy positions on south Bougainville; these had been going on for some weeks. He watched the fighters until they were out of sight, then went back down the hall to where the new WAC secretaries were being introduced to life in the Pacific Theater.

The man doing the breaking-in was eminently qualified to train clerical workers. Maj. Howard D. Flagg was one of General Thompson's four aides. His bailiwick was personnel, and he was cut from the same cloth that makes petty bureaucrats, pushy real-estate salesmen, and office managers everywhere. Flagg was a peacock, pompous and bristling with irritation that he had been four times passed over for promotion to lieutenant colonel. Flagg especially bristled over McLeane's having the same rank as he, when he thought himself decidedly superior. To be honest, McLeane did nothing to soften their relationship and occasionally neglected to include the "l" in the man's last name when typing up reports to the general.

Flagg turned perceptively pale when McLeane strode into the room. The WACs were clustered around half a dozen desks, some sitting, some standing, and all enduring a tedious lecture on office procedures. McLeane clapped Flagg on the back hard enough to make him cough. "Hiya, Howie."

The girl with the auburn hair smiled. All the others looked horrified.

"*Major* McLeane," Flagg said when he had recovered. "Can't you try to be at least a *little* civilized?"

"We're not here to be civilized, Flagg. We're here to fight a war."

There was a note of resignation in Flagg's voice. "What do you want now?"

"I need an assistant for my new unit."

"Oh, *McLeane's Rangers*. As if you weren't enough of a showboater before, now you need an elite unit. How many headlines will it take to satisfy you, McLeane?"

"How many teeth can you go without and still eat your cornflakes every morning?" McLeane snarled. Flagg took a step backward, and once again the girl with the auburn hair was the only one to smile.

"All right, all right, I'll find a secretary for you."

"I can find my own," McLeane said. "Just let me have a look at their files. I'll go back to my office and pick one out, and you can go about your lecture on the proper way of stacking pencils."

Flagg was livid. "Wait a minute, Major. *I'm* in charge of personnel here!"

"Not in this case. Ask the boss if you don't believe me."

"That's exactly what I mean to do." Flagg stormed out of the room.

McLeane sighed and shrugged. "Welcome to the Solomon Islands. I suggest you read Joseph Conrad's version of life here before you take Major Flagg too seriously. It's not all stacking pencils and shuffling papers."

The assembled WACs laughed nervously, with one exception. Margot Thomas's eyes were scorching McLeane's. Clearly, she was as fascinated with him as he was attracted to her.

"Now, can anyone here show me where the files on you people are?" He looked down in dismay at a desk covered with stacks of files.

Without hesitation, Private Thomas stepped forward and pressed a long and rather elegant finger atop the right stack. They exchanged wry smiles.

"Thank you, Private . . ."

"Thomas. Margot Thomas . . . sir."

McLeane hefted the stack and tucked it under one arm. "I'm temporarily headquartered in Room 3K if any of you feel particularly inclined to work for a man who specializes in sneaking behind enemy lines and getting shot at." Then he left the room, nearly colliding with a red-faced Major Flagg returning from General Thompson's office.

Flagg glared at McLeane, who said, "I'll have these files to you in a little while. I don't think it will take me long to find someone."

Indeed, it took him almost no time at all. Half an hour later, he had gone through all the files and had his feet propped up on his desk, when Margot Thomas walked in, snapped to attention, and saluted.

"At ease. What kept you?"

She laughed, and he motioned for her to have a seat. She took the only other one, which was at the other desk.

"Tell me, Private Thomas, what in the world makes a woman with a B.A. in art history from Sarah Lawrence want to join the WACs?"

"What makes a man with a B.A. in history from Columbia want to sneak behind enemy lines and get shot at?" She explained: "I had a little time left after I was taught how to stack pencils. *I* looked up *your* file."

McLeane was thrilled by her boldness and initiative. So she had brains as well as well as beauty.

"Adventure. I came for the adventure. And because I thought I might be able to contribute to the war effort."

"The same here," she replied.

"You were president of the wireless radio club. Do you know Morse?"

"Of course. I plan to work in radio after the war. That's another reason for my being here—to learn all there is to know about radio."

McLeane slammed her file shut and tossed it onto his desk with the others. "Do you have any idea what you might be getting yourself into?"

"I read your file."

"You won't be living in the relative luxury of the womens' barracks at Henderson. You'll have a tent by the edge of Tango Lagoon. You won't be going on missions, but you will have to be on call at all hours of the day and night to handle radio messages."

"I prefer it to stacking pencils and shuffling papers. Major . . . may I ask a question?"

"Only if you agree to drop the title bull and call me 'Mack,' I'll call you Margot. O.K.?"

"You're the boss."

"What's your question?"

"McLeane's Rangers . . . just what kind of outfit will it be?"

"A small, extremely mobile reconnaissance and sabotage unit. We'll be operating out of Tango Lagoon, using a PBY Catalina to get where we're going. Those going out on missions will be myself and five other guys. One I already have picked—an Aussie pilot I shanghaied. He'll probably bunk in his plane. And I have a line on another guy—a Brooklyn street-fighter type named Vince Contardo. He's a lance corporal. We'll have to look up his file. Apart from that, I need a demolitions expert, a crack marksman, and—this one may be tough—someone who's fluent in Oriental languages, especially Japanese and Melanesian dialects."

"There' can't be too many of *them* around," she mused.

"At least he'll stick out in a crowd."

"How much time do we have to round up these guys?"

"All the time in the world—I would say a week."

"So I guess we'd better get started," she said, pulling the top drawer of her desk open and staring at the emptiness inside. She sighed. "At least I know where the pencils and paper are stacked."

"I'll tell you what—if you can find the file on Vince Contardo by five o'clock, I'll take you to dinner tonight."

She laughed. "I was wondering how long it would be before you asked. Where are we going? The Zoo?"

"Never," McLeane said. "I'm taking you to the finest seaside restaurant in the Solomons."

Tango Lagoon sat at one of the mouths of Lunga River and just to the west of East Kukum Beach. It was nearly one hundred fifty feet wide, but too shallow even for PT boats and didn't extend far enough inland to be deemed a worthwhile candidate for being dredged out and made into a deep-water port. Consequently, it was used mainly for the small launches that took naval officers to and from their warships anchored a mile or two offshore, and the launches were berthed entirely on the west bank. The east bank was solid palm grove, save

53

for a narrow dirt road that ran down to the beach, passing within two hundred feet of the east bank of Tango Lagoon.

During the day, the Seabees had managed to hack a one-lane road from the beach road to the east bank of Tango Lagoon, a carpet of moss and ground-hugging vines that sat three feet above the high-water mark. McLeane had his old jeep parked with the grill nearly overhanging the still water of the lagoon. There was no activity on the launches across the lagoon, and a full moon provided enough light for Margot and him to eat the meal he had spent the better part of two hours rounding up: cold sliced turkey sandwiches, fresh oranges and bananas, and a bottle of cognac.

"So this is the best seaside restaurant in the Solomons?" Margot asked, between eagerly taken bites of sandwich.

"It has the advantage of being the only one."

"And this is where we'll all be staying? If the food stays this good, it looks like heaven to me. Do you have any idea of the slop they serve at my barracks?"

"I think I can guess. Fried Spam on toast. SOS. Rubber eggs and Bakelite toast."

"You got it. Where'd you get all this stuff?"

"Here and there. I have contacts all over these islands."

"I can just imagine. A major who can march into General Thompson's office and call him by his first name."

"You really do have eyes and ears everywhere, don't you?" McLeane asked.

"I like to know what I'm getting myself into," she replied.

"Well, let me point out the architect's design. Where we're sitting will be the dock. That will allow us access to the Catalina's aft blister canopies without having to

54

clamber over the fuselage.

"My tent, which will also serve as HQ for the first mission, will be right by the land side of the dock. Yours will be next to mine, to the sea side. The rest of the bunch will sleep two men to a tent, all to the land side of my tent."

"Do I sense that you're protecting me from the rest of the unit?"

"They *are* apt to be a rowdy bunch," McLeane said with a smile. "Besides, your tent will be nearest the beach. It gets pretty beautiful here on the beach some nights."

"It's beautiful now," she said, putting aside her paper plate and resting her head on McLeane's shoulder.

"When do the tents go up?" she asked. "I can't stand living in the barracks."

"Have you ever lived in a tent?"

"Only at camp."

"Camp, this ain't. But these will be good tents, twelve-by-twelve umbrella tents, with mosquito netting, three windows, and canvas flaps for privacy."

"Privacy is important," she replied.

"And hard to find in the armed forces. You see what good I've done for you?"

"I saw that a long time ago, Mack."

"Thanks for finding Contardo for me, by the way. He looks like just the man for the job."

"He sounds like a creep to me."

"Brooklyn street fighters are apt to sound that way," McLeane explained. "I was looking for someone who doesn't know how to spell 'fear,' and I think you've located him for me."

"It wasn't all that hard. It only took four hours and that letter of authorization from General Thompson to let me into every file on the island."

"You're a resourceful lady," he said, turning toward her.

"I can be a lot more resourceful than that," she responded, turning her face up to him to be kissed. He kissed her, their tongues touching briefly.

Soon they were in a passionate embrace, hands exploring bodies, mouths locked, until at last they broke apart, out of breath.

She took a minute to catch her breath, then asked, "Do you have a girl back home?"

"No."

"You have to be kidding."

"No. I never had the time. What with working hard to get my grades up so I could get into the college where Lou Gehrig played ball, I never had much time for girls."

"There must have been a *few*."

"Oh, yeah. A random encounter. The occasional broken heart. Ships passing in the night. All that sort of stuff. But nothing serious. What about yourself?"

"My story is pretty much the same as yours," Margot said.

He laughed and hugged her. "Well, shall we get married now or can it wait until morning?"

"Morning. I'm half an hour away from curfew. I'm sorry, Mack."

He shrugged. "The chaplain's probably at the Zoo and dead drunk by now anyway."

"Try to get those tents up as soon as possible, would you?" she asked.

"Oh, you can count on that," McLeane said, starting his jeep.

Six

McLeane let Lance Corporal Contardo stand at attention for a full two minutes, which must have seemed like a lifetime, before closing his file and looking up at him. At the other desk, Margot was busily making phone calls and going through other files.

McLeane characteristically put his feet up on the corner of his desk. "At ease, Corporal," he said.

Contardo let out a sigh and relaxed.

"You have quite a record, Contardo," McLeane said. "Two Bronze Stars in only a year. A commendation for valor. You're a good marksman and in the campaign to take the island upon which we now reside you distinguished yourself by taking out two enemy machine-gun nests single-handedly. . . ."

"Thank you, sir."

"After having been specifically ordered not to do so," McLeane added.

Impatient and nervous, Contardo shifted his weight from one leg to the other.

"Your CO wrote in your file, and I quote, 'Corporal Contardo is absolutely fearless, a superb hand-to-hand fighter, but apparently incapable of taking and following orders.' "

Contardo's complexion turned a deeper shade of red, and his fists tightened. "Can I speak frankly, sir?"

"Yeah. Get on with it."

"When I joined the marines, I wanted to fight. You know what I mean, *fight?* Instead I find myself marching through the jungle, up to my ass in mud." He turned to Margot, and said, "Begging your pardon, ma'am."

"She knows what an ass is," McLeane said sharply. Margot did not look up from her paperwork.

"So we come to these machine-gun nests and get hung up. The sergeants and officers go into a goddamned huddle for an hour. A fuckin' *hour!*" Again he turned to Margo and apologized for his language.

McLeane said, "They lady has heard the word before, Corporal. Please go on." This time, Margot smiled.

"And I gets me to thinking, what the fuck are we wasting all our time on, sitting in the fuckin' jungle up to our asses in mud? So I just kinda snuck off and took care of the machine-gun nests myself. These big shots think it's such a big deal. To me, it was like taking out a couple of candy stores in Bensonhurst."

"I see. How did you do it?"

Contardo looked embarrassed with pride. "Aw, I kinda just snuck around behind 'em and dropped a few grenades into their ventilation ducts. The yellow bastards were so sure of themselves they never bothered to protect their air-supply system."

"That must have put your sergeants and officers on Alka-Seltzer, right?"

"Yeah," Contardo said proudly. "They were really pissed off at me but couldn't show it because I had taken care of their problem for them."

McLeane thought a minute. "What *did* you have in mind when you joined the marines?"

"To fight, sir, like I said."

"What kind of fighting?"

"The kind I did when I took out those machine-gun nests. But I don't wanna have to take any guff for having done it."

"Corporal, do you know why you're here?"

"Well, I, unh . . . knowing your reputation, sir. . . ."

". . . and knowing I saw you beat the shit out of that sergeant at the Zoo . . ."

"I just can't take hearing the Bums knocked."

Margot looked up. "The Bums?" she asked.

"The Brooklyn Dodgers," McLeane translated.

"Well, maybe I'm gettin' kinda outta line, but when you called me in here I thought maybe you had me in mind for your unit."

"What do you know about it?"

"Scuttlebutt has it you're puttin' together a four- or five-man elite reconnaissance and sabotage unit to sneak behind enemy lines and raise hell."

"That's about the size of it and, yes, I had you in mind."

"Thank you, sir." Contardo beamed.

"You know what I'm looking for—an all-around backup man with a taste for adventure."

"I'm your man, sir."

"So you say. But you have to pass a test."

"Name it."

"You've got to put me on my ass. You'll have three to five minutes to do it."

"Sir? Are you asking me to take on a major?"

"You're a smart boy, Contardo."

"That's a breach of regulations, sir."

"I don't recall your being too worried about regulations in the past."

"But taking on a major . . ."

"You have two choices, Contardo. You can spend the rest of the war up to your ass in swamp, or you can sign on with me."

Contardo looked both frightened and thrilled. McLeane sensed he had long wanted the chance to beat up an officer. "You're the boss."

"Outside," McLeane said. "We don't want to mess up this place the general gave me."

"Are you sure this is the right thing to do?" Margo asked.

"Absolutely. I need a backup man I can rely on, and there's only one way to be sure."

"But what will General Thompson say?"

McLeane thought for a moment. "He'll probably give you three-to-one odds on me."

The scraggly lawn that separated the Administration Building from the road that paralleled Henderson Field seemed like a good enough spot for a test. Both McLeane and Contardo stripped to the waist.

Contardo said, "Are you sure you . . . ?"

His speech was cut off when McLeane tossed a mammoth left hand, catching the lance corporal on the jaw and sending him to the ground. That answered the question. Contardo came off the ground with a scissors takedown, a karate move that caught McLeane's legs between Contardo's at knee level and threw him onto his back. McLeane knew the move, and blocked its normal follow-up, a chop to the throat, by rolling toward Contardo and planting a solid right on the side of his head.

While Contardo was still stunned, McLeane jumped to his feet. Back up in the Administration Building, a crowd of onlookers was gathering in the windows. Two secretaries were watching from the file-room window when Major Flagg saw them. "Are you admiring the sunshine or are you working?" he snapped.

"There's a fight going on outside, sir," one said.

Flagg went to the window and a broad grin crossed his face. "I've got him now," he whispered, and he dashed out the door. Margot, who had been watching the fight from her window, saw Flagg go by and followed him quickly into the general's office.

The general looked up from a chart of Bougainville. "Yes, Major?"

"Sir. Major McLeane is having a fight with a noncom."

Thompson looked back down at his chart and drew a circle around a spot to the south of the island. "Who's winning?" he asked.

"Sir?" Flagg asked, astonished.

"It was a simple question requiring a simple answer. Damn it, Flagg, you're the one who's always bragging about how you always get your facts straight!"

Margot slipped into the room and saluted the general, who acknowledged it with a nod.

Flagg said, "I . . . I don't know who's winning. But it's going on right outside the window."

"Why didn't you say so right off?" Thompson snapped, slamming down his pencil and going to the window. Margot joined him.

"Having a little training session, is he?" Thompson asked.

"He's trying out a new man, sir," Margot replied.

"Five-to-one on McLeane."

Margot searched her pockets and came up with a dollar bill. Thompson produced a fiver and handed the stakes to a stunned Major Flagg. "Hold the stakes, Major."

Thompson clucked his tongue. "Betting against your boss. That's shameful, Private. He'll never forgive you."

"I don't know about that, sir. He thought you'd only give me three-to-one."

Thompson smiled and lit his meerschaum. "Come on, let's go down there."

Outside on the scraggly lawn, McLeane tossed a left jab which grazed Contardo's jaw and a massive right which the smaller, more agile man ducked entirely.

"If Mack lands that right, his boy is gonna be lights-out for a week," Thompson told Margot.

McLeane tossed another combination, both blows of which Contardo ducked under, ramming a fist into McLeane's gut. McLeane grunted, but was not staggered. "You're running out of time, Contardo," McLeane said.

Contardo tried a tiger-tail kick, where he did a complete feet-over-hands and tried to nail McLeane in the head with an outlashed foot. McLeane hadn't seen that one before, but was so much taller than the corporal that the latter's blow landed on Mack's chest. McLeane stood his ground. Contardo leaped up and tried a simple round kick. It was then that McLeane stepped inside the blow and delivered his crusher. With Contardo on one foot and unable to get away, McLeane hit him with a left to the gut and a sharp right jab to the chin. Contardo seemed to hang in midair for a moment, then slumped to the ground, flat on his back, not moving.

McLeane walked to the general and Margot. She said, "I guess he flunked out."

McLeane spoke instead to the general. "Five bucks says it comes from the left side."

"You're on," Thompson replied.

"What are you guys talking about?" Margot asked.

"Just shut up," McLeane said.

Suddenly, Contardo leaped into the air and hit McLeane with a karate chop to the right side of his neck. McLeane slumped to the ground, unconscious.

"Mack!" Margot exclaimed.

Contardo was out of breath and barely able to keep his feet, but he managed to salute the general. "I'm sorry, sir, I . . . it was his idea. I really didn't want to fight the major, but . . ."

"Yeah, yeah," Thompson said, ordering Flagg to pay

Margot the six dollars she had won.

Contardo said, "I didn't hit him hard enough to hurt him, sir. He'll be jake in a few minutes."

"I know that. Look, Corporal, do you seriously think you're the first one to take this test? You passed, but just barely."

"Just barely?"

"He let you hit him. He deliberately turned his back on you."

"Why?" Contardo was astonished.

"He had to know if you had the killer instinct. A Jap soldier wouldn't have let you lie there without knowing you were dead. He would have stuck a bayonet in you before turning his back."

McLeane was coming around, and Contardo helped him to his feet. McLeane rubbed his neck. "Right side, right?"

"Right," Thompson said.

With a frown, McLeane handed over a five-dollar bill.

"How'd you make out on the betting?" he asked Margot.

"He gave me five-to-one. I'm up five bucks."

"So you're buying the beer. Contardo, you in the mood for a brew?"

"Yes, *sir,*" the corporal said, still out of breath.

"Then let's go to the Zoo. General . . . you care to join us?"

"No. I have things to do. And I broke even on the day, so I'm happy."

Thompson and Flagg went back into the building. Both McLeane and Contardo picked up their shirts and caps and, with Margot beside them, headed off in the direction of the Zoo.

McLeane draped his weary arms around both their shoulders. "Welcome to McLeane's Rangers, Contardo."

Seven

The dock wasn't up, but the Seabees had cut away enough of the palm forest to put up the tents, which stood in a row along the bank of Tango Lagoon. Corrigan's Catalina was tied up just offshore, but there was no sign of life aboard. McLeane called Corrigan's name a few times, to no effect. By the time Margot, Contardo, and he got back to the lagoon, it was after dark and all three were drunk.

Margot's tent was labeled with a marine stencil indicating it was #1. McLeane's was #2 and Contardo's, #3. Two others were erected and numbered, but as yet unmanned. Contardo, a good fighter but a sloppy drunk, was helped to his bunk and was snoring happily within minutes.

McLeane inspected his tent. It was laid out to his specifications, and lit by an oil lamp that gave off a soft orange glow. There was a double bunk on one side of the tent. McLeane always remembered General Thompson's advice that "having a bed that has room for only one person is a sure sign of pessimism." On the other side of McLeane's tent were a desk, a chart table, and the beginnings of the unit's radio equipment: a receiver, which Mack quickly tuned so it got jazz. He flopped on the bunk and pulled off his shoes, Margot, staggering a little, sat beside him. "Tough day, sailor?"

He replied: "War is hell."

She helped him pull off his socks.

"Nice HQ you have here, Major."

"Yeah. All the comforts of home. Does this remind you of dorm living or what?"

"It reminds me of dorm living."

He lay back on his elbows. She said, "That took some courage for you to let Contardo hit you."

"Not really. I knew it was coming. And I also knew that when you want to get into a unit, you don't start by killing its CO."

"Still, Mack ..."

"O.K., I knew it would hurt. But I knew the worst that would happen is that it would cost me five bucks and a bruise on my shoulder. I also knew it would give me the ideal backup man. He's over there, happily sleeping off his drunk, probably feeling as proud as a pig in shit."

"And how do you feel?" she asked.

"Tired ... very tired."

"Relax. Take off your shirt and lie down."

McLeane took off his shirt. "Where'd you get that scar on your right shoulder?" she asked.

"It's a long story," he replied.

"And the one on your right chest?"

"An even longer story."

"You've got lots of interesting things, don't you?"

"Some more interesting than others," he said, perking up.

"I can just imagine," she replied, her retort just as saucy as his remark.

"Where's Corrigan? He can't be asleep. It's a national law in Australia that you can't be in bed before four in the morning."

"No fooling?" she asked, ingenuously.

"Federal law," he said, getting up and shedding clothes as he headed toward the tent flap.

65

"Mack ..."

He called out, "Corrigan, you Aussie son of a bitch," where the hell are you?"

She said plaintively, "Mack."

There was no use in her arguing. McLeane stripped naked and dived into the lagoon, swimming underwater until he surfaced near the fuselage of the Catalina.

He pulled himself up waist-high near the aft starboard blister canopy, which abruptly slid open to reveal Corrigan's bleary-eyed, unshaven face. At the same time, there came the splash of another body into the lagoon.

"Corrigan!" McLeane said happily, recognizing his pilot.

"I've been asleep for two hours, McLeane. What do you want?"

"I just wanted to see how the hell you are."

"Tired. Bloody tired."

Margot, having shed her clothes and swum to join McLeane, said, "Hi, Corrigan."

"Who's this, then?"

"The unit's new aide-de-camp, PFC Margot Thomas."

"Welcome," he said, without enthusiasm. "Nice to meet you, Redbird."

She asked, "Redbird?"

"That will require some explanation. Hey, Corrigan, I shanghaied the new man, Contardo. He's passed out in the tent to the south of mine."

"Bloody greaseballs can't take their liquor," Corrigan said, and slammed the canopy shut.

Margot turned to embrace McLeane. "Not very friendly, is he?"

"He's an Aussie. Who knows what they're gonna do from one minute to the next?"

"*I* know what *I'm* gonna do."

"And what might that be?" he asked, although he knew.

66

"I'm going to . . ." She was at a loss for words, and instead wrapped her hands around McLeane's neck and pulled him to her. He felt the softness of her nudity against the roughness of his skin.

McLeane grasped her, running his hands down her body to grasp her ass and pull her against him. Of course, in letting go of the Catalina they both sank beneath the surface of the water. They surfaced, out of breath. "I know what you're gonna do—drown me," McLeane said.

She laughed, and they swam to shore. McLeane was on the bank first, and he helped her up. They embraced again, and he felt himself swelling against the moistness of her pubic hair. Their tongues parried until both were out of breath once again.

"Is it . . . is it against Marine Corps regulations to fuck one's commanding officer?"

"Every one in the book. Flagg would have you flogged."

"I'll take my chances."

McLeane swept her up in his arms and carried her into his tent.

He tossed her onto the bunk and paused just long enough to zip up the flap of the tent. Hanging prominently on it was the *do not disturb* sign filched from a hotel in Sydney. She was laid out beautifully on the bunk, bathed in the soft orange glow from the kerosene lamp. McLeane slid alongside her, and at once they were locked together.

Margot had the most perfect features he had ever seen on a woman; or was it just that he hadn't been with a woman in so long? He preferred the former. She had large, round breasts with plum-colored nipples, a soft, round stomach, and a fine arch to her hips. McLeane slipped a hand between two of the most beautiful legs he had seen in a long time. He sought her out, and she opened her legs to admit him.

He probed her with a finger until she pushed his hand away. "Wait," she said breathlessly. She pushed him onto his back and slid down his body, kissing his chest and stomach. Then she cradled his balls in her hand, kissed the tip of his cock, and slid her lips over it, taking it halfway into her mouth. He gasped and ran his fingers through her hair. She sucked him for a minute or two until he swelled and her jaw ached. He lifted her head from him.

"You're too much for me," she gasped.

"Let's see." He pushed her back onto her back and rolled onto her. Margot reached down with both her hands to guide him, then cried out as he drove into her.

McLeane awoke in a haze, the sound of a man's voice calling to him. It was dawn, and Corrigan was outside his tent.

"Hey, McLeane?"

"Yeah, whaddya want?"

"You and your Sheila left your laundry on the riverbank. Would you have the MPs find it? They come by every now and again, you know?"

"Hang it on a tree."

"Shove it up your ass."

"Then tuck it under the tent flap. That won't be too much trouble for you, will it?"

There was some grumbling and cursing, but several handfuls of clothing made their way beneath McLeane's tent flap.

Margot yawned and rolled against McLeane, one of her breasts resting on his chest. "What's a 'Sheila'?"

"Aussie slang for 'girl'."

"Charming man, this Corrigan."

"You'll learn to like him in time."

Margot reached for McLeane's cock, but he caught

her hand. "Hold on. I'm still sore from last night."

"Me too. I just thought I would make it feel better. She reached down and took it into her mouth for a moment, warming it with her tongue, then released him. "Feel better?" she asked.

"A whole lot. You know, I could grow fond of you, Redbird."

"Redbird! What's this Redbird stuff?"

"Corrigan gave you the name. You came into the Zoo one night with two friends. Red-haired bird, you know."

"And 'bird' . . ."

"Is another Aussie term for girl. Also British."

"I don't have red hair. It's auburn."

"So he's color blind," McLeane said.

She yawned again and asked what time it was. McLeane turned so he could see the clock. "Seven o'clock."

"I have got to get to my tent, if I can remember where it is, and throw together some clothes. We have a full working day ahead of us, remember?"

She slipped out of the bunk, knelt, and examined the pile of wet clothing that Corrigan had shoved under the tent flap.

Margot frowned. "This will never do. Do you think I can make a run for my tent starkers?"

"What?"

"British term for 'naked,' " she said with a smile.

"No. Put on one of my uniform shirts—the dry ones over in the chest. Then make a run for it."

"See you in the office, Major."

Margot put on one of McLeane's uniform shirts, which hung nearly to her knees, and sneaked out of his tent. She hadn't gotten but half a dozen feet before the launch crews, on the opposite side of the lagoon, alerted by Corrigan, let loose a chorus of applause.

McLeane's office was piled high with file folders. They were everywhere: on the desks, the filing cabinets, and the floor. Those on the floor were arranged by category, with paths left between them so Margot and McLeane could get in and out of the room without too much trouble.

McLeane perused a file on a marksman from New England while Margot finished sorting things out. At last she was done.

"How's our Yankee rifleman look?" she asked.

"No good," McLeane said, closing the file.

"Why?"

"He's had range practice only, for the most part. Only been in combat twice. I want someone who learned his art in the woods or in combat."

"Well, that makes one hundred-seventeen you've turned down. Care to try an easy one? The expert in Oriental languages."

"I thought he'd be the hard one to find."

"Not so. There's only one of him. And you're gonna love this one, baby."

McLeane asked for the file and it was dutifully given him. "Eric Heinman ... Jesus, a goddamned Kraut."

"His father was a professor of literature in Wurzburg before the war. Fled the Nazis with his family in 1934. Is Heinman a Jew?"

"Nope."

"Good. It means their decision to run was a matter of principle. Let's see, Heinman got his A.B. and Ph.D. at Oxford. Can't ask for much better than that. Doctorate in Oriental languages, 1939. Postdoctoral fellow, Columbia ... well, well ... from 1939 to 1941 when he enlisted in the marines. My God! Perfectly fluent in Japanese and can get by in at least eight Melanesian dialects."

"The Solomon Islanders are almost all Melanesian," Margot said, unnecessarily. "He was posted to the Pacific Theater ..."

"... Because he's a Kraut. Yeah, the same old story. There are guys I know from back home who had their shortwave radio receivers confiscated by the FBI after Pearl Harbor. The Feds were afraid they were receiving sabotage instructions from der Fatherland. Yeah, nearly every American soldier or sailor stuck with a German surname is fighting in the Pacific. What's this guy's record? I can't read his old CO's writing."

Margot looked over McLeane's shoulder. "He's a first lieutenant. Hobbies are reading and naturalism."

"A butterfly collector." McLeane sighed.

"The only other item I might point out is that his old CO typified him as "an insufferable son of a bitch and a know-it-all.""

"*That* he got at Oxford," McLeane said assuredly.

"He also has a British accent."

"How do you know that?"

"He's been waiting out in the hall for half an hour. He knows you'll have to see him eventually."

"Well," McLeane said with a shrug, "Send the insufferable son of a bitch in."

Eight

Heinman was thin and sported a pencil-thin mustache and black hair that was parted in the middle and slicked back. He stood at attention until McLeane told him to stand at ease.

"Lieutenant Heinman reporting as ordered, sir."

McLeane stared at the man's file in silence, giving Heinman the same treatment he had given Contardo. Only, while Contardo sweated, Heinman kept his cool for the first two minutes before getting annoyed.

"Are you having trouble with your hearing, sir? This beastly tropical air can do that to you."

"I beg your pardon." McLeane didn't look up.

"I said, 'Lieutenant Heinman reporting as ordered . . . sir!'"

McLeane slowly closed the file, set it on the desk, and looked up at Heinman. "You really think you're something, don't you?"

Heinman let out an exasperated sigh, as if to say he had been confronted with another superior officer who was, in fact, beneath his dignity. McLeane saw the gesture and didn't like it. "Heinman . . . who owns New York?"

"What?" the man replied, astonished.

"I said, and quite clearly, 'Who owns New York?'"

"Major McLeane, I . . ."

"Damn it, *who owns New York?*"

McLeane got to his feet, towering over the diminutive German.

"I don't know what you mean, sir."

"You know damned well what I mean, and you have ten seconds to tell me."

"Sir ..."

"Nine."

"I really don't think ..."

"Eight."

"Heinman gave in. "*We* own New York," he said.

"And who is 'we'?"

Heinman's eyes were downcast as he spelled out C-O-L-U-M-B-I-A.

"Sing it," McLeane ordered.

"Really, Major. I was a postdoctoral fellow, not an undergraduate in a raccoon coat."

"Sing it!"

Margot went running from the room fighting back tears of laughter as Eric Heinman stumbled his way through a chorus of Columbia's football fight song.

Heinman was humiliated, but at least he knew who was boss. When he was done, McLeane said, "Very good, Heinman. Have a seat."

Margot reentered the room, wiping her eyes. "Was it really necessary to humiliate me, Major?"

"Yes, it was. Your last CO called you 'insufferable.' I intend to make you less so. In the meantime, tell me how good you are with the dialects of southern Bougainville."

Heinman was visibly glad to be back on more comfortable ground. "Well, they're all slightly different, but in the South, a mix of Fijian and Polynesian. The vowel *i* is pronounced always like the *i* in well, 'marine.' The letter *e* is pronounced as our *a* in 'shake.' Some examples: the sea is *keno;* sand is *mesalo-lanum;* a

73

mountain is *olo,* and reef is *aru-oshe.*"

"O.K., I'm impressed."

"I'm most familiar with the natives of the Siwai, Baitsi, and Lokutu districts."

"Perfect. It says in your file that you're a naturalist."

"Correct."

"Does your knowledge extend to the flora and fauna of Bougainville?"

"It most certainly does. Of course, there is a bewildering array of plants, and the natives have six names for each of them. But I daresay I can tell you what plant's useful for what."

McLeane tossed his hands up. "You're my man."

Heinman beamed with pride. For all his stuffiness, he really did want to be one of the boys. "What will we be doing, sir?"

McLeane told him.

Heinman thought in silence for a while. "If this *Australian* knows the territory as well as he claims, and if the *Italian* gentleman and you are as tough as your reputations, and considering my knowledge of native languages, customs, and flora, and fauna, I think we might just be able to do it."

"Welcome to McLeane's Rangers, Heinman. Margot will show you to your tent. I want you there as soon as possible. We're an elite unit, and I want us kept apart from the regular fighting men."

"Yes, sir. Thank you, sir." Heinman headed for the door, but was called back.

"You seem to have some strong opinions on the strengths and weaknesses of the world's ethnic groups. Where would you look for a demolitions man."

"A bomb maker? Well, bombs as a means of assassination have traditionally been the province of east central Europeans ..."

"... But as they're rather occupied at the moment ..."

"I would look for an Irishman. Preferably a veteran of the Easter Uprising."

"Uh-huh. Thanks, Heinman."

When they were gone, McLeane poured himself another cup of coffee, adjusted his crotch where it was still sore from the night before, and muttered, "An Irish demolitions man. That must narrow the list down to nine thousand at least."

Two days and not quite nine thousand files later, Patrick J. O'Connor stood before McLeane's desk, getting the same silent treatment as the others. Unlike Contardo and Heinman, he didn't seem to mind. He was about five-ten, with a freckled red face, bulging biceps that nearly matched his beer belly in size, and a benign smile on his face.

After McLeane learned that this guy wasn't responding to the silent treatment, he shut O'Connor's folder and put it on the desk. "Have a seat."

O'Connor did.

"Let me summarize your career. You're twenty-eight. Been in the army two years. Before that you were a bartender in Chicago. How does that make you a demolitions expert? I thought demo men had to have steady hands."

"Did you ever have to mix a stinger for Al Capone?"

"I get your point," McLeane said. "So you have steady hands."

"And the big brains in the army tell me I have a natural talent for blowing things up. They taught me to make bombs out of practically nothing."

"And then stuck you in the Seabees ..."

"Where I had the fine and grand opportunity to destroy what the Japs had built, pausing now and again to rid the world of a mountain so's we could build an airstrip."

"I take it you'd like to do something more interesting."

"My exact thought, Major."

"Your record says you're only a fair pistol shot."

"That's not what I'm best at. Let's say that I can manage to hit the narrow side of a barn. But you show me something you want sent to its reward, give me the equipment to do it, and it's as good as done."

"You want in, Private?"

"Yes, sir ... assuming the army will let you have me."

"I think that can be arranged. Let me tell you what this unit's all about."

When he was done, McLeane once again asked if O'Connor was interested. O'Connor said, "Let me put it this way, Major. If Betty Grable were to walk into this room right now and make an indecent proposal, what would you do?"

After a quick glance that told him Margot had no apparent opinion of that possibility, McLeane said, "Welcome to the club, O'Connor. Margot will take care of the paperwork. I expect you to show up tomorrow morning at Tango Lagoon. You'll have a tent mate. Do you have preference between a Kraut with an English accent, an Italian from Brooklyn, or —"

"Jesus, Mary, and Joseph," O'Connor said.

"We'll work it out some other time," McLeane said quickly.

McLeane had gone through the entire stack of sharpshooters considered desirable for his purpose by the powers-that-be. There were a few possibilities, and he interviewed half-dozen of them. Still he was dissatisfied. He stood, stretched, and announced he was going for a walk in the woods.

"What woods?" Margot asked, while cleaning up the

latest pile of rejected files.

"Any woods."

"Do you want company?"

"Not this time, if you don't mind. I don't want to hurt your feelings, but there are times when walking in the woods has to be done alone."

"Well, it's not as if I don't have things to do here," she said, looking askance at the piles of papers."

"I'll be back at the base by dinnertime."

"I'll be waiting."

McLeane commandeered one of the staff jeeps and drove east down the main road leading away from Henderson Field, past Fighter Strip One and Tenaru Beach, toward the "safe" perimeter along the Balamora River. He parked the jeep with the sentries, assuring them he would be doing nothing more dangerous than sitting against a tree, smoking cigarettes, and drinking the beer he had picked up at the Zoo on the way. Then he walked across the rickety wooden bridge over the river that separated the Allied military area on north central Guadalcanal from the coastline native villages and inland forests and fields of the eastern part of the island.

McLeane walked around a swamp lining the east bank of the Balamora, then made his way through a small mangrove forest laced with native trails. Knee-high in wild grass, he crossed a wide field and climbed a hillock atop which sat a dozen lontar palms. From his hilltop vantage point, McLeane could see all the way to Tasimboko Bay. Two native outriggers were crossing it, heading east, looking for fish. McLeane sat down with his back against a palm, lit a Lucky Strike, popped open a bottle of beer, and leaned back to meditate.

There was no wind, and relatively little bird noise. McLeane drank two bottles of beer, smoked three cigarettes, and took a leak at the base of another palm.

Then he sat back down in his original spot and had nearly fallen asleep when he was awakened by a queer feeling. It was a feeling he had had many times when something was about to happen. The birds, which had been fairly quiet before, had stopped singing entirely. Sitting stock-still, McLeane watched as a lone man, dressed in army camouflage gear, stalked a herd of wild boar across the field below. The boar must have been barely visible to the man, who was himself short and stocky, built like a barrel, and carrying an M1.

McLeane could see the herd clearly. There were two mature males, each bearing razor-sharp tusks, and a dozen females and juveniles. The adult males were big animals, and dangerous, and almost as McLeane had that thought the wind picked up ever so faintly. The boars picked up the scent of the man stalking them. Boars were dangerous critters, especially when protecting their herd. They turned on him, fanning out to his right and left. McLeane wondered if the short, stocky guy could see them in the tall grass. He thought of yelling something, but then realized that the soldier—whoever he was—had gotten himself into a situation with which he must have some familiarity or he wouldn't have gotten into it at all. McLeane opened another beer and leaned back to watch.

The hunter pulled the bolt on his M1. McLeane could hear the sharp click, and so could the boars. They homed in on the sound, moving toward it, slowly at first, then with increasing speed. The soldier appeared unconcerned. He stood straight up, his rifle at his hip, and at the last moment as the beasts charged him, he fired two shots, wheeling left then right, dropping both animals, each with a single bullet squarely between the eyes.

McLeane was astonished, and fumbled for his cigarettes. Silence still reigned over the pastoral setting, the rest of the herd having fled to the cover of the trees.

McLeane lit a match on the sole of his boot.

The sound must have carried, for the hunter whirled toward the hillock, his rifle pointed at McLeane, who froze.

There was a moment of portentous silence, then McLeane called out, "You do that every day, soldier. Is it some kind of hobby or what?"

The hunter's shoulders dropped, as did his rifle. There were still Japanese holdouts on the loose in Guadalcanal, and the hunter seemed relieved to find out that the man watching him was a friend. He was less relieved, though, when McLeane walked down the hill and his major's uniform became apparent. The hunter snapped to attention.

"Take it easy," McLeane said. "At ease."

"Permission to speak freely, sir."

"Granted," McLeane said, noting that the man's eyes seemed transfixed on McLeane's nametag.

"Shoot, Major, I hope this doesn't get me in a big passel of trouble."

"Why should it?"

"Heck, I was just out gettin' a little extra vittles for my unit. Y'see, we just can't live on army food."

"I know what you mean."

"Trouble is, I got one more vittle than I needed. I was stalking one boar. It wasn't until too late that I saw the other one. Shoot, I don't know what the dickens I'm gonna do with the other one."

"I can think of something. Private, you just gunned down two dangerous animals coming at you from opposite directions with two head shots, hitting both squarely between the eyes, firing from the hip. And you did it in under two seconds."

"Well, they was movin' kinda fast, Major, sir. Hell, that ain't really nothin'. My daddy once popped four 'coons outta the same tree with four shots firing from the hip, and I think he did it in less time than I took."

The man had a thick southern accent, and McLeane asked him where he was from.

"Gator Creek, Alabama, sir," the man said proudly.

"Do you have a first name, Private Wilkins?" McLeane had taken pains to examine the hunter's nametag.

"Tommy Joe. Sir, I know it ain't none of my business, but are you *the* Major McLeane?"

"Yeah," McLeane said. The fame business was getting tiresome.

Wilkins pumped McLeane's hand. "Wait till I write m' daddy to tell him I really met you."

"You met me. Look, there's something I'd like to talk about."

"Y'see, m' daddy tore this here picture of you outta *Life* magazine and sent it to me." Wilkins produced an oft folded and unfolded picture of McLeane being pinned with a medal. "When he found out I was posted to Guadalcanal he figured I might run into you, and I sure as the devil have. Would you mind autographing it so's I can send it home? It would make him feel right proud."

McLeane nodded dumbly and signed the photograph.

"Shoot, sir, I can't tell you how happy I am. They're gonna be flappin' their gums about this for years and years, and—"

"Can I get a word in here?"

"Y'see, I learned how to shoot from m' daddy, and —"

"Goddamn it, *shut up!*" McLeane yelled. Off in the distance, a hawkbill yelled back.

"Yes, *sir.*" Wilkins snapped back to attention.

"At ease. Everything but your mouth, that is. Now Wilkins, I just spent the past couple of days ruining my eyesight reading files on guys who are supposed to be the best shots on Guadalcanal. How come I never read a file on you? You just get here?"

"No, sir. I been right here from the beginning. Came in with the first wave."

"Then why the hell don't we have a file on you?"

Wilkins looked down and pawed the ground with a foot. "It's probably because I don't go to the practice range, sir."

"You don't go to the practice range?"

"Hell, no. I mean, I'm not braggin' or nuthin', but I can shoot the balls off a boll weevil at a hundred yards without touching a hair on his ass. Could ever since I was ten. M' daddy—"

"I don't want to hear about your daddy. I want to find the best sharpshooter in this war." McLeane looked around, and found a baseball-sized rock. "I'm gonna throw this in the air. If you can blow it to hell, then I have a proposition for you."

Wilkins shrugged. McLeane threw the rock as far and as high as he could. Wilkins rifle barely seemed to move. He fired again from the hip and the rock flew into a thousand pieces before it was fifty feet away.

"You're hired," McLeane said. "And this is one job they're really gonna be flappin' their gums over back home in Gator Creek."

Nine

There was nothing madder than a Heinman whose opinion had been ignored, McLeane found out.

It was just past sunset, and a fire was roaring between the unit's tents and the edge of the beach. The members of the unit—save Corrigan, who was fiddling with the elevator linkage in his Catalina—were gathered around the fire repairing a metal frame while Heinman paced back and forth, ranting and raving.

"Guppy would be *outraged,*" he said.

"What?" Wilkins asked. Like O'Connor and Margot, he was leaning against a convenient palm, drinking beer.

"He's talking about a fish that's gone daft," O'Connor said.

"Oh."

Heinman overheard. "I am *not* talking about a fish. I am talking about H. B. Guppy, a surgeon in Her Majesty's Navy and an amateur geologist who explored these islands in the latter part of the nineteenth century. He described in perfect detail how a wild boar is to be cooked, and what you gentleman are preparing to do has no bearing on what he described."

McLeane and Contardo had built a fine log fire in a pit dug in the sand and were busy fixing the spit over it. The spit was jury-rigged from the skeleton of a Japanese radio antenna bombed to bits before the invasion of

Guadalcanal. There were uprights hammered deep into the sand and wired to horizontal struts that extended over the flames to form the rack upon which the boar had been cooking for nearly a full day.

"What did he describe, Heinman?" McLeane asked, wiring the last horizontal in place.

"Henry Brougham Guppy—there is an island and a snake named after him, by the way—was very specific on the matter of cooking boar. After skinning and gutting, the animal was quartered then placed directly on a fire made of a pile of logs built up three feet high. A tripod of poles was erected over this to help in pulling the flames up over the carcass. *This* is how you're supposed to cook a boar—not with a contraption that I suppose is meant to resemble a grill."

"I don't like ashes in my boar, Heinman," McLeane said.

"I think if you're going to bother to kill and butcher a native animal, you ought to have the common decency to cook it in the native manner."

"Where'd you get this guy, Major?" Contardo asked. "Some kinda library or something?"

"No, I just sorta found him wandering around the base, being insufferable."

"What's insufferable mean?" Wilkins asked.

"Thick-skinned, lad. It means he can feel no pain. Like Superman, you might say." O'Connor winked at Margot, who smiled.

"I am *not* being insufferable. I am merely trying to educate my colleagues in the *rudiments* of life in the Solomons."

His repair work on the grill finished, Contardo wiped his hands on his pants and walked slowly toward Heinman. "How's a Kraut wind up with an English accent."

Heinman sighed. "That's an *Oxford* accent, and kraut

83

is fermented cabbage that has been spiced with caraway and juniper berries."

"I bet you know just about everything, don'tcha?"

"Is there a point to that question, Corporal?"

"Yeah, how'd you like a little Flatbush education?" Contardo said, moving on Heinman and abruptly lashing out with a right cross. With an agility matching Contardo's own, Heinman side-stepped the assault and tossed Contardo to the ground with a simple foot-throw.

Contardo was surprised, but quickly regained his footing and got ready to fight.

"Knock if off, the both of you," McLeane snarled. "We came here to fight Japs. You can fight each other when we're finished. Heinman?"

"Yes, sir?"

"That move wasn't in your file. Nowhere did it say anything about your knowing judo."

"Nobody asked me, sir."

"Unsurprising," McLeane said, shaking his head.

"Besides, it was a simple *oguruma* foot takedown I picked up last year in Burma."

"How good are you at judo?"

"I'm no expert, in all honesty, sir. But in a pinch I think I can hold my own."

"Thank you, Heinman, for admitting to being less than perfect. That was a nice takedown. Now let's get this show on the road before the general gets here."

"The general?" Contardo asked. "He's coming here?"

"In about an hour. So let's haul it."

"What's he coming here for?"

"I asked him. Besides, he likes pork."

The prepared boar was roasting away, sending clouds of cooking smoke into the night air.

"It smells delicious," Margot mused.

"Yeah, and it's gonna attract half the guys on Guadalcanal."

"So what? We can't eat it all ourselves anyway."

"Just as long as there's enough for the general and us," McLeane said.

"Is the sauce ready?"

"As ready as it'll ever be."

She stood, picked up a five-gallon tin pot half-filled with a syrupy liquid, and carried it to the edge of the fire. McLeane helped her shove it close enough to be heated by the flames.

"What's in this anyway?" he asked.

"Basically, a lot of butter. I tried to find a gourmet spice shop, Mack, but ran out of luck."

Heinman said, "You might try tossing in some brown sugar, capers, and lemon. In Burma, we used to—"

"We're not in Burma," McLeane interrupted.

"But I might be able to dig up some brown sugar and lemons," Margot said. "Capers I doubt they keep at the PX."

McLeane said, "You have an hour."

Margot went trotting off toward Henderson.

"I know of a very interesting plant the natives call *kuraka*. Its leaves are used to make a savory broth. I just might be able to find some," Heinman said.

"Go."

He headed off down the beach, inspecting the ground shrubbery with a flashlight.

Both Magot and Heinman were back within half an hour with their hands full. She had found half a pound of brown sugar and eight lemons. The sugar and chopped lemons were stirred into the sauce, along with two handfuls of *kuraka* leaves that Heinman had managed to gather in the shrubbery living amongst the beachside palms.

The boar had taken almost twenty-four hours to cook, including one flip-over that involved the use of two pitchforks. By the time General Thompson arrived with two jeeps filled with hungry aides-de-camp, the members of McLeane's Rangers were seated against the palms, their bellies full of roast pork, bread, and beer. Still, they managed to jump to attention.

Thompson waved them to fall out, and they very nearly did, collapsing back against their trees.

"A first-class fighting force, General," McLeane said with a smile.

"I can see them. Presumably a bit more lively when they're not stuffed."

"You have my assurance."

"I'll meet them now. Let them stay on their duffs, Mack. They've got some hard work ahead of them, and I won't ask them to get up twice in a minute and a half."

McLeane escorted Thompson down the line, introducing all but Margot and Contardo, both of whose talents he had seen at close range.

When they were done, Thompson said, "They look fine to me, and your reports on all of them read just right. I don't know how you're managing to get along with this guy Heinman. No other CO has lasted a week with him."

"Simple. I try not to pay attention. Besides, he can be surprisingly useful. Try the sauce. He found some native leaves that make it taste like something out of the Ritz."

"It's about time you got around to asking. I didn't come here just for conversation, you know."

Using his bayonet, McLeane hacked off a chunk of meat and slapped it atop a piece of bread lying on one of the ubiquitous metal dishes found in the armed forces. Thompson poured on his own sauce, and ate as he walked McLeane away from the rest of the men. In a minute they stood by the surf's edge.

"This is sensational. I take back everything I said about Heinman. Mack, did that cracker really nail those two porkers the way you said he did?"

"Every word was gospel."

"I have to see him in action someday. Look, I brought you away from the rest for a reason. I just got back from that meeting with the big shots I told you about, and we have to move faster than planned."

"Has an invasion date been set?" McLeane asked.

"Yes. November 1 at 0700 hours."

McLeane whistled through his teeth. "That's eight days off!"

"Right, and it means you and your boys won't have time for practice maneuvers. Tomorrow I want you to come up with a practical plan of attack and have it on my desk by three P.M. You'll brief your men in the evening, and take off early enough the following morning to have reached your target lagoon on Bougainville by dawn."

"I was hoping for a few practice sessions up in the hills right here."

"Sorry. MacArthur wants those landing strips on Bougainville as soon as possible so he can use them to neutralize Rabaul. We're not going to try to take Rabaul as originally planned. We're going to by-pass it, but we're gonna use those strips on Bougainville—and the one on Vella la Vella—to bomb the shit out of it first. So you have to be on Bougainville by the day after tomorrow. If we've got a D-Day of 1 November for Bougainville, I want that munitions bunker knocked out at least three days ahead of time. No more, no less. I don't want the Japs to have those munitions to bring up to reinforce their garrison at Cape Torokina."

"O.K." McLeane sighed. "You got it."

"And another thing. Nobody knows what I just told you until they're on the plane and in the air."

"Corrigan has to know. He'll be picking the lagoon we're going to land in."

"O.K., but he stays in that plane until you take off."

"And hopefully for a little while longer."

Thompson smiled.

"He spends all his time there anyway," McLeane said.

"You can do your planning in the plane. But I want you in my office tomorrow at three."

"And my radio equipment?"

"It will be installed in your tent, as requested, by noon tomorrow. We'll run a patch up to the big antenna at Henderson. It won't be too much trouble."

McLeane picked up a smooth shell and skimmed it across the surface of the Pacific unil it disappeared into the darkness.

"Behind enemy lines a week before the invasion with no tune-up," he mused.

"This time you have strength behind you. You have a unit."

"I just hope I don't get them all killed."

Thompson elbowed McLeane in mock anger. "Knock off the maudlin bullshit, will you? And get me another helping." He handed McLeane his plate.

"Get it yourself," McLeane grumbled, handing it back.

Thompson smiled. "Now, that's the kind of attitude I want to see."

The light in McLeane's tent burned with a special softness, as if it had been veiled.

The wick was turned down until it barely left enough cotton exposed to burn. Margot was in bed with the covers pulled up to her neck. McLeane zipped up the front flap and tossed off his shirt. Off toward the beach the party raged on, and, in fact, several dozen Guadalcanal denizens showed up, uninvited but welcome, to partake of the leftover pork.

McLeane had only to awake in reasonable shape the following morning. He'd had five bottles of beer, which to a man of his dimensions was like using mouthwash with a little bit of ethyl alcohol in it then spitting it out. He felt as wild as the boar he had just cooked and eaten and four times as horny.

He sat on the edge of the bunk. "It sounds like the party will go on all night," Margot said.

"It will," he replied, removing his boots and socks, "but the *real* party will be in here."

Margot blushed, which McLeane found endearing.

"How did you get to be such great pals with General Thompson? I mean, there aren't that many majors who can call a general by his first name."

"We go back a few years." McLeane leaned back across the bunk and rested his head on her belly.

"Take it easy," she complained. "There's a lot of pork in there."

"There's gonna be a lot more before the night's over."

She gave him a playful slap on the head. "That's not nice to say," she said. "But it's a wonderful thought."

McLeane took off the rest of his clothes and bounced them off the tent wall.

"If we wind up married, am I gonna have to pick up after you?" she asked.

"How did we get to marriage?" he asked.

She replied, "How come you and General Thompson are such great pals?"

"I pulled his brass ass out of a burning jeep at Pearl. A Jap bomb went off about fifty feet away and blew the goddamned thing upside down. Driver was killed outright. Never knew what hit him. I happened to be running down the side of a hangar looking for a place to hide *my* ass when it happened. Anyway, I pulled Archie out of the jeep unconscious and got him to a safe spot. He was grateful."

"I should think it only appropriate."

McLeane laughed. "He sent me a gift."

"Flowers or champagne?"

"Flowers. In a manner of speaking." McLeane laughed again.

"What's funny?" Margot asked.

"The gift. Her name was Lotus Blossom. Her professional name, of course."

Margot sighed. "He sent you a hooker."

"She would be offended by the term, but . . ."

"She was a hooker."

"Yep. Does that upset you?"

"Mack, if I was easily upset, I would stay a good ten miles away from you and your entire unit."

"She was more like a geisha. Japanese girl. I think she's been interred in California along with her family."

"War is hell," Margot said, staring at the ceiling.

McLeane turned toward her and suddenly yanked the covers entirely off. Margot sucked in her breath in anticipation. He touched her thighs, and they parted. He knelt between them. She reached down to pull him into her, but he had other ideas. He said: "Lady, what I am going to do to you is illegal in all forty-eight states." And he sank his face into the warm, moist hair between her legs.

Ten

The first rays of dawn filtered through the seams of McLeane's tent, awakening them. Margot was lying with her head nestled on his arm, her luxuriant hair spread across his chest. He played with it idly. Somewhere nearby, a male crocodile was making a racket, bellowing to herald the new day.

"What's that?" she asked, yawning.

"A crocodile."

"Those things can come on land, can't they? And eat their way through tents?"

"He'd never make it. I have a secure system."

"What? Anticroc nets spread across the entrance to the lagoon?"

"No. Corrigan. If the croc is in the lagoon, he'll have awakened Corrigan. One rule of living in the South Pacific is never to piss off an Aussie."

Almost immediately, they heard a burst of fire from one of the 20-mm Brownings mounted in the stern blister canopy of the Catalina.

"What did I tell you? I wonder how you cook a crocodile."

There was a chorus of obscene protest from other members of the abruptly awakened unit.

"You don't have to eat *everything* you shoot. Besides, I doubt crocodile meat is very good."

"Only one way to find out."

"Come on, William, not another cookout. I'm still full from last night."

"O.K., I'll have it made into a pair of shoes for you—and a purse."

"Much better idea," she said.

"I guess we had better get up."

"Why? I could stay here all day."

"There are things I have to do—important things."

"You're leaving on the mission soon, aren't you?"

He nodded.

"When?"

"Early tomorrow morning."

"That's what you and General Thompson were talking about down by the surf."

Again he nodded.

She sighed and hugged him. "You *will* be coming back, won't you? I mean, what will I do for pork and purses without you?"

"Of course I'm coming back. I lead a charmed life."

She thought a moment, then asked, "Why were you at Pearl when the attack came? I thought you were with the AVG."

"Chennault kicked me out. I wrecked three of his planes, and he didn't have that many. I guess I was never cut out to be a fighter pilot."

"Did you get *any* enemy planes?"

"Four."

"That's all? Four?" Her voice was impressed, nearly incredulous.

"At five hundred bucks apiece it wasn't bad money. . . ."

"Certainly enough to keep you in Lotus Blossoms," she said.

"I'll pretend I didn't hear that. Anyway, it takes five kills to make one an ace, and I didn't qualify. Boyington

92

did. A couple of others. Some of them are around here someplace. But I was a little impetuous, and our Mustangs were outclassed by the Japs' new Zeros anyway. I wrapped three Mustangs around palm trees and Chennault sent me to Pearl for rest and recuperation. Some rest. Some recuperation."

"And you decided to stay on the ground."

"I parachute on occasion, but most of the time, yes, I stay on the ground. I can fly pretty well in a pinch, but I prefer to restrict my pinches to select targets." He pinched one of her nipples.

"Hey," she protested.

There was a rustling at the tent door. It was Corrigan. "Hey Yank, haul it outta there, if you don't mind. There's a war on."

"Yeah. A war on crocodiles."

"I was thinking of leaving him for you to deal with. He was swimming for your tent. I guess the noise attracted him. You know, for a single man, McLeane, you make more noise at night than—"

"That will be quite enough, Corrigan."

Margot giggled.

"I'll join you in half an hour. You got coffee in that flying boat of yours?"

"Tea, mate. Take it or leave it."

"I'll make coffee," Margot said.

"Half an hour, Corrigan. And I expect your brain to be functioning as well as your mouth. We've got a lot of planning to do today."

"Don't you worry about planning. I've got it all figured."

"Terrific. The world's first Australian military genius—Corrigan of the Outback."

"I'll be in the plane," Corrigan said, and stomped off.

"You have some talent for making friends," Margot said.

"Don't I just?" He pressed his lips against her neck and soon her arms were around him.

Corrigan had put several crates together and slapped a couple of boards on top of them to form a worktable. Upon it were spread the latest detailed topographic map of southern Bougainville and a stack of the most recent aerial reconnaissance photographs.

McLeane had his mug of coffee with a sweet roll.

"*Now* can you tell me the intricate details of your precious mission?" Corrigan asked.

"Sure, as long as you're prepared to stay aboard this craft until we're in the air—and for a bit longer, maybe."

"I have everything I need. Food. Beer."

"A pot to piss in?"

"No, but I've got a funnel hooked up to a hose running through the wall of the fuselage. Don't worry about my personal conveniences."

"You're an ingenious man, Corrigan. We've been assigned to take out a munitions dump north of Kara Airstrip." He placed a fingertip on the airfield, which was about twenty miles inland from the southernmost tip of the island.

"I thought it would be something like that. Why can't we just send in a couple of B-17's and bomb the piss out of it?"

"Because the munitions dump is protected by six feet of concrete and steel."

"Which is why you've hired that bog-trottin' barkeep to stick some dynamite under it."

"Right."

Corrigan examined the chart at length. McLeane said, "Kara is the heart of enemy-held territory, and I don't see any good, secure place on the nearby shore to hide the Catalina."

"*You* don't see, but then that isn't your specialty, is it?

94

Your specialty would appear to be quail hunting."

McLeane smiled.

Corrigan placed one of *his* fingertips over a spot on the coastline. "Tauvi Lagoon, fed by the Tauvi River."

McLeane looked at the chart and saw nothing but unbroken coastline. "No lagoon. No river." He consulted the aerial photos of the region and likewise found nothing. Corrigan's alleged lagoon was at the heart of the East Siwai section of Bougainville, which the charts showed to be a solid mangrove swamp unbroken by trail or river. On either side of the vast swampland were Japanese outposts, one at Marnagawa and the other at Tokuaka, about thirty miles apart and connected to inland roads by newly cleared dirt roads.

Corrigan said, "The lagoon is where I said it is. The river runs right through the swamp practically to Kara."

"Then why isn't it on the chart?"

"It's not on the chart because the East Siwai swamp is the most God-awful swamp you've ever seen, inhabited only by a tribe of natives who are, to put it mildly, unfriendly."

"Oh."

"They hate foreigners, and prize alien scalps. Especially Japanese scalps."

"I see." A ray of sunshine had entered the case. "So the place is uncharted because of the vegetation and unpatrolled by the Japs for the reason you just mentioned."

"Yeah, even the Japs are smart enough to recognize a hunk of real estate that just ain't worth botherin' with. You see, they've made the presumption that if they can't go into it, we can't either."

"And we can?"

"Yeah. The Tauvi natives hate Japs, but they will tolerate white men. In fact, they have a particular fondness for a certain Australian I could name."

"God help them."

"They have simple needs, McLeane. I think that in order to lay our hands on two of their river canoes and four oarsmen it would cost us . . . let's see . . . a dozen steel knives, a dozen cooking pots, a few dozen solid fishhooks, and ten or twelve aluminum pipes with an inside diameter of no more than a quarter-inch."

"What's the last item for? Blowpipes?"

"Correct. Bamboo blowpipes don't have the accuracy of the metal rods I've been bringing them over the past few years."

"In exchange for what?"

"Pearls. What else?"

"Boy, you sure get around, Corrigan."

"A man's got to make a living," the Australian said off-handedly.

"So we can land in this lagoon, hide the plane, and make our way up the Tauvi River in native canoes."

"Beyond a doubt. There aren't even crocodiles. A few nasty little things, but you'll survive the journey. You *will* have to cross under two main east-west supply roads shortly before reaching the outskirts of Kara Field."

"Oh, great."

"I'm sure you'll manage. The Japs have built wooden bridges. You can slip through at night. The river terminates in a rather large lake just south of Kara."

"I see it," McLeane replied, consulting the chart. "Kofu Lake, kidney-shaped, with a kidney-shaped island at the center."

"That's the one. I've never seen it myself and have no idea if the Japs use it for anything. You can find that out for yourself."

McLeane used a magnifying lens to examine an aerial photo of the lake. "There seems to be some sort of structure on the island."

"Probably a Jap teahouse. It's your problem, not mine."

"This lagoon . . . can you slip into it before dawn?"

"I've done it a dozen times before, mate."

"And the natives . . . ?"

"I only know a few of their words. We'll let Heinman handle the linguistics. The important things is that they hate the Japs and trust me. And all we have to do is come up with the knick-knacks they want in return."

McLeane leaned back and wondered out loud where he was going to get a dozen aluminum pipes of the required dimensions.

"Try the electronics dump at Carney Field. The antenna components for walkie-talkies are what the black little devils like the best."

"Am I gonna have to steal this stuff, or do you have a formal arrangement with the operators of the establishment?"

"The latter. Would you call me a thief? There's a Sergeant Wyan. Slip him a twenty and he'll give you anything you want."

"Do you have everything you need?"

"Yes, sir. Fully provisioned, armed, and fueled. I'm just gonna park my bum out on the bow and, as you Yanks like to say, 'catch a few rays' for the next few hours."

"As long as you don't talk to anyone."

"If they're anything like you or the rest of your lot, they won't get anything but scorn from me."

McLeane got up, stretched, and yawned.

General Thompson poured two glasses of scotch over ice and handed one to McLeane. It was three o'clock in the afternoon, and the general had just finished going over McLeane's report, charts, and photos.

He proffered a toast: "To the sunny South Pacific."

"Amen to that."

They touched glasses.

"It looks good to me," Thompson said.

97

"Thank you, sir."

"You know that you're staking a lot on that Aussie pilot's knowledge of the terrain."

"He's spent a lot of time learning it—trading with the natives. Probably a lot of stuff he wouldn't admit in front of a court."

"Unquestionably." Thompson paused. "Mack . . . your plan looks good. But how do you *feel* about it? If you have any doubts, I want to hear them now."

McLeane thought for a while. "Doubts? Who doesn't have them? I've always worked alone before."

"You wanted an elite unit. You got it."

"Yeah, and now I have six headaches instead of one. But also a fuck of a lot more firepower. Yeah, I have doubts, but I think we'll pull this one off."

"There's less than a week to do it in. On 1 November all hell breaks loose on Bougainville."

McLeane drained his glass. "I'll try to give the enemy a little less hell to break loose with," he said.

"And what shall I do with Private Thomas?"

"Margot can take care of herself."

"And you as well, I hear."

McLeane smiled.

"She'll run the radio link between the unit and here. She's trained in radio—wants to go into it after the war. We may see her turn up on the Fred Allen show someday."

"I'll try to keep the wolves away while you're gone nonetheless," Thompson said.

Eleven

The smell of freshly brewed coffee filled McLeane's tent, as did the sound of radio static and random signals.

He opened his eyes reluctantly, and with foreboding, as he did at the start of every mission. McLeane saw Margot, completely dressed, fixing breakfast with one hand and fiddling with the radio with the other.

"What time is it?" he asked.

"Two in the morning."

"I'm going back to sleep."

"No you're not. McLeane, I went to bed—with you—at ten in the evening for the first time in my life just so I could have you up and around by two in the morning."

"You have me *up*."

"That will have to wait until your mission is over. Sorry, William. Business before pleasure."

He grumbled and rolled out of the sack. "Off to get my ass shot off again," he muttered, not intending to be heard. She heard.

"As long as you don't get anything more important shot off," she said. "I don't mean to be insulting, but your ass I could do without. Especially when it decides to speak for itself."

"I'm not sure, but I think I've been insulted."

"You have. Will pancakes be O.K., or do I have to run off in search of bacon as well?"

"Pancakes will be fine," he replied, pulling her to him and kissing her on the behind.

"*That* is the most beautiful ass I have ever seen. I think I'm gonna have it bronzed and hung on the wall."

"*William!*"

"Perhaps even silver-plated."

She pulled away from his grasp. "Do you want your pancakes or not?"

"O.K., O.K., I'll behave. Do I have time to wash and shave first?"

"Twenty minutes."

He yawned, stretched again, and stumbled off in the direction of the showers.

When they were done eating, she sat next to him while he finished putting on his camouflage gear. After their mild wise-cracking over breakfast, Margot was strangely quiet. It was only after he had made his final gear-check that she said, "I won't be seeing you for a week, maybe two."

"I'll be back. Ask Thompson. He knows I always come back."

She nodded, though without conviction.

He noticed her despondency, and lifted up her chin. "Hey . . . I'm immortal. Didn't Archie tell you that?"

She shook her head.

"Ask him tomorrow. He'll tell you."

Suddenly there were tears in her eyes, and she stood to embrace him. "William . . ."

"It's just another mission, and this time I have a small army behind me." He brushed aside her tears.

"I always thought I was immune to attachments. At school, I avoided them like the plague. But you . . . it's different somehow."

He kissed her on the forehead, then on the lips. "I'll be back, Redbird."

"Promise?"

100

"I promise."

They heard the sound of the Catalina's twin, twelve hundred-horsepower Pratt & Whitney engines turning over and, before long, roaring to life. "Duty beckons," he said. "I'd better get going."

She pulled herself together and nodded in compliance with the inevitable.

He hefted his pack. "Look at it this way. If we pull this one off, maybe I can get *your* picture in *Life* along with mine."

"The only magazine my parents read is the *New Yorker*." She laughed through what was left of her tears.

"I'll send them a goddamned clipping," he growled, kissing her passionately and then storming from the tent.

All of the unit but Contardo were aboard the plane. The Italian stood by the dock, nervously shifting his weight from one foot to the other, as if he couldn't wait to get on with it. "Come on, Major. Corrigan says we got to haul our butts outta here."

"That's only because the guys in the launches on the other side of the lagoon will start shooting at him if he doesn't knock off the racket."

McLeane hurried up the dock, tossed his gear into the starboard stern blister canopy, and followed it. Contardo slipped the stern and spring lines, then went forward to let go the bowline. McLeane closed the blister canopy.

The members of McLeane's Rangers were seated on the starboard and port benches, some sleeping, others idly sipping on cups of coffee. Heinman and Wilkins were engaged in a hot conversation about the correct nomenclature to be given the flora and fauna of the Tombigbee and Mobile, Alabama, rivers. A friendship appeared to be developing between the unlikeliest of people, McLeane noticed. Heinman, the Oxford-educated know-it-all with a fondness for nature, and Wilkins, who had been brought up in the woods, seemed to hit it off with

101

no trouble at all.

McLeane made his way to the copilot's seat and occupied it.

"I haven't rushed you, have I, mate?" Corrigan asked sarcastically.

"Fly the goddamned plane. All lines are clear."

"I mean, I wouldn't want to take you away from your Sheila before the deed was done, you know."

"Shut up and fly."

Corrigan switched his radio to the main flight operations channels for Henderson Field. He brought the microphone to his lips. "Henderson, this is Lone Ranger preparing for takeoff from Tango for cargo run to Malaita."

The answer came swiftly. "Lone Ranger, you are cleared for takeoff. You have clear skies, a northwest wind of seven knots, and no incoming or outgoing traffic. Proceed."

"Roger, Henderson."

Corrigan pushed the throttles forward slightly and eased the Catalina away from the dock and out of the lagoon. McLeane switched on the copilot's radio to the special high-frequency band assigned to the unit.

"Redbird, this is Lone Ranger."

Margot's voice came back instantaneously. "This is Redbird, go ahead Lone Ranger."

"Sheila," Corrigan said.

"We should be back from Malaita by noon. Just the same, let's make it a dinner date. Your place or mine?"

"Mine. Yours is a mess."

"You have a deal, Redbird." McLeane signed off. "So our special frequency works," he said to Corrigan.

"I thought you proved that yesterday."

"With the walkie-talkies, but not with the gear on the plane."

"Didn't want to blow her darlin' little ear off, did you? I

must admit, McLeane, for a Yank you have fine taste in women."

"Since all Australians think about is whiskey and women, I'll take that as a compliment."

"We think about other things," Corrigan said, as the Catalina cleared the lagoon and was out in the Pacific.

"Yeah. Sheep."

Corrigan said nothing, but scowled and shoved the throttles all the way forward. The Catalina raced across the placid sea, until at last she burst up into the air and soared above all that was common and human. Soon the water was but a blur and the stars above were glowing with increasing brightness.

Corrigan said: "I figure we'll bank northwest off Florida Island, then head straight up the Slot at ten thousand feet. . . ."

"The optimum crusing altitude for this bird."

"You've been doing your homework, Yank. We'll go on that course until we get within one hundred miles of Shortland island where the Nips still have a small base."

"Then?"

"We'll drop to wave-top level and skirt them to the west, landing in my lagoon at about quarter to six."

"That's just a little before sunup," McLeane said.

"My people will be waiting with torches to guide us in. They can hear me coming twenty miles out, and assemble like locusts."

"What about the Japs?"

"They fly patrols—one Zeke—at dawn, noon, and sundown. Their dawn patrol is as sloppy as some of ours. Most of the time it's at least half an hour late. By then, we'll be well-hidden within the lagoon."

"God, Corrigan, I hope you know what you're doing. My ass is on the line here."

"*All* our asses, mate. And tell me, where did you dig up this 'Lone Ranger' bullshit?"

"Lone Ranger has been my code name for years. We're using it to let them know we're coming—or at least *I'm* coming. The idea is to let them expect another solo visit by me. Which means that if by some chance they pinpoint the landing spot they'll send ten men, not an army, which they'd need to deal with this lot I've assembled."

"Smart, McLeane, smart. I didn't think you capable of it."

"I'm grateful for your confidence," McLeane said, closing his eyes and going back to sleep to dream of Margot.

The two-hour flight from Guadalcanal to Bougainville was uneventful. Corrigan spotted no planes and only one surface vessel, an American destroyer. Over the command frequency, Corrigan heard the phony radio message "confirming" his arrival at Malaita, an island to the northeast of Guadalcanal.

"Bleedin' spy bullshit," Corrigan said, waking up McLeane.

"What did you say?"

"I said we're nearly there. Fifteen miles out. We should be able to make out the coastline in a few minutes."

McLeane stared out the copilot's side window.

"I can't see anything but water and stars."

"You also can't see any Nips, so consider yourself lucky."

The Catalina's V-bottom was nearly touching the wave tops.

"How far offshore are you gonna put her down?" McLeane asked.

"About a mile. We'll go in very slowly to give my shore party time to assemble."

"What about coral reefs?"

"There's one, but her top is a good eight feet below the low-water mark. We'll clear her even if the tide's out."

"And the lagoon?"

"Big enough for two of these birds. I'll get her inside and we'll swing her around so her bow's pointed straight out to sea. That's just in case you fuck up and we have to make a fast getaway."

"Your confidence in me is overwhelming."

The predawn glow had begun to appear, and there was a slight surface fog.

"We're coming up on the landing point," Corrigan said.

"I can't see a thing but fog."

"Trust me."

"That'll be the day. The day the king trusts you with the crown jewels, I'll trust you with my life."

McLeane turned and shouted down into the fuselage, "Landing point within a minute or two. Everybody braced and ready?"

Corrigan was offended. "Everybody braced, my ass. I mean to set her down as soft as a baby's bum. Your grimy lot can go about jerking off or whatever it is they're doing."

McLeane said, "I can make out the coastline."

Corrigan peered through the windscreen. "I can see Cape Tauvi off to the right. The lagoon is about two degrees to port. Adjusting."

He adjusted.

"You were right on the mark, Corrigan. Congratulations."

"Thanks."

"I guess you Aussies learn your precision from all the practice you get fucking kangaroos."

"Sheep, mate, sheep. Kangaroos are too fucking dangerous, not to mention too fast. Sheep you can get a good grip on."

"Land the goddamned plane," McLeane said, and yawned.

Corrigan throttled back and the plane slowed, dropping the final few feet to the glassy surface of the Solomon Sea. The V-bottom of the Catalina cut the water like a knife, and spray flew up and back, pouring over the stern blister canopies as if they were in the midst of a torrential downpour.

"I have a good view of the coast now," McLeane said. Contardo had invited himself into the cockpit and was hunched over between Corrigan and McLeane, straining for a view.

"No Guineas allowed," Corrigan snarled.

"Where'd you find this bum, Major?" Contardo asked.

"In the woods."

"Under a rock I bet."

"Nope. Behind a sheep."

Contardo laughed. Corrigan said, "Don't knock it until you've tried it. The worst Australian sheep is better than the best Italian woman."

"Hey," Contardo said sharply.

"I see lights on shore," McLeane interrupted.

Corrigan squinted through the fog, then nodded. "That'll be my shore party. One set of torches on either entrance to the lagoon."

"These natives can really hear you twenty miles out?" McLeane asked.

"Mate, these birds can hear a chickadee getting a blow job in the middle of a monsoon. Sure, they can hear my engines, and tell 'em from anything the Japs have got as well."

The Catalina slowed nearly to a stop and Corrigan pulled the throttles back almost as far as they would go. The huge seaplane crept slowly toward the shore, which gradually became clear in detail through the waning mist.

"So this is Bougainville," Contardo said. "It looks like every other island."

"They're all the same, lad. The only difference is who

106

owns 'em at a given time, and whether or not the natives are friendly.''

A quarter-mile from shore they could see the lagoon. The entrance was wide, but covered like the rest of the lagoon with a canopy of coconut palms and mangrove trees.

McLeane said, ''No wonder this joint doesn't show up on the recon photos. It's like a goddamned cave.''

''Yeah, a cave made of trees,'' Contardo added.

A group of natives stood beneath palms on either side of the entrance, waving torches made from twisted palm fronds that had been dipped in the flammable resin of the katari tree. All along the banks of the lagoon, small knots of Tauvi warriors waved excitedly at the arrival of the airplane that they knew always bore gifts.

Corrigan swung the plane around and shut off the engines. Abruptly, the silence of the rain forest regained control. He shut off all the switches and climbed out of his seat. ''I'd better have a word with 'em before they see any of you,'' he said. ''The little devils are suspicious.''

''On an island full of Japs, that ain't difficult,'' Contardo said.

As Corrigan walked aft, McLeane told Heinman to listen in on the conversation and get a line on the local dialect. The German nodded and hid himself beneath one of the blister canopies, where he could overhear but not be seen. Corrigan flipped open one of the canopies and, smiling, waved his hands in a gesture of welcome. Shouts of greeting came to him from the shoreline.

Corrigan said, awkwardly, *''Fantellao . . . papalana . . . A-ili . . . kore . . . tapoina teletafela.''*

McLeane, who had ducked down beside Heinman, asked what Corrigan had said. Heinman replied, ''I bring you fishhook, knife, pot . . . many gifts.''

From the shore came the reply, *''Ahana pe-una? Borotulu?''*

Heinman translated, ''What do you want? Pearl?''

"Can you talk their langauge better than Corrigan?" McLeane asked.

"Of course. It's a dialect typical of the Bougainville straits."

McLeane called to Corrigan, "Tell them you've brought friends who are going up the river to kill Japanese. Tell them we need to borrow two canoes."

Corrigan did as he was told. There was some discussion on the shore, but the tone of it didn't strike McLeane as being alarming.

"Corrigan, introduced them to Heinman. Heinman, try not to insult the sons of bitches, would you? I realize it will be a strain."

Heinman gave his CO a pained glance, but said nothing to him. Instead, the German stood beside Corrigan and began chattering away with the natives.

After a few minutes, Corrigan stuck his head back into the plane. "Fuckin' Adolph here speaks their language better than they do. They're impressed."

"Did he get us our two canoes?"

"Four. *And* rowers to go with them."

"We don't need four canoes," McLeane said.

Corrigan smiled. "The other two," he said, "are to use in bringing back Japanese heads."

Twelve

McLeane sat in one of his favorite positions—propped up against a palm tree, sipping a cup of herbal tea Heinman had induced the natives to brew. The German had proved invaluable. He not only spoke their language as well as they, he knew their customs, protocols, and most of the flora and fauna that surrounded them. The Tauvi were at work preparing four canoes. Two war canoes, each about thirty-five feet long, and two smaller canoes, each about fifteen feet, were being outfitted with native weapons and food. A number of the Tauvi had decided to take up the Raiders' cause. The outbreak of war having interrupted their customs of raiding the native villages of competing tribes on nearby Shortland Island, the Tauvi were spoiling for a fight—and prize skulls. The chief, Lalafa, had decided the battle plan. One war canoe manned by Heinman, himself, and a dozen warriors would lead the way up the river. The two small canoes, carrying the rest of McLeane's Rangers, would follow. The second war canoe, manned by about a dozen Tauvi, would bring up the rear.

All the canoes were built of planks hacked out of the native trees and sealed together with resin. Both stems and sterns were carved with figures of sharks, birds, lizards, or other animals, and the canoes reminded McLeane of miniature Viking ships. The natives were short, the men averaging five-three and the women seldom reaching the five-foot mark. They dressed in skins and wore assorted decorations, including necklaces and wristlets made of sea shells and sharks' teeth, and braided armlets to protect them from enemy arrows. But what struck McLeane most was the color of their hair—brilliant magenta.

"Red ocher from the earth," Heinman explained, helping himself to a seat next to McLeane. "They mix it with water and rub it into their scalps."

"Sort of a native beauty salon, right?"

"In a manner of speaking. However, the primary motivation is that the red ocher helps keep their hair free of vermin. The natives of the eastern Solomons use lime for the same reason, giving their hair a light brown appearance. Really, Major, how can you expect to fight a war on terrain where you don't have the foggiest notion of native customs."

"I hire experts. You, for example. How much do you think Patton knows about Sicily?"

"As he is an American general, probably nothing."

"What's this brew you've concocted? It's pretty good."

"It should be, but I wouldn't have too much of it before going into action."

"And why not? I thought the British drank tea before doing *anything.*"

"This particular tea is brewed from the kernels of the plant called *Nipa fruticans.* It's accepted as being quite alcoholic among the Malays, but these local chaps apparently are—or were—unaware of its properties. I have enlightened them."

"And what was their response?" McLeane asked.

"They appear to be most grateful," Heinman said proudly.

"Terrific. We've created a race of drunken headhunters and are going to use them to go up the river. Nice work, Heinman."

"I didn't make enough to endanger the mission,"—
Heinman sniffed—"but I gave them the recipe in the
event we feel in the mood for a celebration upon our
return."

"Good thinking. Brew me up a gallon to take along just
the same."

"Done."

"It gets rough out there in the field, you know,"
McLeane said.

"Beyond a doubt. You might also want to bring along a
pocketful of betelnuts, or *olega* as they're called in these
parts."

"What for? All they do is make your mouth turn red."

"Not true. When chewed in moderation, betelnuts have
a pronounced stimulant effect. Such an effect may
become necessary."

"O.K., Heinman, I place my body chemistry in your
hands. Have betelnuts collected and make sure each of my
men gets a pocketful."

"Yes, sir."

McLeane sipped at his tea with renewed interest.

"You're a true wonder, Heinman."

The German seemed embarrassed, and McLeane
picked up on it. "No, I mean it. I think the problem you
had with earlier COs is that they didn't realize just what a
storehouse of information you are. And the reason they
didn't understand was that you have this way of talking
that makes people feel inferior, so of course in defense
they write you off as being full of shit."

Heinman was thoughtful. "Full of shit? Well, I wouldn't
put it *quite* that way, but ..."

"See, you're doing it even now."

Heinman sighed. "It's the Oxford accent, I suppose."

"Yeah, that's a contributory factor. You're stuck in the
South Pacific with a couple of million guys who might
describe a certain street corner in the Murray Hill section

111

of New York as being 'Toity-toid and Toid.' "

Heinman chuckled.

"Naturally they're gonna think you're some kind of self-styled big shot, and since you don't have the general's stars to back it up, they're gonna come down on you. Hard."

"I suppose you're right."

The natives appeared to have finished working on the canoes. The chief—Lalafa—came over and had a long conversation with Heinman, most of which McLeane ignored. When Lalafa had gone, McLeane asked what had transpired.

"They're ready to go. All our equipment—and theirs—is packed and ready."

"Then let's go." McLeane got to his feet. "Oh, and there is a slight change. I'm riding point with you and Lalafa."

"That's not in the plan."

"I just changed the plan. We'll keep in touch with the other canoes—the two small ones anyway—by walkie-talkie. I had 'em adjusted so they don't have a range of more than a quarter-mile. There's no chance of the Japs picking up our signals, even if they had the equipment to receive the frequency we're broadcasting over."

"It makes no sense for the CO to be riding point in an operation of this sort," Heinman said, back on his high horse. "I realize there's a precedent in military history, but . . ."

"But *this* CO wants to see what happens first, *and* to be in immediate contact with his native guide and the man's translator. Besides, Heinman, I'm a better shot than you are."

Heinman's shirt was now fully stuffed. "That's not been proved."

"Heinman?"

"Yes, sir?"

112

"How would you like to entertain the assembled with a few choruses of 'Who Owns New York'?"

Heinman leaped to his feet. "No, *sir.* I would not like to do that, *sir.* May I have your permission to carry out your previous orders?"

"Yes, Heinman, you may."

The man turned away from McLeane and began walking off. McLeane stopped him. "Heinman."

"Yes, sir." Heinman did not turn around.

"You really *are* an insufferable son of a bitch."

"Yes, sir," Heinman said, and went on his way.

Corrigan was lallygagging atop the bow, a fishing line dangling over the side of the ship, when McLeane came to make his farewells.

"I'm hoping a small bonito will wander into the lagoon and take my bait. More likely the crabs will wander off with it."

"Why don't you just heave a grenade over the side? That'll get you fish."

"It'll also give the natives ideas I'd rather they did not have. It's trouble enough supplying 'em with fishhooks."

"I see your point. Besides, they might discover how useful a handful of grenades might be in dealing with their tribes on Shortland Island."

"They might indeed."

Corrigan's face abruptly took on a quizzical look, and McLeane asked what the trouble was.

"Jap dawn patrol, mate. Have a listen."

McLeane froze as the sound of a Japanese fighter plane become louder and nearer.

"Relax," Corrigan said. "They fly at five thousand feet and will pass straight over us. The bastards are looking for our invasion fleet, not a solitary band of loonies in a Catalina."

McLeane looked up at the canopy of broad leaves that

113

hid them. Corrigan was true to his word. The enemy plane could not be seen even as it passed directly overhead.

"Do the Japs ever use patrol boats?"

"I don't know. I've never been here long enough to find out. Two days was the longest."

"You'll be here up to a week this time. Better have the Tauvi put up something to block the entrance to the lagoon so any Japs that happen along in a picket boat can't see inside."

"The reef is a mile offshore, McLeane. Any Jap boat big enough to patrol this coast will have to stay outside it, and nobody can see in this lagoon from a mile out."

"You know everything, don't you? You're as bad as Heinman. Humor me, would you?"

"O.K., I'll get the Tauvi to stick a couple of their war canoes—decorated with human heads—in the entrance. That should discourage prying eyes."

"Good idea. I have to go. Enjoy your vacation, and try not to work too hard."

"I'll give it my best effort. Oh, and McLeane . . ."

"I know, be back on schedule or you'll leave without me."

Corrigan smiled. "You *do* learn fast for a Yank."

McLeane left the plane through the stern blister canopy to allow fast access to shore. An impromptu raft had been rigged from lashed-together logs. Corrigan, who trusted no one, planned to roll up the raft at night.

McLeane found the four canoes in line at the entrance to the river. The Tauvi River was wide at its entrance, wide enough for two of the big canoes, and was about five feet deep. McLeane climbed into the lead canoe and joined Heinman and the Tauvi chief at the bow. The stempost, he noted, was carved to resemble the head of a shark. McLeane asked if they would be able to travel all the way to Tofu Lake by canoe, and Heinman conferred with the chief.

"He says these canoes have been there before," Heinman reported. "It appears that the Tauvi have had their quarrels with inland tribes as well as those on Shortland Island. The river *will* narrow, and it may be necessary to hack away some foliage, but the chief assures me we'll make it."

"O.K.," McLeane said, "let's move out." He waved the formation to proceed. Heinman spoke with Lalafa, who shouted to his men, and slowly, with more than a few creaks, the small armada began to move into the jungle.

"How long before we reach the first Jap bridge crossing?" McLeane asked.

The reply was "Eighteen hours."

"That will be at about midnight. Good. It will give us time to think of a way to sneak past without being noticed. Did you brew that gallon of 'tea' I asked for?"

Heinman said that he had.

"I'll have it now, if you don't mind."

Heinman reluctantly produced a gallon-sized jerry can and handed it over.

"I believe I'm corrupting you," he said.

"I was corrupted long before you stumbled into my life, Heinman. Is there a place where I can recline, and is there any protocol against my so doing?"

McLeane had his answer in a moment, and relaxed on the forward bench, the one normally reserved for the chief and his sons. He took a swig of Heinman's brew, then shut the jerry can and brought the walkie-talkie to his lips.

"Contardo?"

"Yo, boss," was the electronic reply.

"Just checking. O'Connor?"

"Right on the trail of the Eye-talian gentleman," O'Connor replied.

"First Jap bridge by midnight. We'll start worrying about it around ten. In the meantime, relax. You may not have another chance for a while."

Thirteen

McLeane watched intermittently as the scenery changed in a way that was getting to be familiar to him: palms gave way to mangroves which gave way to enormous banyan trees. Lianas were everywhere, and now and again the splash of the Tauvi oars was joined by the swish of a crocodile's tail. It was not possible to see more than ten feet past the riverbank except in spots. No wonder the enemy ignored the place, McLeane thought. Between the terrain and the Tauvi it just wasn't worthwhile.

McLeane, Heinman, and Lalafa took turns at the prow, just as the dozen oarsmen worked in rotating shifts. At several points the river narrowed and machetes were used to hack a path. Eventually day turned to night, and McLeane took charge, directing the boat with the assistance of an infrared spotlight and special goggles. The red glow thus given the rain forest made the trip seem eerier yet.

At ten o'clock, McLeane woke Heinman from a light sleep.

"We should be coming up on the first of the bridges in about two hours," McLeane said.

Heinman spoke with Lalafa.

"The chief says less than an hour. Apparently we've been making better time than anticipated."

"O.K., Heinman, you're back in Burma. Do you see any

rationale an enemy CO would have for posting a guard on those bridges?''

Heinman thought for a long moment, then shrugged. ''Absolutely none.''

''I want to hear reasons.''

''The Japs think the East Siwai swamp is impassable except to headhunting natives who certainly would have no reason for attacking a Japanese bridge. They might want to remove the head of a Japanese *guard,* however, and perhaps have done so.''

''Ask Lalafa.''

Heinman did, and was rewarded with a self-satisfied grin.

''O.K., no guard on the bridge. That means all we have to worry about is the possibility of traffic.''

''At midnight it seems hardly likely.''

''Nonetheless, let's get some firepower up front.''

''Do you want me to have our men brought up to join us?''

''Yes. No, wait a minute. These Tauvi guys are pretty good with bows and arrows and blowpipes, aren't they?''

''I would think that something of an understatement, sir.''

''Better to have any wandering Japs taken out by our native *amigos.*''

''Good idea, sir. That will make them happy, and deny the enemy the knowledge of our presence.''

''Ask the chief to bring up his best talent, would you?''

In due course, with an amount of jostling, four archers and three natives armed with blowpipes arrived near the bow of the lead canoe. Through Heinman, McLeane explained the situation and gave them instructions to fire only on his command. They nodded, and McLeane rewarded them by giving each a peek through the night-vision equipment.

''Lalafa says that the first bridge is just around the next

117

bend in the river," Heinman said.

McLeane got on the walkie-talkie and explained the situation to the other members of the unit.

"No shooting except on my order; you got that?" McLeane said.

Two reluctant acknowledgments came back over the airwaves.

"Coming around the bend, Major," Heinman said.

McLeane ordered the oarsmen to be as quiet as possible, and after translations had been made, they complied.

McLeane peered through the night-vision equipment as the bridge hove into view. It was a simple, wooden structure, wide enough for a small truck and protected by a short, bamboo handrail. The Japanese—no doubt prompted by earlier losses of men to the natives—had cleared the forest within fifty feet of the bridge in all directions, but there was no guard. There also appeared to be no traffic.

"Let's go," McLeane said, and the four canoes started forward swiftly and silently.

McLeane was a little disappointed. But just as the first war canoe passed under the bridge there came the sound of an auto engine. "Enemy jeep," McLeane said.

The jeep spotted the other three canoes in an instant and screeched to a halt. McLeane heard the sound of three men jumping to the floor of the wooden bridge right over his head. He said to Heinman, "A hotshot of some kind, one driver, and two guards. The hotshot is still in the jeep."

There was a loud order in Japanese. It translated as "Halt or you're dead. You in the small boats. Who are you?"

McLeane whispered to Heinman, "They've seen our men. Can the chief fix them?"

Quick exchanges were made in Melanesian. Soon six Tauvi warriors were climbing the bridge railing, carrying their bows and blowpipes in their teeth. A few seconds later, the midnight air was ripped by the sound of screaming. McLeane climbed up to have a look. The sight was ghastly. There were indeed four Japanese, including one who wore the uniform of a colonel, but all had been relieved of their heads. The Tauvi warriors held the heads up, grinning proudly and babbling about their accomplishment.

Heinman peeked over the side of the bridge. "My God," he exclaimed.

"Yeah. Let's get out of here before the late colonel is missed."

"And let's hope that the Japs feel the Tauvi, satisfied with four heads, have gone south into the swamp."

"I couldn't say it better myself. Come on, Heinman, tell our friends to haul ass."

Soon they were all back aboard the lead canoe, and the armada moved swiftly toward the second bridge, five miles to the north.

"I think we can be past the second bridge before the Japs miss their colonel and by some stroke of luck have the imagination to put a guard on the second bridge," McLeane said.

"I hope so," Heinman replied, wiping the sweat from his brow.

"What's the matter, Adolph? Unnerved by a little simple butchery?"

"I just wish they didn't insist on bringing the heads along."

"They're prizes, remember, and unmistakable indications to the enemy that the work was done by the Tauvi."

"Well said. But I wish you wouldn't join the others in calling me Adolph simply because I have a German surname."

"Have some tea and shut up," McLeane said, fumbling around the bilge for the jerry can.

McLeane's Rangers passed the second bridge unnoticed by all but an insomniac crocodile, and by dawn had reached the southern reaches of Lake Tofu.

The river broadened as it approached the lake, but the vegetation likewise increased. The Japanese had, in fact, blockaded the entrance, perhaps fearing a Tauvi attack. Several trees had been cut down and formed a rude blockade that, when covered by heaps of branches over which lianas had rapidly grown, gave the impression of a natural barrier.

"The chief says the blockade is new. It wasn't here last year. He says it is man-made," Heinman reported.

McLeane nodded. The prow of the lead canoe nearly touched the blockade, the boat held in place by the oarsmen. It was two hours before dawn, and the predawn glow was beginning to lighten the scenery. Lalafa abruptly rose, said something in his native tongue, and went as if to strike at the blockade with his long machetelike sword.

"No," McLeane snapped, and caught the chief's arm before it could fall.

Lalafa was both surprised and a little angry. One didn't go around stopping the blows of a Tauvi chief and do it lightly. Heinman looked quizzical. "Major?" he asked.

"Get on the radio and tell O'Connor to haul his bogtrottin' ass up here. And tell the chief that that blockade may hide a trap."

"Done."

Heinman spoke to the chief, who seemed mollified, then by radio to O'Connor, who obeyed.

McLeane showed O'Connor the blockade. "Would you just barge through that?" he asked.

O'Connor laughed.

"O.K., find it for me."

"I'll be needin' your night-vision equipment, Major," O'Connor said. He was given it, and went about the task of examining the blockade.

It didn't take the Irishman long to find the thin copper wire which ran through the lianas from one bank to another. "There it is, Major. I would guess more than three ounces of pressure would set off a couple of sticks of dynamite on the left bank."

"Why the left bank?"

"Well, that's right lookin' at it from their side. The Nips read from right to left, don't they? People are instinctual. Westerners in the same situation would pick the other bank."

McLeane shrugged. "You're the expert. Defuse the goddamned thing."

"Bring the bow over to the left bank and I'll see what I can do."

O'Connor followed the trail of the copper wire with his infrared spotlight until it terminated in a pile of dried leaves on the left bank.

"This dingus has been left here a good while," he said.

"Take care of it."

"Hold the spotlight."

McLeane held the spotlight while O'Connor brushed and blew away the leaves. Beneath was a simple switch tied both to the copper wire and to six sticks of dynamite that had been hooked up to four dry-cell batteries.

Chief Lalafa peered at the alien device and shook his head.

"Can you defuse it?" McLeane asked.

"Is the Pope a Catholic? Come on, Major, a four-year-old could defuse it. This here device was left as protection against natives who wouldn't think to look for a trap. This trap was never set in expectation of us."

"Good. Get rid of it. I hate bombs."

O'Connor took wire cutters from the multiplicity of tools on his belt and peered at the red and blue cables running from the batteries to the switch.

"What's your favorite color, Major? Red or blue?"

"Solitude," McLeane said, and closed his eyes.

O'Connor cut the red wire, then put the cutters back on his belt. "Done," he said.

McLeane opened his eyes. "It was that easy?"

"Like I said, the Japs weren't expecting Yanks. The thing is totally defused." To accent the point, O'Connor slammed his fist down on the copper wire, producing no explosion whatsoever.

"You made your point. Nice work, Pat."

"Thanks, Major. Say, this dynamite's a bit unstable. The slants must have left it here for six months to a year at least."

"So they don't patrol this side of the lake."

"Would you mind if I pitch the sticks into the water? They'll float downstream, and within two hours will be harmless as Oxford dons."

Heinman's face went as red as the defused wire, but McLeane shut him up with a wave of his hand.

"Pitch 'em in," McLeane said.

When O'Connor had returned to his canoe, Heinman said, "Frankly, I didn't think the man had it in him. I was rather impressed."

"You should be. You would have been blown to hell without him."

"And you as well."

"I hired the man, Adolph. I know his capabilities."

"And I must say that you performed admirably, sir, in stopping the chief's blow. Your instinct that the blockade was booby-trapped . . ."

"Could have been had by a booby."

Heinman got on his high horse again. "A booby, sir, is a waterfowl with either blue or red feet that is typically found in the Galapagos Islands. These fowl are known as either red- or blue-footed boobies."

McLeane snarled, "Adolph, one of these days I'm

122

gonna take your ass and fry it like I fried that porker back at Guadalcanal."

"That was broiling, sir, not frying."

McLeane suddenly became as unstable as the deep-sixed dynamite. "Adolph, there is a point where a rational man becomes irrational. I am nearly there, and the fault is yours. I am now at the point where the thought of you on an *untraditional* spit that would have driven Guppy *mad* gives me no end of delight. I might even turn cannibal myself for the occasion."

Heinman was horrified. He turned pale, and sat down on the leading bench.

McLeane laughed and clapped him on the shoulder. "Take it easy, Heinman. Ask the chief here to hack us a way large enough to fit one of the small canoes. Then we'll take the lay of the land. There's something on that island. With the coming of dawn, I should be able to see it, and I intend to know what it is."

The Tauvi chief did as he was told, his men pushing several of the tree trunks far enough apart for one of the small canoes to fit through, yet leaving sufficient foliage to give the impression nothing had changed. It took the natives an hour, and in that time dawn approached.

McLeane got out his regular binoculars and focused them on the island. Heinman hedged alongside, eager for a view of the structure that seemed to hold so much mystery.

McLeane said "It's made of bamboo ... looks like a stockade. But there don't seem to be any guards."

"There is no need for guards," Heinman said.

"Oh?"

"The lake is lousy with crocodiles. There's almost no chance of making the swim to shore; that island must be at least half a mile away."

"So they only send a boat out—probably from the north bank, near the airstrip, which we can't see from here—once or twice a day to feed those in the stockade."

"A POW camp, sir?"

"We seem to have stumbled over the notorious Japanese hospitality," McLeane said.

"That could be useful."

"Indeed it could, Heinman. The prisoners on that island—assuming they're ours—may have a knowledge of the airstrip."

"We'll have to take one of the small canoes out."

"We'll take *both* the small canoes. I want all my men with me in case this is another trap."

"We can't do it during the day."

"No, we'll have to cool our heels right here until sundown. In the meantime, I would suggest we hack away some of the bank-side bushery so those of us unaccustomed to spending two days in a canoe can get back our shore legs."

"Good idea, sir, I'll ask the chief for some helpers."

"Let's leave a discreet barrier of flora between our new base camp and the lake shore. Say about twenty feet."

"Right, sir. No point in making a point of one's arrival, what?"

McLeane sighed. "This time let's give the natives a hand. We can't expect the Tauvi to do everything for us, can we? I mean, Corrigan's relationship will be ruined."

"We can't let that happen. Where would the world be without Australian blockade-runners?" Heinman asked.

Fourteen

From the seclusion of the bushes that lined the south bank of Lake Tofu, McLeane kept a day-long surveillance of the kidney-shaped island at the heart of the kidney-shaped lake.

While the lake was perhaps five by two miles, the island was barely a mile long and perhaps half that wide. Upon it was indeed a POW camp, containing maybe two dozen prisoners, nearly all of them Caucasian. The prisoners remained unguarded most of the day, the prevailing theory apparently being that there was no place for them to escape to that wasn't teeming with crocodiles.

They were visited twice daily, at nine in the morning and five in the afternoon, by a provision boat bearing food and what appeared to be medical supplies. McLeane couldn't be sure what they were being given, but it didn't seem like much. While the prisoners ate and submitted to the cursory ministrations of Jap medics, an enemy bigwig—probably a lieutenant general—strutted around the perimeter of the stockade, occasionally whacking its bamboo poles with his walking stick.

"My God, a Jap MacArthur," McLeane muttered at one point, but no one heard him.

The enemy stayed no longer than an hour each visit, then left in what McLeane could not see but judged to be an old, single-engine launch. The chorus of obscenities that accompanied both Japanese departures witnessed by McLeane convinced the major that the POWs were, indeed, on his side. When darkness fell, he ordered both small canoes brought out into the lake.

Heinman said, "Lalafa wants to come along."

"Tell him he and his men are needed to guard the canoes, and that we're just taking a look-see anyway. Killing Japs will come later," McLeane said.

McLeane got into one canoe and took the position in the front, his Winchester in one hand and the night-vision equipment in the other. Heinman and Contardo manned the oars behind him.

O'Connor and Wilkins were in the boat that followed in the wake of the first.

"Row as quietly as natives. There may be Jap guards we can't see on the far side of the stockade," McLeane ordered.

It was dark, but the water was illuminated by a partial moon. The stockade looked like a building made of Tinker Toys. The men inside it were walking around, and one or two were still berating the guards. McLeane heard a British accent, and an American.

Abruptly there was silence. All the men in the prison stockade stood at once and looked in McLeane's direction; Contardo apologized for having made a loud splash. "Sorry, Major. They make oars different on Flatbush Avenue."

The canoes were a hundred yards from the island. McLeane turned on the infrared spotlight and trained it on the stockade. Men, some of them in pretty sorry shape, lined the wall, all looking in his direction.

One of the prisoners could be heard in the night's quiet. "It's the bloody natives they told us about. No wonder they didn't leave guards."

Another prisoner said, "They're gonna let the natives have us."

"Shit," McLeane swore, putting aside his night-vision equipment.

"Row faster," he said.

A voice from the island screamed, "Guard! Guard!"

McLeane shouted back, "Shut up, asshole. We're here to rescue you."

There was stunned silence, then, "It's a Yank!"

"Yeah, a whole bunch of 'em. Now will you hold it down?"

A quieter voice said, "Don't worry. There're no guards on the island, only on the north shore of the lake, and they ignore us."

The bows of the two canoes touched the soft earth of the island.

"Are there any traps, any mines?" McLeane asked.

"Nothing. The Japs figure we won't try to escape."

"Logical," Heinman said.

The Rangers hopped onto the bank and pulled the bows of the canoes after them. They walked the dozen yards to the south edge of the stockade. Grimy but grateful fingers welcomed them, and their hands were shaken dozens of times. Finally, McLeane asked, "Who's the senior officer here?"

"I am."

The voice belonged to a Britisher of medium height with thinning hair and the tattered uniform of a lieutenant colonel. He stepped to the wall and announced himself as being Walter Biggins of the Royal Air Force. "Our transport was shot down over the Slot en route from Darwin to Guadalcanal. We had to ditch near Shortland Island, and the Japs picked us up. Most of the men here are mine."

"How long have you been here?" McLeane asked.

"Nearly seven months."

"You don't look like you've been too well-treated."

Biggins seethed. "The yellow bastards leave us here unguarded knowing that if we try to escape either the crocs or the natives will get us. The blasted crocs crawl up on the island and nip at the stockade trying to get at us. The Japs think it's funny."

"Cute, really cute," Contardo said.

"And your name, Major?"

"William McLeane, United States Marines."

Biggins' eyebrows arched to the heavens.

"Your reputation precedes you, Major. I had no idea that Headquarters would send such an illustrious man to get us out."

McLeane smiled and rubbed his chin. "Well, Colonel, in all honesty . . ."

". . . You didn't come for us."

"We had no idea you were here at all. We came to blow the munitions dump at Kara. But I think we may as well take you home with us when we're done."

"That sounds good enough to me." A murmur of agreement went through the prisoners. "You say you're going to blow the munitions dump at Kara? I suppose that means the invasion's on."

McLeane said nothing.

"So it is, and probably not too far off. Well, it's about time, if you ask me. How the devil did you get here? The Japs say that the jungle is impenetrable."

"They say that to further discourage escape attempts, I guess. Anyway, there's a perfectly navigable river that runs straight through East Siwai."

"But what of the natives? The headhunters."

Heinman said, "They show a marked preference for Japanese heads."

"They brought us here. There are a few dozen of 'em in the bushes to the south, along with two big war canoes capable of carrying all you fellows once we get our job done."

Suddenly a voice said, "Not all of us are fellows."

There were a few laughs as a slender, busty woman in

khaki shorts and an army shirt knotted beneath her breasts pushed through the crowd.

"Major, this is Janice Blythe, corporal in the Australian Army and one of the finest coastwatchers on God's green earth."

McLeane shook her hand, which felt soft and nice.

"Corporal. It's a pleasure."

"Blythe may be able to help you," Biggins said. "You see, she's the only one of us who's gotten a good look at that base."

"I was kind of hoping there'd be someone here with firsthand knowledge of the joint," McLeane said.

"That's me," she said, sticking her hands on her hips and affecting a nonchalant look.

"All I know is what I've seen on the aerial photos and old charts, and that's not much."

"Let me out of this jail, and I'll draw it for you."

"Sorry ... can't let you out until after we blow the dump. The Japs will notice your absence tomorrow morning."

"Yes,"—she sighed—"I suppose I *do* stand out around here."

There were a few bawdy remarks. She immediately turned and snapped, "Though not as much as some of these so-called soldiers would like."

Jesus, McLeane thought, another Corrigan. This was one tough broad, despite the pretty mouth and slender limbs.

"Give me pencil and paper," the woman said to McLeane, and they were quickly produced. She knelt by the side of the stockade wall and, by the light of a small flashlight, drew an outline of the Kara base, including the location of the munitions dump and several small trails the Japanese had cut within recent months.

"They have single-file trails cut halfway around the lake," she said. "These are patrolled every four hours.

We can see them from here. I suspect they're looking for natives."

"And hoping not to find any," McLeane cut in. "They may soon have to be disappointed."

"The trail to the east end of the lake terminates near a small cove. The trail to the west end stops at a mangrove swamp."

"What do you know about the dump itself?" O'Connor asked.

"It's the size of a large gymnasium, buried almost entirely. Only the top six feet project above ground. There's a service entrance—for loading and unloading—midway along the north wall, and a regular entrance midway down the shorter east wall. I imagine they're guarded, but I doubt by very many men. The Japs don't think the natives are much interested in munitions. They mainly like heads. Really, Major, the enemy seems more concerned with the Tauvi than with the chance of any insurgency by our side. One thing that may help you is the fact that the surface of the dump roof is covered with debris—branches, grass, garbage, clumps of ripped-up vegetation—in an attempt to hide it from bombing by our side."

"Is there enough of this phony cover-up for us to move along the top of the dump undetected?"

"I think so."

"Do you know anything about the reinforcement of the walls?" McLeane asked. "We have no information except that bombing doesn't seem to work."

"The walls and ceiling are made of twelve feet of steel-reinforced concrete," she said.

"Jesus Christ," McLeane said.

O'Connor shrugged. "It doesn't matter a bit, Major. I don't plan to destroy the building . . . only the contents. The bastards won't have time to refill it. If anything, the thick walls will help contain the explosion of the munitions going off. It will give us a more complete effect."

"Sort of like a pipe bomb?"

"Now you're cookin' with gas. Just like a pipe bomb."

"The dump is set a quarter-mile to the west of the main trail leading from the Kara base to the little boat dock they use to supply us," Janice said.

McLeane shut off the flashlight, stood, and thought for a while.

"O.K., here's what we'll do. Tentative plans only. We'll scout the area near dawn. Hide out all day tomorrow, then attack at midnight tomorrow. We'll let the Tauvi, who are hot to have Jap heads to hang on their tent poles, bushwhack one of the Jap patrols as it reaches the end of the east trail. When the patrol doesn't return, they'll send another. The Tauvi can have them too. The Japs will assume there's a massive native attack coming from the west and send all available guards in that direction. Then, we'll move in from the east, cross the top of the munitions bunker, take out the guards, and let O'Connor go to work."

"What about us?" Biggins asked.

"We'll let you have two or three knives. You can hide them when the Japs are here tomorrow, can't you?"

"As you Yanks like to say, it will be a piece of cake."

"After dark tomorrow, start going to work on the south wall of the stockade with the knives. Hack away at the bamboo and its bindings. Before the Tauvi start their attack, they'll leave one of their two big war canoes here. Heinman will stay to translate and show you how to get back to the river entrance."

"I won't be going for the big show?" Heinman asked, very disappointed.

"No. All you'll get to do is save a few dozen lives. Besides, anything I need to say to the Japs from this point on can be said with my Winchester."

"As you wish, sir," Heinman replied dutifully.

McLeane turned to him and whispered, "Besides, I want one of us to keep an eye on the Tauvi. I don't entirely trust them, and we don't want any taking of RAF heads, do we?"

Biggins said, "It's a classic pincer movement, Major, very good. A feint from the east, drawing the enemy's fire, and then the real attack coming from the west. I congratulate you."

"Congratulate me," McLeane said, "once we're safely back at Guadalcanal."

Fifteen

There were two Japanese soldiers patrolling the east trail every four hours, and of course, they stopped at the far end of it to sit on tree stumps and smoke vile-smelling cigarettes.

McLeane's Rangers lay in the underbrush less than twenty feet away, with Heinman by McLeane's side. As the soldiers talked, Heinman whispered a translation into McLeane's ear.

"Stinking weather."

"At least it's warmer than Osaka this time of the year."

"And has more mosquitoes."

"You know, I almost wish the Allies would attack and get it over with. I'd rather have a real fight than this damned patrol duty looking for cannibals."

"They're not cannibals, only headhunters. Here . . . I'll show you a cannibal."

The speaker leaped as if to bite the hand of the other man, but was shoved off. "Come on . . . let's get back. I hate this swamp."

The two soldiers tossed their cigarettes into the swamp and trudged back up the trail.

"They sound bored," Heinman said.

"They won't be for long. Let's see if there's a way to get to the bunker. The Tauvi say there may be a way through the mangrove swamp."

"Yes. A small trail hidden behind about one hundred square meters of sinimi fern between two stands of Nipa palms, somewhere along this trail."

"Let's move out, but stay low and keep it quiet."

"Do you think those two guys patrol both the east and west trails?" Contardo asked.

"Probably, stopping at the main road on each pass to bullshit with their buddies."

McLeane studied his watch as the group moved slowly down the trail. "Let's see, they stopped at the end of the west trail at two P.M. An hour to walk back to the main road. Another hour to reach the end of the east trail. That's four P.M. So the patrols reach the end of the trails at two, four, six, eight, ten, and twelve midnight. I think if we have the Tauvi take out the eight P.M. patrol, the Japs won't get a replacement patrol back to look for them before ten P.M. at the earliest. The Tauvi will take them on. When *they* don't report back by eleven, the Japs will attack to the east. We'll then have an hour clear to attack the munitions dump from the west. It shouldn't take longer than that, and the enemy will be running off to the east chasing headhunters."

"Sounds too good to be true," Contardo said.

"Yeah, that's what worries me."

McLeane's Rangers found the sinimi ferns easily enough. And, as the Tauvi said, hidden amongst the foul-smelling plants was a native trail that led in the direction of the airfield the Japanese invaders had carved out of the jungle they had occupied. Once, the trail was used by Tauvi warriors on headhunting missions against the tribes of the Koromina region east of Kara. Now the Japs had ruined the sport, but the ingenious Tauvi had made up their minds to substitute yellow skulls for brown or black ones.

The Rangers had to duck low, but indeed, there was a passable trail through the mangrove swamp which the

Japanese considered so impenetrable as to ignore. The trail led north-northwest and ended in the black concrete wall of the munitions dump. Incredibly, the Japs were so sure that the swamp was impenetrable that they hadn't bothered to clear away the underbrush from the southern edge of the bunker. O'Connor wanted to see the roof, which was eight feet up.

"Give us a boost," he said to Wilkins, physically by far the strongest of the Rangers.

Wilkins let O'Connor stand on his shoulders and, with a grunt, stood up, giving the Irishman a good look. O'Connor was back down on the ground in a minute.

"The Japs have put so much camouflage atop this tidy little potato cellar of theirs that you could move a tank battalion across it without being noticed," O'Connor said.

"So it's settled. The original plan sticks. Let's get back to the base of the river and let the Tauvi have the good news that the slaughter is soon to begin."

It was just before eight P.M. when the two Japanese soldiers approached the far end of the east trail. They were the same two soldiers the McLeane and his unit had seen earlier in the day. Although the sun had not yet set, it was dark in the rain forest, and the soldiers used a flashlight to pick their way to the end of the trail.

"Thank the spirits it's over for another day," one of them said.

"Yes. Want to stop for a cigarette?"

"No. I hate this place, especially at night."

"What? Are you afraid of a few crocodiles? Or is it savages that frighten you?" The man laughed and poked his friend in the ribs. "Come on, have a cigarette. We're finished for today."

"All right. A quick one. I want to get back to my tent and take a bath."

"You need a bath."

The two soldiers plucked cigarettes from their green packs and stuck them in their mouths. One lit a match. It was the final act of his young life. Two Tauvi arrows made faint swishing noises and then dull thumps as they embedded themselves six inches into the chests of the Japanese soldiers.

The men gasped, then fell to the jungle floor. Lalafa and one of his sons emerged from their hiding places, grinning from ear to ear and bearing long knives.

Two Japanese soldiers guarding the small boat dock which serviced the prison camp and which was at the southern end of the main road to Kara Field were also at the end of their long, ten-hour tour of duty and eager to get back to the base. Their replacements had already arrived, but it was 9:15 P.M. and the patrol that had gone down the east trail had failed to report back on schedule.

"They're fifteen minutes overdue," one soldier said.

"And on their final patrol. Who is ever overdue after his final patrol of the day?"

"Maybe they're taking their time."

"Sato and Kiraku? When have they been a second late when it was time to go off duty? You know they wouldn't laze around on their own time. Get on the telephone and have a patrol sent to look for them. Make it four men this time. Something may be wrong."

"You're an alarmist. Sato probably fell in the swamp and got lost."

"Do what I said nonetheless."

Within fifteen minutes, a jeep carrying four Japanese soldiers came to a halt by the dock. "What's the matter?" the unit commander asked.

"Sato and Kiraku are half an hour overdue from their last patrol of the day. Down the east trail."

"And this is unusual?"

"Very."

"Natives?"

"Or crocodiles. Who knows?"

"All right, we'll go looking for them. If we're not back by eleven, put out a general alarm."

"Yes, sir."

"Come on, men, double time." The four soldiers began jogging down the increasingly dark trail, their flashlights disappearing like fireflies into the forest.

The two guards who had waited half an hour for their comrades to appear had run out of patience. "Come on, let's get out of here," one said. He turned to the two replacements. "Now this palace is yours for the night."

"Thank you," one of them said, without conviction.

"Just remember to put out an alarm if those four heroes aren't back by eleven."

The replacements nodded, and the two weary guards went trudging up the main road toward Kara Field and what they were certain would be a restful night.

An hour later, at 10:30, the guards at the boat dock heard what they thought was the sound of far-off gunfire. They talked about it for a while, then decided that the noise was the sound of a "Betty" bomber, notorious for the roar of its engines, getting a tryout by the flight engineers at Kara. The matter was forgotten until eleven P.M. when, as instructed, they put out a general alarm warning of a possible Tauvi attack coming from the northeast side of Lake Tafu.

At eleven P.M., half a dozen armored personnel carriers rumbled down the road from Kara. From the passenger's side of the first vehicle stepped a short, rather fat Japanese colonel.

"I am Colonel Nakajima. You put out a general alarm. Why?"

"I was instructed to do so by Major Nakanishi. He left an hour and a half ago to investigate the failure of our last

137

patrol to return from its reconnaissance of the east trail. He, too, is now to be considered missing.''

''How many men in all?''

''Six, sir.''

''And nothing from any of them?''

''Not a word, sir.''

''Any problem from the island?''

''Nothing. They're as quiet as sheep. Sure, there were the usual insults after out last inspection tour, but apart from that . . . nothing.''

''I see.''

''There . . . there was one thing.''

''Tell me.''

''About half an hour ago we heard what might have been gunshots coming from the east.''

''And you didn't report it?''

''We dismissed it as the sound of engine repair. You know the racket they make over in the bomber sheds.''

''Yes, I know. Very well, Corporal. Stay at your post. I'm going in with my squadron to find out what the devil is going on here. I—''

The colonel's speech was cut short by the appearance of one of the four men who had gone down the trail after Sato and Kiraku. He was staggering from the trail, blood dripping down his chin. Without uttering a word, he fell flat on his face. There was a Tauvi arrow projecting from his back.

''That does it,'' Nakajima said. ''It's a massive native assault. Call out all available men and have them move on the east! Quickly!''

As Japanese klaxons sounded on the far side of the lake, Heinman stood poised, like Washington crossing the Delaware, in the prow of a largely empty Tauvi war canoe. He had with him only four native oarsmen, the rest of the tribe having slipped through the mangrove swamp to join the battle brewing to the northeast of Lake Tofu. His job was to ferry the POWs from the island to the river and keep them safe until the show was over and it was time to flee back downstream. At first Heinman minded being left out of the main action; upon second thought, he realized it made him responsible for rescuing some two dozen Allied POWs—without having to get shot at in the process.

Biggins had used the knives given him by McLeane well. After the Japs had left following their final visit of the day, Biggins and two of his men had set about the task of cutting through the ropes, wire, and palm strips that bound the bamboo bars of the stockade together. It took them only two hours to cut away four of the bars, enough for the prisoners to squeeze through, and they were waiting when the bow of the native canoe touched ground on the island.

Heinman gave Biggins a formal salute. "Lieut. Eric Heinman, United States Marine Corps."

"With a British accent?"

"My personal history is rather on the complicated side, sir. Suffice it to say that I was educated at Oxford."

"My Lord! Well, we can't ask for better than that, can we?"

"Is everyone here?" Heinman asked.

"That's right, Lieutenant. We even have a few Yanks and Aussies to help with the rowing."

Biggins peered suspiciously at the natives, who grinned at the POWs.

"Unh ... Lieutenant ... can they understand English?"

"Not a word."

"And can you speak their tongue?"

"Fairly well, sir."

"Heinman ... can we really trust these birds? One hears so much about their fondness for skulls."

"They've been perfect so far. Besides ..." He patted his M1, which was slung over his shoulder.

139

"Well, I'm certainly glad to hear that."

"Really, Colonel, all the Tauvi seem interested in is getting the Japs off their island so they can go about their business unhindered. When they heard we came here to kill the Nips their eyes lit up like Piccadilly Circus."

"All right, men, into the boat." As they complied, Janice Blythe stopped at the water's edge just long enough to wash her face and hands. Biggins said, "I assume we'll be going down the Tauvi. Where will we emerge?"

"In an uncharted cove about halfway between Cape Moila and the settlement at Marnagata."

"And how do you plan to get from there to Guadalcanal?"

"We have a Catalina waiting for us. The cove is totally covered with a canopy of leaves."

"I can't fault you fellows for not planning ahead. Major McLeane deserves his reputation."

"Begging your pardon, sir, but we'd better get on with it. Major McLeane wants us to get a good head start. As this boat is heavier with passengers than any of the others, they'll catch up."

"Right you are," Biggins said, and let Heinman give him a hand over the gunwale.

Sixteen

Even from their position behind the gymnasium-sized munitions dump, McLeane could hear the pounding feet of the Japanese soldiers rushing down the main road and, from there, into the east trail.

Starshells lit the jungle off to the east as hundreds of enemy soldiers went after the elusive Tauvi.

"I sure hope those Indians know what they're doin'," Contardo said.

"They've been doing it for centuries. They can hide behind a mushroom, then come out with their goddamned blowpipes blazing," McLeane said.

"Yeah, but up against an army?"

"An army that can't see them, starshells or no starshells. Look, Lalafa and his men will knock off a few dozen of the bastards then hightail it deep into the woods. The Japs won't be able to keep up with them."

The pounding of feet faded into the distance. McLeane said, "They're gone. I'll bet most of the on-duty personnel on that base are chasing the Tauvi now. Let's blow this goddamned thing and get the hell out of here."

He helped Wilkins onto the roof, and in turn, he pulled the others up. With McLeane and Contardo in the lead, their Winchesters fitted with silencers and held in front of them, the Rangers moved slowly across the roof of the bunker. Wilkins and O'Connor were behind, with the

141

burly Southerner helping the Irishman with his several heavy packs of explosives, fuses, and timers. The roof was nearly waist-deep in every form of litter imaginable, mainly branches and dead leaves. The sound of gunfire in the distance drowned out the noise the Rangers made as they pushed the debris aside.

When they neared the east end, beneath which the personnel entrance was to be found, they dropped to their knees. McLeane crawled to the edge and cautiously peered over. Two Japs guarded the entrance. They were smoking cigarettes and talking. No other enemy soldiers seemed to be around, and the main road was hidden from view by a sharp curve in the dirt trail that led to it.

McLeane crawled back to his men. "Two guards. Wilkins, get 'em."

Wilkins walked to the edge of the roof, pulled the bolt on his rifle, and fired twice in the space of a second. Nonchalantly, he walked back to the others. "Two dead Japs, Major."

Contardo looked at McLeane. "Ain't you even gonna check?"

McLeane shrugged. "Why waste effort? O.K., here's what we'll do. Contardo and Wilkins stay on the roof and cover us. O'Connor, I'll go down first and you lower your stuff to me. Then you follow."

"As you say."

McLeane lowered himself over the edge and dropped to the ground. Two enemy soldiers lay face-down in the dirt, their heads blown half apart. McLeane dragged them into the bushes.

O'Connor lowered four packs, each one weighing about forty pounds.

"You really need all this stuff?"

"No. I could probably take out this place with two grenades. But in that case I wouldn't get out myself."

"Who needs another Irish bartender anyway?" Mc-Leane said.

"Thanks a lot, Major." He joined him on the ground.

The entrance to the bunker was an unlocked metal door. "I'm gonna stick my head in to see if there's anyone in there," McLeane said.

He did so, his carbine in front of him. The door opened slightly, revealing a cavernous interior lit by dim ceiling bulbs and packed nearly to those lights in places. The crates were marked in Japanese, but McLeane, with Heinman's help, had taken pains to memorize the Japanese characters for danger and munitions and several other similar warning signs. The crates were arranged along four rows, and no one else appeared to be inside.

McLeane went back outside and helped O'Connor carry in his packs.

"How long is this gonna take?"

"Ten, maybe fifteen minutes if you don't mind lendin' a hand."

"Just tell me what to do."

Contardo and Wilkins were lying down on the roof, their guns trained down the dirt road. McLeane yelled up: "Contardo, I don't like surprises."

"Ain't no one here gonna get surprised but them Japs," Wilkins said.

McLeane rejoined O'Connor, who was already removing the straps from one of the four packs. He said, "They're color-coded, Major. It goes this way: blue, twenty minutes; yellow, seventeen minutes; red, fourteen minutes and green, ten minutes. Each pack holds six ready-to-go bombs. Each bomb has four sticks of dynamite, a dry-cell battery, a blasting cap, and a timer. The timer is set off by a red button. I sure hope you're not color-blind."

"Rather late to worry about it, don't you think? No, I'm not color-blind."

"We'll set the blue ones at the far end of the building. Don't be fancy. Just shove them anywhere and press the button. Then we'll move down the aisle and set the yellow ones. Same deal."

"O.K., I got the rest figured out on my own."

"The idea is that by the time we get done we'll have ten minutes to get the fuck out of here."

"By running across the roof of a building about to be blown sky-high. Terrific."

"Aw, it's a mere stretch of the legs. I figure we'll be off the building and halfway through the swamp before the building goes. All the bombs should go off more or less at the same time, but it doesn't really matter. The munitions will have something to say as well."

"Let's hope the Japs don't have anything to say. O.K., I'll take the blue and yellow. Let's make it fast."

"Oh, you can count on that, Major."

McLeane hefted the two packs and, struggling a bit under the eighty-pound weight, jogged down the main aisle to the far end of the dump. He ripped open the packs and pulled out two bombs. He stuck one behind a stack of crates which looked as though they contained artillery shells, and the other behind a larger stack of grenades. Before two minutes were out, he had the six blue bombs set in place along the ends of the four aisles and their timers ticking.

"Come on, Major," O'Connor shouted.

McLeane hauled the yellow pack a quarter of the way down the line of stacks and repeated his performance, hiding the bombs and pressing the red buttons. Then he ran as fast as he could to the entrance, where O'Connor was touching off the timer on the final bomb, which he placed right by the door.

"Done," the Irishman said proudly.

"Haul it," McLeane snapped, but just as the words were out of his mouth the sound of gunfire came from outside the building.

"Oh, *fuck,*" he said.

McLeane crept to the entrance and peeked out. Contardo shouted, "We got four guys, Major, but it may only be the first wave. You'd better haul ass."

McLeane and O'Connor hauled ass. They let Wilkins pull them up to the roof while Contardo kept his rifle trained down the dirt road.

"I hear an engine," McLeane said.

"The second wave."

McLeane and O'Connor readied their Winchesters and lay down beside Contardo and Wilkins.

"Eight minutes, Major," O'Connor said.

"Yeah, yeah. I just want to get the second wave. We can spare a few seconds."

An enemy jeep raced around the bend in the road. It carried four men and a Type 93 heavy machine gun.

"Fire," McLeane said.

The four Rangers fired almost as one, and another four enemy soldiers went to join their ancestors. The jeep went out of control, careened off a palm, and flipped over, blocking the road.

"Toss a grenade in it," McLeane said.

"Nix, Major," O'Connor shot back. "Too close to the bomb I planted by the entrance."

"O.K., let's go."

With Contardo in the lead, since he could see best in the dark, McLeane's Rangers ran across the roof of the munitions dump, following the path they had made on their approach.

"Seven minutes," O'Connor said.

"Shut up and run, you goddamned bog-trotter," McLeane yelled back.

There was the sound of another vehicle approaching the building; no matter, its way was blocked by the overturned jeep.

"If they get that machine gun up here they can sweep us off the roof," Contardo said.

"Somehow I don't think they want any more to do with sticking around this dump than we do. The Japs must have got it worked out by now. If they don't, they will as soon as the see O'Connor's first bomb. It's right inside the door."

"Yeah, and if they've got any brains they'll run like hell in the other direction."

"Six minutes."

Contardo snapped, "Here's the edge, jump!"

After he hit the ground, Contardo switched on his flashlight for a few seconds while the others found soft spots on which to land. Then darkness reigned again.

"Five minutes," O'Connor said.

"Contardo, I hope you're as good as you say at seeing in the dark." McLeane's voice was calm.

"Hey, don't worry, Major, there's lotso' dark alleys in Brooklyn. Follow me."

Contardo started jogging down the path through the mangrove swamp. It would take them to the far end of the west trail and, ultimately, to the lake. The others followed, with McLeane bringing up the rear, constantly looking over his shoulder for the chase that was yet to come.

"Four minutes."

"Let's say that whole thing goes sky-high." McLeane asked, "How far away should we be?"

"I wouldn't mind a mile," O'Connor replied.

"Well, you're not gonna get it."

"The jungle will give us partial cover. We'll hit the dirt with thirty seconds to go."

"The starshells stopped a couple of minutes before you guys got out of the building," Contardo yelled back.

"That means they gave up on the Tauvi. I hope the little bastards got away all right. Let's keep it quiet from here on. There may be a party waiting for us at the end of the west trail."

"Three minutes."

"Just let us know when to hit the dirt," McLeane snapped.

146

The sour, unpleasant smell of rotting vegetation assaulted their senses, as the tough leaves of sinimi ferns slapped at their arms and faces. They were nearing the half-mile point, not far from the lake.

"Coming up on the trail," Contardo said in a loud whisper that was passed back down the line. "I don't see anyone."

"Get ready anyway."

There was no enemy party waiting in ambush. The Japanese had not yet figured out from which direction the Rangers had come; they were preoccupied with trying to decide whether there was a chance of saving the munitions dump. The time for that decision was quickly running out.

The Rangers ran down the trail and slipped back into the mangroves, the same way they had come.

"Two minutes," O'Connor said, determined to give a countdown no matter how much abuse he had to take in exchange.

McLeane said, "At least now we're on ground the Japs don't know about. All we need is a little more real estate between us and that little explosion we're about to make."

"One minute, Major."

McLeane took a sharp slap on the face from a low-hanging palm frond, and swore. The bright waters of the lake appeared through the bushes. O'Connor shouted, "Hit the dirt!"

The four men did just that, falling into the dirt and marsh and covering their heads with their arms.

The thirty seconds left them by O'Connor seemed to go on for an hour. McLeane consulted his own watch. "I'm waiting," he said.

"Ten seconds," O'Connor replied.

The time came and went. Another thirty seconds passed.

"O'Connor, if you fucked up . . ."

At that moment the earth shook as if hell itself was erupting. All four men couldn't help but turn and look.

147

What they saw was a fireball that soared a quarter-mile into the sky and lit up the jungle as if it were noon. Exploding munitions . . . rockets, bombs, grenades, curled into the air like Fourth of July fireworks.

"Heads back down!" McLeane ordered.

The Rangers covered up again as debris began to rain down on them. Bits of concrete and shards of blown-out shell casings peppered the forest for several minutes before stopping.

Looking up again, then finally getting to their feet, McLeane and his men turned to see a gigantic fireworks show as shells continued to burst and rockets continued to curl high into the night air.

"We did it," Wilkins said. "My good Lord, we did it!"

"Yeah," McLeane said. "Now let's get back to the canoes before the Japs figure out which way we went. I have this incredible sixth sense that tells me they're a little pissed off right about now."

Seventeen

The two small canoes had been pulled into the bushes lining the extreme western edge of the lake, just to the north of a crocodile-infested swamp that was truly impassable, even for the Tauvi.

The Rangers found them and pushed them back into Lake Tofu. They only had to traverse a half-mile of lake front to reach the entrance to the Tauvi River. It sounded easy. It was not to prove so.

The Japanese, having watched their munitions dump and several dozen of their men disappear into the night air, were indeed pissed off. They had half a dozen men aboard the launch that normally ran twice daily to the prison island, all of the men armed to the teeth.

Once they learned that the prisoners were gone, they began a sweep of the lake. Fortunately for the Rangers, they headed counterclockwise, thereby missing the Tauvi warriors, who had already escaped down the river in their war canoes. The Rangers were nearly as lucky. They were just entering the river when the enemy spotlight picked them out.

McLeane and Wilkins were in the last of the two canoes. "Let 'em have it," he snapped.

Wilkins whirled around in a crouch and, as usual, fired from the hip while McLeane kept rowing. The spotlight was the first thing to go, disappearing in a hail of splinters. Two more shots resulted in two screams and one splash.

"I don't know how you guys lost the Civil War," McLeane snapped.

"Beats me, too, Major, sir."

The canoe disappeared into the Tauvi River despite a hail of Japanese fire. McLeane stopped rowing just after the barrier had been passed.

"Whatcha doin'?" Wilkins asked.

"Inviting incaution," McLeane replied, pulling the pin on a grenade. Imitating his CO, Wilkins did likewise.

When the Japanese patrol launch drew close enough, both Wilkins and McLeane tossed their grenades over the log barrier and into it. There followed two, perhaps three, seconds of shouting before the launch was turned into flaming matchsticks.

"Time to leave, gentlemen. Contardo?"

"Yo, boss."

"Can you see O.K., or should I be up front with the sniperscope?"

"I can see terrific. The moonlight is enough."

"Then let's row like hell. I want to put as much mileage as possible between us and them."

"How are they gonna come after us?" Contardo asked.

"Swim. I don't know. I'm just not counting out their having a trick up their sleeve. One thing's for sure, though. We have to catch up with the other two boats before they reach the first bridge."

"The Japs will have the bridges blocked. I never thought of that," Wilkins said.

"That's because you got nuthin' between your eats but turnips," Contardo replied.

"You care to say that to my face, Yank."

"Anytime. And don't call me Yank, you goddamned shit-kicker."

"You're not from the South. That makes you a Yank,"

Wilkins said.

"I'm from the South."

"Yeah. Where?"

"South New York." Contardo laughed at his own joke.

"I thought it was South Alcatraz." O'Connor didn't want to be left out.

"We just fought the Japs, and we're gonna have to do some more. Do we have to fight each other?" McLeane asked, then quickly added, "Contardo, what doesn't make you a Yank?"

"What doesn't make me a Yank is that Yanks are Yankee fans. I don't wanna be associated with them bums."

"No. You got your own Bums, right?"

"You bet your ass."

"What's he talkin' about, Major?" Wilkins asked.

"The Brooklyn Dodgers are known locally as the Bums."

"Most likely on account of their fans."

"Watch your mouth, plow-face," Contardo said. "Hey, Major . . . what's your team? I mean, they don't got one in Nebraska, do they?"

"Only semipro. I'm a Yankee fan."

Contardo muttered something McLeane couldn't hear.

"What did you say?"

"Nuthin'."

"He said 'fuckin' college boy,' Major," O'Connor said gleefully.

"You're a rat, O'Connor. A real stool pigeon. I'm gonna get you one of these days. What's *your* team?"

"Cubs, who else?"

"Terrific. What was their won-lost record last year?"

"I don't bother with trivia," O'Connor replied, a bit defensively.

"It was sixty-eight wins to eighty-six losses, that's what it was. I pegged you as a loser from the word 'go,' O'Connor."

151

"Boston and Philly did worse," O'Connor said.

"I thought you didn't bother with trivia. So the Cubs were third from the cellar. Three times nuthin' is still nuthin'."

O'Connor said, "Will you listen to him, Major? He can count, after all—without using his fingers."

"How'd you get the bad luck to be a Yankee fan, Major?" Contardo asked.

"Yankee Stadium is two bus rides and fifteen minutes from where I went to school. Besides, Gehrig was a Columbia man. He used to knock windows out of the Journalism building—this one professor's classroom in particular. I don't know why Gehrig picked on this one window, but I swear they had a crew on hand day and night to replace the glass."

"O.K., O.K., so the Yanks had a few good players . . ."

"A few good players! Shall we start with the Babe? Gehrig? And what about this new wop they got, DiMaggio?"

"Hey, watch your mouth."

"Might I bring your attention to last year's World Series?" McLeane asked.

Contardo said, "Luck, just luck."

"Yeah, the Dodgers were lucky to win one game. If Camilli hadn't gotten that lucky single off Murphy in the sixth and driven in Walker, the Bums would have stayed in the gutter where they belong."

McLeane was getting into the swing of things. For the first time in days, there was something nonlethal to fight over.

"That was no lucky single. That was the most beautiful shot you've ever seen. It stopped the Yankees' string of consecutive series wins at ten games."

"And that's just the point, isn't it, Contardo? You just admitted that the Yanks had rolled up ten consecutive World Series game wins. Did the Bums ever do that? Let's face it, Contardo, the Yanks had three men batting over .300 in last year's series—Rolfe, Keller, and Gordon. They outbatted Brooklyn .247 to .182, team average. And do you want to discuss the ninth inning of game four?''

Contardo turned nervous. ''I don't know, Major. Maybe we're makin' too much noise with all this chatter. The Japs could be following us.''

''Kiss my ass. The Dodgers were leading 4–3 in the top of the ninth with two outs. *Two* outs! You hear that, Contardo? You hear that, Japs? Then your center fielder lets a ball get away from him, letting Tommy Heinrich reach first. Four runs later gives the Yanks a 3–1 series lead. They wrapped it up the next day at the stadium without working up a sweat.''

''Awright, so they got lucky. Anybody who plays ball in the Bronx has got to be lucky even to stay alive.''

''You're an asshole, Contardo.'' McLeane laughed.

''Even for a Yank,'' Wilkins added.

There was silence for the shortest of moments, until McLeane put up his hand and told the others to shut up. ''I hear something.''

All listened.

''An engine,'' O'Connor said, ''a boat engine.''

''Back on the lake,'' Contardo chipped in.

''I thought they only had one launch on the lake,'' McLeane said.

''So did I,'' Contardo said.

''Did anybody bother to take a look at their boat dock?''

McLeane's answer was shakes of the head all around.

''So they have a second boat. Holding how many men?''

Contardo speculated, ''Twenty . . . maybe more.''

''All armed to the teeth and in full possession of our escape route. O'Connor, how long do you figure it will take them to bring down that log barrier they built between the lake and the river.''

O'Connor thought a moment, then said, "If they use grenades, an hour. If they use dynamite . . . assuming there's any left at their base . . . also an hour; it will take them half an hour to forty-five minutes to set up. If they can get two or three clear shots with an 88-mm gun—they can blow their way through right away."

"That's out of the question. It'll take them an hour to move an 88-mm gun within range. So we're talking about an hour, no matter what."

"It seems that way," O'Connor said.

"O.K., we're about a mile downstream now. In another hour we'll be three or four more miles downstream. That gives us a five-mile lead. Assuming their second boat is like the first, it has a deep draft and its captain certainly isn't familiar with the twists and bends of the river like we are."

"But they're faster and better armed," O'Connor said.

"And more likely to run aground. I think we have a shot."

"I hope so."

McLeane said, "We're at least a mile away from them now. I'm gonna try the walkie-talkie; it's set for a quarter-mile range. I want to raise Heinman and see if the Kraut is still alive."

McLeane put down his oar and let Wilkins do the rowing. He brought the mouthpiece of the bulky radio to his lips. "Lone Ranger to Adolph. You still with us?"

There was no response but static. McLeane tried twice more, with no better result.

"Switching to one-half mile range," McLeane said, and repeated the message. Still there was no reply.

"Three-quarters of a mile."

That one got a response. McLeane heard the reply. "Lone Ranger, this is, if you insist, Adolph. Come in."

"Adolph, we have finished our mission. . . ."

"We noticed, Lone Ranger. Nice fireworks."

"Thank you. We're about an hour behind you and gaining. Stop one-half mile before first bridge to await our catch-up. Rendezvous approximately 0500 hours. How are Tauvi?"

"They lost three men, but gathered a passel of heads. They are on top of the world."

"And the POWs?"

"Some serious malnutrition and several cases of malaria. Have two dozen healthy British men ready to fight, though. And one Australian woman who won't be kept by hearth and home."

"I think I met her, Adolph. Tell her she'll get her chance to fight yet. See you at 0500 or thereabouts."

Eighteen

McLeane had indeed moved his canoe into the van by the time the two small canoes caught up to where the large war canoes were moored, side by side. In the predawn hours, McLeane needed the infrared sniperscope to help him see more than a few dozen yards ahead. When he rounded the last bend and saw the war canoes, he also caught sight of half a dozen Tauvi warriors pointing blowpipes and bows at him.

McLeane struggled to remember the few native phrases Heinman had taught him. *"Mai-ito ahampeo?"* What is this?

The Tauvi lowered their weapons. Some smiled and raised severed Japanese heads high. "Mack! Mack!" they said.

O'Connor said, "I've seem some tough birds in my days on the south side of Chicago, but these guys beat 'em all."

"Don't they just?"

The clamor roused Heinman, who was sleeping in one of the war canoes. After his eyes cleared, he saw McLeane. "Major!" he exclaimed. "You're still alive!"

"A brilliant deduction. Attributable to your Oxford education, no doubt."

Colonel Biggins could be heard chortling from a position farther back in the same war canoe. The Tauvi were in one canoe with their trophies. The POWs and

Heinman were in the other. It had taken Heinman the better part of two hours to explain to the Tauvi why they felt less than comfortable falling asleep in the same canoe with three or four dozen severed craniums.

"I'll ignore the insult, Major, but only because it was the royal will of King George that set up that boarding house you call a school in the first place."

"Uh-huh. Tell me about the Japs. Have they fortified the first bridge? Do you know?"

"They have." The answer came from Janice Blythe, who had stepped over sleeping POWs to get to that portion of the war canoe nearest McLeane.

"How do you know? Reconnaissance by river is out of the question, and the swamp is impassable even to the Tauvi."

"Maybe the East Siwai swamp is impassable to the Tauvi, but it's not to me. I spent ten years here working for the Royal Geographical Society. I had the time to spend mapping trails and counting types of flora, a luxury the Tauvi could scarcely afford."

"They were too busy taking skulls," Contardo said.

"And after the war broke out I busied myself making charts of the whole territory."

"These charts . . . where are they?"

Janice tapped a fingertip against her temple. "In here."

"And for me to get them out . . ." McLeane said.

"You'll simply have to take me with you," she replied. "I suggest a land assault on the two bridges, with you and me taking the western bank and two or three of your men taking the east."

"Can you handle a gun?"

"Does a bear shit in the woods?"

"I can't claim personal knowledge, but I assume the answer is yes. What are the fortifications on the first bridge?"

"One light tank. A jeep mounted with a 6.5-mm Type II

machine gun. And about a dozen troops. All muzzles are pointed upstream."

"Which is?"

"A half-mile away."

"We'd better do it soon," McLeane said, "because there's a Jap river boat about an hour behind us and gaining, I have to assume, pretty fast."

"Jesus."

Biggins stepped back to where the two boats met.

"O'Connor?" McLeane called.

"Yeah, Major?"

"Do you have enough fireworks left over to turn that bridge into a dam?"

"Major, I can make a fine mess of it with just a few grenades. But it just so happens I have a few sticks of dynamite left."

"Good. Let's see if we can't give the Japs in that boat chasing us a few more obstacles to cut through. We'll take this bridge and move right on to do the same to the next. That should give us enough time to get downriver to the Catalina before the enemy catches up."

"There are two 20-mm Brownings mounted in the Catalina," Heinman explained.

"O.K., let's move. Wilkins and Contardo, you take the left bank. Janice, can you tell them a way to get to the bridge?"

"There's a trail . . . a wild-pig trail . . ."

"Perfect for these bums."

" . . . leading south along the bank of the river. It twists and turns a bit, but it will take you to the bridge. Now, there's a very thick patch of small nipa palms and sinimi ferns. The trail turns to the left there. If you go through the patch you'll be able to approach the bridge undetected."

"Got it," Contardo said.

"Off you go. Let's take those guys out and get going."

Biggins interrupted. "I don't mean to intrude on your battle plan, Major, but I have at least a dozen fit men perfectly capable of fighting and, in fact, rather eager for a little revenge."

"That's fine, Colonel, but we didn't bring extra arms. Heinman will stay with you to provide firepower if it's needed. I suggest you make a little noise starting in about fifteen minutes . . . say by starting to move up the river with as much noise as possible."

"In effect, to make the enemy concentrate on us."

"Yeah. I wouldn't come into firing range, though. Stop by the last bend in the river and let us do the rest. We'll contact you by walkie-talkie when we're done."

"Nonetheless, Major, if you could lend us your sidearms . . ."

"O.K., I don't suppose we'll need them. Contardo, Wilkins, Heinman, would you mind? Janice will be using mine."

The three Rangers handed over their .45's and a sufficient quantity of ammunition. McLeane gave Janice his handgun and an ammo belt, which she unhesitatingly strapped around her waist.

"Contardo, I'll give you the word by walkie-talkie when we're set. I think the most likely scenario is that we open fire from a secure position, drawing the enemy's attention from the river to us."

"You're gonna be duckin' a lotta lead."

"I said a *secure* position. To shoot at us they'll have to turn their backs on you."

"Gotcha, Major."

"We'll pluck their tail feathers, don't you worry," Wilkins said.

"Were I a worrier, I wouldn't have hired you guys," McLeane said.

Janice Blythe *did* know the East Siwai, and nearly tree

by tree. McLeane led the way, but at her direction, picking his way along a pig path similar to the one Contardo and Wilkins were traversing. Dawn was coming, and with it the seemingly inevitable ground fog. It would help cover their approach.

"The palms on this side of the river are older and bigger," Janice said. "There won't be any trouble finding a secure position. In fact, I think I recall one."

"Photographic memory?"

"So I'm told. I *do* keep notes when I can, though, just to be safe. The Royal Geographical Society likes to see reams of paper in exchange for its funding."

"They're not alone."

McLeane was once again slapped in the face by a sinimi leaf. "Did you rally spend ten years in this swamp?"

"In and around it. Until the Japs caught me a year ago."

"How'd they get you? I mean, you lasted out two years of their occupation."

"I got clumsy. I decided I just had to take a swim after three straight months in the woods. A Jap patrol boat came along and caught me starkers."

"Got you with your pants down, eh?"

"And a good deal more than that. The bastards thought it was funny."

"It was."

"Yeah, well you wouldn't have thought so if it were you. At least it saved my life."

"How'd getting caught swimming in the nude save your life?"

"The Japs assumed that any Australian woman crazy enough to be swimming starkers in shark-infested waters off a Japanese-held island—and off Tauvi territory at that—had to be too nuts to be a threat. And I had left my sketchbook on the bank with my clothes, the one I used to draw flora. I convinced them I really *was* a naturalist, and not a coastwatcher as well."

"Nice touch."

"Quiet now, we're getting close to the bridge. The stand of palms is just around the next bend.

McLeane cocked his Winchester and crouched down, moving with caution around the last bend. Before him the trail skirted the promised stand of old, thick nipa palms. Janice moved up beside him.

"I can't see the bridge," he said.

"That patch of woods is maybe a hundred feet across. We can go through half of it before we have to start thinking about being spotted.

"O.K. If we can't see them, they can't see us. Let's go."

They had just entered the stand of palms when McLeane heard a clamor of enemy voices and barked orders.

"Heinman has started to move downstream. O.K., the Japs are looking upriver. Let's find the biggest couple of trees near the bridge and open up."

McLeane and Janice found a triangle of thick palms not at all unlike the one he had used as a fortress during his solo mission along the Numa-Numa Trail. From behind it, they had a clear view of the enemy position. The force was exactly as Janice had described it.

The Japanese commander, a major, was on the radio. "He's calling for reinforcements," McLeane whispered. "Let's go to work before they get here."

McLeane got on his own radio. "Contardo . . . you in place?"

The reply was, "As our cracker friend here would say, in place and loaded for bear."

"I'm gonna try to pick off the guy manning the 20-mm and whoever moves in to replace him. Have Wilkins get that Jap major. We're secure. I'll get off enough shots to let them know where we are, then you guys open up."

"You got it."

McLeane put the radio aside and edged around the side

of one tree. To Janice he said, "You stay down and keep an eye out for anyone trying to sneak around to the side of us."

She nodded.

McLeane had a good view of the enemy jeep. The 20-mm machine gun, projecting from the rear of the vehicle, was aimed downstream; its operator, like all the enemy soldiers on the bridge, paying attention only to the river and the noise Heinman was making with his oars.

McLeane sighted in on the machine gunner and pulled back on the trigger. The man was caught in the chest and hurled right off the jeep. Confusion ran wild in the enemy ranks. McLeane stepped from behind the tree and picked off the man standing by ready to feed ammo belts into the 20-mm, then put two slugs into the mechanism of the gun itself. He then jumped back behind the tree as a hail of return fire ripped into the palms.

"They found us," he said.

"No kidding." The air was filled with splinters. Then, suddenly, another hail of fire filled the jungle air as Wilkins and Contardo opened up. There was more confused screaming as the enemy, now pinned down in the open and under fire from two sides, searched for guidance. There was none coming. Wilkins' first shot had severed the enemy CO's head as neatly as if it had been done by a Tauvi.

"My turn again," McLeane said as the fire that had been aimed at him began to go in the other direction. McLeane took a quick look. Three Japs had taken refuge from Contardo's and Wilkins's fire by hiding on McLeane's side of the jeep. McLeane put them down with one slug each, then picked off another Jap who was bravely trying to man the wrecked 20-mm.

Another storm of splinters ripped up McLeane's palm shelter.

"Enough already," McLeane said, picking up his radio. "Heinman?"

"Yes, sir?"

"Time to open up a third front. Stick the nose of your canoe around that last bend in the river and open up. I want the chance to move up and put an end to this."

"Right away, Major."

"Make sure everyone who isn't armed stays the hell down in the bilge."

"What are you going to do?" Janice asked.

"When the Japs realize they're under fire from three sides, they'll either break and run or hit the dirt behind the bridge railing. In any event, it will give me the chance to move closer and put an end to this bullshit."

"I'm coming with you."

"The hell you are. You stay right here."

"I can take care of myself," she insisted.

"Just do as I told you before. Don't let anybody get behind me I wouldn't drink with."

Janice was not happy, but gave in. McLeane peered around the tree. The fire aimed in his direction was slackening, then stopped entirely. Heinman and the British had opened up from the river. Two enemy soldiers broke and ran, but were cut down by Wilkins. The rest—and there were only four or five remaining—hit the dirt as predicted.

McLeane picked a large, single palm about fifty yards from what was left of the enemy force and ran full tilt toward it. He was noticed, but too late. A solitary slug embedded itself in the trunk of the tree after McLeane was safely protected.

He pulled the pin on a grenade, stepped out from the other side of the palm, wound his quarterback's arm and hurled a perfect strike. The Japanese resistance ended in a blast of fire and blood.

McLeane waited two, three, then four minutes and heard nothing but silence. He walked cautiously out onto the bridge. The carnage was dreadful; bodies and parts of bodies were everywhere. The CO's radio was still alive, presumably with requests for information. McLeane shut it off, and shouted, "All clear. Heinman, come up and join the party. Wilkins, Contardo."

He turned and was about to head off Janice before she could get to the bridge and the awful sight upon it when he was distracted by a sound from the river. McLeane turned to see the lead war canoe come around the bend in the river, the others close behind; the distraction nearly killed him.

A shrill Japanese war cry sounded, and then the roar of a .45. McLeane whirled as a blast from Janice Blythe's handgun cut down an enemy soldier who, though wounded, had gotten up the strength to try to put a knife in McLeane's back. Janice strutted up, proudly sticking the .45 beneath her belt. She seemed unmindful of the carnage.

"You were saying something before about being caught with one's pants down?" she asked.

"Yeah, yeah. So nobody's perfect."

"You could at least say thanks."

McLeane pulled her to him and gave her a quick kiss on the lips, earning a chorus of applause from the POWs. "Thanks," he said.

Janice was caught off guard by the kiss. For a moment she had nothing to say, and McLeane sensed she wanted more. But it was hardly the time or place, and she turned tough again. "Watch it," she snapped.

McLeane ordered Heinman up into the bridge. "My God," he said when he saw the bits and pieces of bodies.

"Yeah, the Major here has a real talent for making a mess," Janice said.

"Heinman, the Jap CO's radio is in the jeep and still functional. Find the nametag of some obscure private and radio in a quick call to their HQ. Sound like things are under control, but you're too busy to talk. Tell them 'This is Private So-and-so. The major is dead, but the enemy is routed. Some have fled into the swamp. We are pursuing.' Then sign off."

"Right you are."

Before long, Heinman was on the radio sounding as though he had been born in Tokyo. There was a brief, faint reply.

"They want to know if 'we' need help."

"Tell them we will if they don't shut up and let us get going after the enemy."

Heinman did it, then shut off the radio.

"Put a slug in it."

Heinman aimed his M1 at the dashboard-mounted radio and turned the instrument into garbage.

McLeane said, "In case there's anybody we missed, he won't be able to call home and tell them the truth. Do you think they bought it?"

Heinman shrugged. "There's no way to tell, sir, but I think so. The fact that we used the name of a real soldier will lend some credence to the fabrication. I will say, though, that their signal was rather on the faint side."

"It must be coming from Karamoku," Janice said. "That's the nearest Jap encampment."

"How far?"

"Twenty miles."

"They never go over twenty-five miles an hour on this dirt road. O.K., we've time, but not much. Heinman, how far do you make it to the next bridge? In hours and minutes."

Heinman thought, then said, "Five miles. We've got the current behind us this trip. The current is about three miles per hour, and we can row at least that fast. We might even make seven or eight miles an hour if we put our backs to it. I would estimate forty-five minutes to the next bridge if we leave immediately."

"O.K. O'Connor, you have five minutes to turn this

bridge into a fine dam. Let's move those boats through. Janice, back into the lead canoe. No need for you to revel in this pretty scene anymore."

"For once I agree with you," she replied, climbing over the bridge railing and, with the help of the men below, into the lead boat. Slowly, the four canoes moved under the bridge as O'Connor went about setting two packs of dynamite bombs at strategic points on the bridge. Contardo and Wilkins kept watch on the road and river in the event they had missed someone. They did not need another Japanese zealot, eager to do them in.

Instead of a zealot, what they got was the sound of an engine. Instantly, everyone was silent.

"A jeep?" Contardo asked.

"No. The RPMs are too low. A river boat. They've broken through the barrier we left by the lake."

"And are about a mile away, I should think," Heinman chipped in.

"O'Connor!" McLeane snapped.

"Hold your horses, Major. I'm almost set."

"Damn, I wish I had left that 20-mm gun intact. I'd take them on right here. Too late for that now. Set the timers for three minutes and let's go."

"Done," O'Connor replied when he had set the second one ticking.

The Rangers clambered over the south side of the bridge and into the last of the canoes. The other three were already well down the river.

"Row like hell," McLeane said, and the Rangers did, while McLeane trained his Winchester upriver.

"Two minutes," O'Connor said.

"Shut up and row."

"I can see my watch while I'm rowing," the Irishman shot back. "The goddamned oar is right in my face half the time."

"It'll be up your ass if you don't shut up and row," McLeane said.

"I don't suppose we'd be lucky enough for that river boat to be under the bridge when she blows," Heinman said.

"That's too much to hope for. Let's just hope the bridge goes down like Jake the Bartender here says it will."

"One minute," O'Connor said.

The canoe was nearing a bend in the river. Despite the splashing of the oars, McLeane could hear the boat growing nearer.

"O'Connor! We're only a few hundred yards from the bridge. Are we in any danger?"

"Not likely, Major. The whole mess should go straight down, what with the weight of that jeep to help it."

"You'd better be right."

"Thirty seconds."

The chugging of the boat engine had come within a half-mile of the bridge. Curiosity overcame the urgency of rowing when O'Connor started counting down from ten. Right on time, the Rangers saw the bridge light up in a brilliant flash of light, hover for an instant, then collapse into a pile of rubble blocking the river. The jeep sat atop that pile of rubble, like a ridiculous ornament.

"It'll take them at least an hour to blast through *that*," O'Connor said proudly, once the cheering from the POWs downriver had subsided.

"That's *if* they have dynamite," McLeane said. "What if they don't?"

"Then the poor dears will spend the rest of the day and half the night digging."

"Let's hope the latter is the case. Come on, gentlemen, let's catch up with the fleet."

Nineteen

McLeane halted their downstream flight at a point roughly midway between the two bridges and called a convocation in the lead canoe, where Heinman had regained his commanding position at the prow.

"We have to assume that by now—twenty minutes since the bridge blew—the Japs in that river boat have inspected the rubble and found only yellow skins."

"Logical," Heinman said.

"And that they have taken the trouble to pass the word on to the local HQ. I think we can expect another welcoming party at the next bridge."

"I consider the matter to be beyond doubt," Biggins said.

"A question. Can we take this bunch the same way as the last?"

"Why not?" said Contardo.

"Because there are no trails that I know of on the left bank," Janice said. "I know of one on the right. It's the same pig trail we were on before."

"So we go down that one," Contardo said. "We can get 'em in a crossfire between us and the men in the boat."

"No," said McLeane. "The guys in the boat would be wiped out. The enemy has to have at least one 20-mm on the bridge . . . same as the last time."

"Maybe the Indians know of a trail," Biggins suggested.

"Heinman . . . ask the chief."

Heinman complied, but Lalafa shook his head and said something that translated as "The forest is much too thick on that side river. Not even pig fit through. Full of crocodiles, too."

"So much for using the Tauvi as our left flank. It's just as well. We can't ask guys with bows and arrows to go up against machine guns . . . at least not during the day."

"We could fortify the bow of this canoe and plow straight through," Biggins suggested.

"That's a thought. We ought to fortify the bow anyway, though these planks must be two inches thick. Still, we'd be no match for them. What we need is a whole new tactic. Heinman, is there any of that tea left?"

"Tea?" Biggins asked.

"In a manner of speaking." McLeane was handed the jerry can and took a mighty swig. "You're welcome to a sip or two, Colonel, but I'll warn you . . . Earl Grey it ain't."

Biggins had a drink; his eyes rolled around in their sockets. "My word!"

"Enough," McLeane said, taking back the can. "We have to keep our wits about us. Let me think." He took another swig, then screwed the top back on the can.

"O.K., here's what we'll do. Heinman will take the canoes down the river to a spot just out of sight of the bridge. You recall that bend where the sand bar came out?"

"Yes, sir."

"The rest of us will go down the trail and get the lay of the land. If there's a Jap force on the bridge, and it's too big for our combined efforts to handle, Contardo and I will go up the road a mile or two and see what we can find that might be useful."

"What?" Contardo asked.

"An enemy jeep!" Biggins said. "If they've called in reinforcements based on evidence found at the first bridge, as is likely, you could take one of their jeeps intact.''

"Right, and hopefully it will be one carrying a 20-mm gun."

"That's a long shot, Major," Contardo said.

"You have a better idea?"

Contardo shook his head.

"If nothing happens along that we can grab, then we'll cross the road and take up positions behind them. That way we'll have fire from both sides."

"It sounds like the only feasible plan to me," Biggins said.

McLeane picked out a sand spit that jutted ten feet into the river from a small clearing on the otherwise fern-choked bank and ran the lead canoe gently aground.

"O'Connor, you stay with the boats."

"Hey, I may be out of dynamite, but I can still shoot and I got a left hook you wouldn't believe," he objected.

"Do as you were told. I want Heinman with us this time. There just may be some bit of information he has on the terrain that Janice doesn't. And I'm gonna need all the information I can get from here on in."

"I'm ready, Major," Heinman said proudly.

"O.K., same as the last time. I'll give a shout on the radio when we're set. O'Connor, you make some noise with the oars or something. Pick a fight with one of these limeys."

"That will be a pleasure."

"I don't care what you do as long as it gets those Jap gun barrels aimed your way and gives us the chance to get the jump on them."

"You're not going without me," Janice said.

McLeane smiled. "I can't think of anyone I'd rather get lost in the woods with."

McLeane helped Janice out into the sand spit. Contardo, Wilkins, and Heinman quickly followed, pausing just long enough to shove the bow of the war canoe back into the water. O'Connor took up Heinman's position in the bow.

"Watch yourself," McLeane said.

" 'Watch yourself,' he says, to a man who's out on a fine river cruise while you're risking your neck in the jungle."

"Nonetheless."

"O.K., Major, I'll be careful."

McLeane started toward the bank, then turned back. "O'Connor? Weren't you too young to have made a stinger for Al Capone?"

O'Connor smiled. "You're right, Major. I lied."

"I thought so."

"I made it for Frank Nitti, the wop that took his place."

McLeane shoved Contardo into the woods before a ruckus could break out.

The pig trail that Janice had described was, fortunately, wider than the last one. Apparently the animals traveled in greater numbers the nearer they got to the coast, trampling down more underbrush in the process.

McLeane led the way, with Janice right behind him. As he bent low to get under the branch of a katari tree, she said, "you know, McLeane, I'm getting tired of staring at your bottom all the time."

"Hey, you go up front. I'll stare at yours for a while."

"What I *meant* was, I'd like something to *do* around here." She smiled and gave him a friendly poke.

"Well, I think you made a nice contribution at the first bridge. This time . . . you can tell me how long it will take us to get to the road."

"At this pace . . . an hour, no more."

"Does this trail go all the way to the coast?"

"Yes and no. It gets rather complicated after we pass the next road, but don't worry, I know the way."

"I'm gonna get that Paddy bastard when this is over.

I'm gonna get him good." Contardo's statement made them all laugh.

The pig trail split before reaching the road leading across the bridge that was the last obstacle between the Rangers and the freedom of Tauvi Lagoon. The left fork led toward the bridge; the right led off to the southwest. "It crosses the road about two miles west of the bridge," Janice said.

"And the left trail?"

"Same as the last one," she replied. "It skirts a palm grove a few score yards from the bridge."

"Is that grove as thick as the last one?"

"Just about."

"O.K.," McLeane said. "Heinman and Wilkins, you creep up the left fork and hide yourselves in that grove. Janice, Contardo, and I will find our way up the right fork and see how the pickings are."

"Roger, boss," Wilkins said.

"When we move, you'll know."

"How will we know?"

"Trust me," McLeane said.

He led the way up the right-hand trail. The forest seemed to be thickening as they moved closer to the coastline. The occurrence of mangrove was more frequent, and the bellowing of crocodiles nearly constant. Janice provided direction, and McLeane obeyed. She indeed knew the territory well.

The trail met the road where Janice had said it would— about two miles west of the river crossing. Its way to the road was blocked, as was so often the case, by a shoulder-high stand of ferns. McLeane pushed them aside.

The dirt road was heavily trafficked; there were many signs of recent activity, both by vehicles and infantry. To the left, he had a clear view of a mile or more. To the right, the road went up a slight grade, then disappeared from

172

sight, perhaps a hundred yards away.

"We'll go up to the top of that hill," McLeane said. "I want to have the best possible view in all directions."

"Is that a good idea?" Janice asked. "To put us in the open like that?"

"We have to see what's coming, and we can't from here. Besides, there's no end of woods to dive into if we don't like what we see."

"Yeah, lots of woods with lots of alligators," Contardo said.

Janice laughed. "They're crocodiles, not alligators."

"Big things with lotso' teeth. Same difference."

"And none of them are close enough to the road."

McLeane started up the hill at a jog, and they followed. Once at the top they could see the trail for nearly two miles to the west and a bit more than a mile to the east. It was, so far, empty.

Janice checked the surrounding terrain. Instead of mangroves there were areca palms and banyan trees, underlined with the usual coating of small vegetation: wild plantain, alpinias, and heliconias. There was, indeed, plenty of benign vegetation to dive into.

McLeane said, "O.K., here we sit until something comes along. If the Japs are as forewarned about our arrival downstream as we think, that shouldn't be too long."

"And if they're not?" she asked.

"Oh, I think that given the little display we left at the first bridge, the enemy will expect us any time now."

"And should be sending reinforcements. Like whatever it is that's coming up the road from the west."

McLeane whirled in that direction and saw a dust cloud on the horizon. He trained his binoculars on it.

"Whatcha got, Major?" Contardo asked.

"Just what we need. A jeep."

"With a 20-mm?"

"Could be, could be. It's hard to tell from here."

"We've got to take that thing intact."

"And it's too late to drag a log across the road. We need a diversion . . . something that will stop them."

"Will I do?" Janice offered.

"No way. I'm not going to let you get killed," McLeane said.

"I have no intention of getting killed. What do you say I let myself 'get caught' in the act of crossing the road?"

"I don't want you caught either. For one thing, they just may blow you apart without asking questions."

"I won't get caught. I'll freeze long enough to let them see I'm a woman, then run into the woods on the south side of the road. You guys take them from behind when they stop to look for me."

Contardo said, "It could work, Major."

McLeane thought fast. "O.K., but you have to promise to find a fat tree to hide behind."

"You can count on it."

"That jeep's coming up fast," Contardo warned.

"Silencers on, and into the bushes. Janice?"

McLeane took her by the shoulders, brushed her hair aside, and kissed her on the forehead. "Be careful."

"Yes." She nodded.

McLeane and Contardo leaped into the bushes to the north side of the road, while Janice stood by the side of it. When the enemy jeep was a hundred yards away she jogged across the road, saw the jeep, and pretended to freeze. One of the two men in the vehicle pointed at her, then rose from his seat.

She bolted into the woods to the south. Predictably, the jeep roared to a halt near the spot where she had disappeared.

The Japanese private, who had gotten up from his seat, was barking orders into the woods. "Now," McLeane said.

Two simultaneous shots were fired. The driver slumped

174

over in his seat. The other soldier was hurled from the jeep.

Quickly, McLeane and Contardo ran to the jeep. "Let's toss these guys into the woods. Get their grenades first, though."

McLeane dragged the body of the driver out of the vehicle and into the woods to the north.

"Janice!"

She came out of her hiding place, shaking her head.

"You guys are really something," she said.

"It was you who did it. Come on, get in the back of the jeep. Contardo, are you a good wheelman?"

"Are you kiddin'? I got me a reputation that goes all the way from Flatbush to Bensonhurst."

Contardo inspected the machine gun, which was mounted where the rear seat would have been. It was smaller than a 20-mm; but there was plenty of ammunition, and the firer was protected by a metal shield.

"I never seen a Jap gun like this before," Contardo said.

"It's a 7.7-mm heavy machine gun, belt fed. Don't worry, I can operate the dingus."

Contardo got behind the wheel and tried out the transmission. "I got no problem with this thing. How do you want to go in?"

"Fast, and at the last moment, just before we reach the bridge, make a sharp left, get the hell out, and use the jeep as a shield. You, too," he said to Janice.

"I want to be with you," she protested.

"Just do as you're told. If you insist on helping, help Contardo chuck grenades."

"Major, what if they've got a goddamned tank down there? We're going in blind."

"Then I would say we're in big trouble."

"No foolin'?" Contardo said and put the jeep into gear.

Twenty

McLeane took the dust cap off the muzzle of the machine gun, fed in one of the long cartridge strips, and cocked the weapon. Contardo had the jeep up to around thirty mph, about as fast as was possible on the dirt road. Janice was huddled down beneath the machine gun, surrounded by crates of grenades and machine-gun belts.

It took three or four minutes before the bridge came into view. McLeane let out a sigh when he saw it. There was indeed a Japanese force, but it was only a bit larger than the force on the first bridge. Notified by the river boat radio that the Allies had escaped, the enemy CO had called in reinforcements. He didn't know, of course, that McLeane had his finger on the trigger of the "reinforcements." A few of the Japs on the bridge looked up briefly when the jeep was heard roaring down the dirt road, but paid its arrival little real attention. It was expected, and was kicking up so much dirt and dust that its occupants were hard to see.

McLeane trained the 7.7-mm on the 20-mm already mounted on the bridge. He wanted to take it out before Contardo made his turn and aim momentarily became impossible. The enemy soldier manning the 20-mm saw the approaching jeep, gave it a toothy grin, and waved. It was the last thing he did in his life.

McLeane hit the man with a burst in the belly that

knocked him clean off the jeep and the bridge as well; then he raked the jeep with fire, killing the 20-mm feeder and the enemy CO, this time before the radio could be used.

Contardo whipped the jeep into a sharp turn. Hugging the 7.7-mm just to hold on, McLeane still managed to free a grenade from his ammo belt, pull the pin, and toss it into the enemy ranks. Four Japanese soldiers, gathered in front of the jeep, were blown to the four winds.

Chaos overwhelmed what remained of the fifteen or twenty Japanese soldiers on the bridge as fire opened up on them from the underbrush to the northwest, from the river to the north, and from their own jeep. Contardo and Janice were hidden behind their commandeered jeep in an instant, McLeane covering them as he raked the bridge with rapid fire.

Contardo tossed two grenades, both falling short of the enemy jeep but clearing out any opposition on that side.

"Try not to blow my fuckin' head off!" Contardo yelled to McLeane.

"What are you . . . ?"

McLeane's words trailed off as he watched Contardo run head-down toward the enemy jeep, a grenade in each hand. Suddenly there was a rustling in the bushes, and Wilkins and Heinman were on his tail, their rifles at the ready. McLeane kept firing, sweeping the bridge to the far side of the enemy jeep but well over the heads of his men.

Contardo tossed a grenade to the far side of the enemy jeep and then huddled alongside it. The explosion filled the air with screams.

Heinman and Wilkins were standing atop the jeep in a flash, firing both from the shoulder and the hip. McLeane grabbed his rifle and ran to join them, but it was all over by the time he got there. Two enemy soldiers ran off down the road to the east.

"Contardo, try to get those guys."

"Yo, boss."

Contardo sprinted up the road in pursuit of the two escapees, but was back in a moment. "They got away into the woods. I couldn't follow 'em."

"Don't worry about it. The crocodiles will get them."

Janice came wandering up, her hands on her hips, shaking her head in disbelief at yet another scene of bloody carnage.

"Did you ever make a count of how many men you've killed?" she asked.

He shook his head. "After a while it all becomes a kind of yellow blur that you pump shells into."

Contardo said, "Actually, ma'am, the major here *does* keep count. He makes notches in his wooden leg."

"You're gonna be countin' boot marks in your ass if you don't watch what you say," McLeane snarled, shouldering his rifle.

Heinman and Wilkins jumped down from the enemy jeep. "I must say, that was a brilliant frontal assault, Major," Heinman said. "How did you manage to take that jeep intact?"

"I had a unique decoy," McLeane said, indicating Janice.

"I see what you mean. Running across a beautiful woman in the middle of the Bougainville jungle must have been quite a shocker to them."

"Not as big a shock as those Japs got when they turned their backs on us to look for her," Contardo said.

"I can quite imagine."

"All right," McLeane said, "enough self-congratulation. Heinman, tell O'Connor to move those boats through."

Acknowledging the order, Heinman ran to the northern rail of the bridge; it was red with blood and torn by 7.7-mm slugs. O'Connor, already rounding the bend, waved his rifle as if it were a triumphant sword.

"Did you get 'em all, lads?" he called.

178

Heinman replied, "Two escaped, but they've fled into the woods. I don't think we need worry about them. The major wants to move the boats through."

"I'll gladly do that." O'Connor waved the boats forward, and both Tauvi and Allies rowed. "But there is something for you to worry about."

McLeane overheard and came to the railing. "What's that?"

"The Jap river boat. She blew the first bridge and could be halfway here by now. I could hear the explosion from nearly three miles off, so it must have been a beauty."

"Damn it," McLeane swore. "And you say you're out of dynamite?"

"I haven't so much as a match."

"We've got to blow this bridge."

"Given an hour, I could rig something up."

"We don't have an hour. Get the boats through and let me think."

O'Connor obeyed orders, bringing the four canoes safely under the bridge.

Heinman said, "Six or seven grenades, properly placed and set off simultaneously . . ."

". . . Might or might not bring down this bridge. Anyway, the Japs have shown themselves perfectly capable of blowing away any obstacle we may put in their path. That river boat of theirs must be armed to the teeth."

Heinman smiled. "And expecting what?" he asked.

McLeane joined him in his smile. "Either a determined but underarmed force fleeing them . . ."

". . . Or a well-armed friendly force on this bridge!"

"Heinman, you're a bloody genius!" McLeane said, clapping his friend on both shoulders at once. "Contardo?"

"Yeah, Mack?"

"That jeep we stole. Bring it up here alongside the other one. Heinman, see if that 20-mm is still functional."

O'Connor looked up from his position in the lead boat. "You're going to ambush that Jap river boat, aren't you?"

"Right you are."

"That may not give you time to catch up with us."

"We'll go by land. Get moving."

"Major," O'Connor protested, "I don't want to leave you."

"Janice can show us the way through the jungle." McLeane turned to her and asked, "You can, can't you?"

She nodded.

"O'Connor, get those prisoners and the Tauvi to safety in the lagoon. That's an order."

"Major . . ."

"That's an order, O'Connor. It may take us an extra day to catch up, but that will just give you all the more time to relax. You might even shoot a boar and have it roasting for us when we arrive."

"Aye, I'll at least do that."

"Get the hell outta here," McLeane barked, and the four boats started on their way back down the river, to the lagoon, and safety. "Good luck, Major," Biggins shouted.

Contardo brought the jeep McLeane and he had captured alongside the other one. Now there were two machine guns facing upstream, toward an enemy river patrol boat whose chugging could just be heard in the distance.

"Heinman?" McLeane asked.

"It's a 20-mm Browning, sir, probably bought before the war. And in perfect shape."

"O.K. Wilkins, Heinman, take up positions near the west end of the bridge. Janice, where's the trail south?"

"Near a mangrove swamp about a hundred yards west. I know it well."

"Then get up there and wait for us. We'll be along soon enough."

"I'd rather—"

"Janice!" McLeane said sharply.

"I know." She sighed. "What can a girl armed only with a .45 and her wits do?"

"You saved my life once, and I'm grateful. Can we debate this later? Right now I'd prefer you leave the warfare to the professionals and wait by the trail."

"Yes, *sir*," she said sharply, and marched off.

"Women."

"You can't live with 'em and you can't live without 'em," Contardo said.

"Amen to that."

McLeane went to both jeeps, pulled out his .45, and put a single slug in the bottom of each gas tank. Petrol began to pour onto the deck of the wooden bridge.

"Whatcha tryin' to do, Major, get us blown up?"

"Yeah. I was planning on having fried—sorry—broiled dago for lunch."

"Hey, I gotta take that from O'Connor; now I gotta take that from you, too?"

"Until the day you outrank me, yeah, you do. Heinman, Wilkins, go set up. That boat is getting closer."

McLeane smashed the radios on both jeeps with the butt of his Winchester. "Just in case those two guys who ran into the woods can get back here after we've left and before this bridge goes up in flames," he explained.

McLeane took up his position behind the 7.7-mm machine gun he had swiped from the enemy.

"When do you want to open up?" Contardo asked.

"Let's see. The bend in the river is about a hundred yards off."

"A piece of cake."

"Yeah, but I want several pieces of cake. Let's let the boat get fully around the bend and then some. By the time her skipper figures out he's been had her momentum, and the current, will have carried her within seventy-five yards. *Then* we'll open up. You take the wheelhouse. I'll

181

take out any machine guns and then go for the waterline. After the wheelhouse, sweep the decks."

"You got it."

"With any luck, we'll drive them aground on the east bank and have them at our mercy. I want that boat out of our lives once and for all."

The twin sounds of petrol flowing onto the timbers of the bridge and the chugging of the boat's engine filled the air for one, two, three, then seven minutes. At last the boat appeared. It was a narrow, fairly small launch only about forty feet long. The only permanent armor on it was a 7.7-mm machine gun mounted on the bow. There was a small wheelhouse which fit three people, but the boat was loaded to the gunwhales with enemy soldiers, many of them carrying light machine guns.

"We have to get as many of those guys as we can while we have this chance," McLeane said.

"Yeah. There must be fifty of the bastards."

The boat came around the bend and turned toward the bridge. "Ready," McLeane said, and he could hear Contardo pulling the bolt on the 20-mm. There was another sound—the river boat's transmission being shoved into reverse.

"They've figured it out! Open fire!"

McLeane opened up first, blowing the machine gunner and his weapon from the deck. Then, before having to change ammo belts, he put a row of holes the entire length of the ship right at the waterline. In the meantime, Contardo turned the wheelhouse to splinters. The boat veered to port, its bow ramming aground against the left bank.

His gun reloaded, McLeane went to work on the midship area, where he figured the engine and gas tank to be. As promised, Contardo swept the deck with his next burst. That sent a few Jap soldiers over the side in an attempt to reach the woods. Only a few did, but the other Rangers picked them off one at a time. The rest of the enemy ducked below decks.

"Only you got the power to shoot through the hull, Mack," Contardo shouted.

"Consider it done."

McLeane peppered the hull with 20-mm fire. There was a chorus of cries and shouts, and a dozen enemy soldiers dove over the far gunwale and into the water before clambering into the swamp. Wilkins and Heinman got a few, but more escaped. Contardo and McLeane continued firing until they were out of ammunition. Despite the best efforts of the other Rangers, another handful of enemy soldiers escaped into the swamp.

The silence that descended was deafening.

"That boat's finished," McLeane said. "It's not going anywhere."

McLeane jumped down from the jeep, and Contardo quickly followed. "Let's not stand around admiring our handiwork this time. Let's haul it."

The four Rangers ran up to where Janice was marking the trail south. McLeane pulled the pin on a grenade and tossed it onto the bridge. When the grenade exploded, so did the spilled gasoline. Soon the wooden bridge was a blazing inferno. As the Rangers followed Janice into the woods, the gas tanks on the two jeeps exploded, and a few minutes later, the whole bridge tumbled into the river.

Twenty-one

Dusk was beginning to settle in. It seemed that they had been walking for days. In fact, they were six or seven miles from the bridge. Janice finally turned to McLeane, who was following her lead, and said, "I've had it."

"What, do you want to be carried?"

"Come on, Mack. We're ten miles downstream from that bridge."

"Well, almost."

"And dusk is settling in. I can't follow this trail in the dark, and if I can't you sure can't."

"The point is, can the Japanese?"

"They never have before."

"They've never been quite so pissed off before."

She turned and faced him, effectively halting the march. "Mack . . . the Japs have been here two years. I've been here ten. I know a hiding place they'll never find, even if they are dumb enough to try to follow this trail in the dark. It's about a mile inland. I used to use it as a base camp when I was making my sketches of the local flora."

Heinman perked up. "Are you familiar with the local flora?"

"And fauna. But after we rest, please."

"O.K.," McLeane said. "We'll camp there for the night and move at dawn."

"I could sleep for a week," Contardo said.

"When we get back to Guadalcanal you can sleep for a month. What's today's date, by the way?"

"October 29. Why do you ask?" Janice said.

"Just wondering. All right, Janice, where's this camp of yours?"

"Follow me."

She led them through a small mangrove swamp that they had to traverse by hopping from clod to clod and, occasionally, crawling on their hands on knees. "Tell me the Japs are going to follow this," she said.

"O.K., O.K., we agree," McLeane said.

Before too long they were on another trail and headed inland, away from the mangrove swamp and alongside a fresh-water stream that Janice said ran all the way from the inland volcanic mountains to the Tauvi River a few miles downstream. Heralding the coming of darkness, a flight of several hundred fruit bats soared overhead, making their usual racket. "We're nearly there," she said.

Janice Blythe's old camp was a thirty-foot-wide clearing between a mixture of banyan and katari trees. The ground was soft and dry, and covered with leaves. The constant trickling of a tiny nearby stream provided a backdrop of rather pleasant noise. The Rangers dropped their equipment on the ground and flopped beside their packs. McLeane put his pack next to a banyan tree, then sat, leaning against it. He lit a cigarette and offered one to Janice, who had joined him.

"The katari bark burns readily, if you want to make a fire. The natives all over these islands use katari resin for their fires and torches, so the Japs will take no notice of it . . . if they see it at all."

"Have a smoke?" he asked.

"Thanks."

She took one of his Luckies, and he lit it for her. "What a day," he said.

"Do you do this all the time?" she asked.

185

"Sometimes I get a few weeks off."

"And what do you do on your time off?"

"Get bored. Play football. Have a few beers with the boys. Write home. What else is there to do?"

"Isn't there someone in your life?"

"A woman? This is a war zone, not the French Quarter of New Orleans."

"Surely a man of your repute . . . and looks . . ."

"I am not now or have I ever been engaged to be married," McLeane said. "I won't lie and tell you I spend all my time alone, but . . ."

". . . You're not precisely halfway up the aisle to the altar, right?"

"Right. What about you?"

She laughed. "How many chances do you imagine I have? And if you think anything untoward transpired while I was locked up with that bunch of limeys . . ."

"It never crossed my mind. Is there anyone home waiting for you?"

"Nope. Ten years is too long to expect any man to wait. And you?"

"Just mom and dad."

"In their comfy little cabin somewhere in the States, right?"

"Nebraska."

"Where's that?"

"Somewhere in the States. In the middle of the States. My dad is a newspaperman."

"Mine's with the navy. The Australian Navy, that is. He's a purser aboard a corvette."

"That's a nice way to get knocked about, at least in the Atlantic."

"The waves are smaller here," Janice said. "He says it's not too bad a life."

McLeane finished his cigarette and stubbed it out. "Are you hungry?"

"No. Just dirty and tired."

"Me too. Is there a place around here where I can take a bath without being eaten by a croc or having to let this bunch of rogues watch me."

Her face lit up with a smile, she got to her feet, and helped him up. "Come with me."

Contardo saw them first. "Where you goin', Major?"

"To the Ritz. You guys stay here. Build a fire if you want. Wilkins, feel free to shoot us something edible . . . using your silencer, of course. Heinman will tell you what's edible and what isn't. Janice and I will be back in a while."

The rest of the Rangers refrained from making provocative comments as McLeane followed Janice Blythe's round little behind out of the clearing and upstream. A few hundred yards upstream—they had traversed these by walking in the two-inch-deep water itself—was a small fresh-water pond almost entirely surrounded by white, yellow, and brown orchids and sinimi palms.

Near the point where the stream departed the pond was a patch of flat, mossy land. McLeane sat on it, Janice by his side. He had brought his shaving and bathing kit with him; this consisted of two bars of soap and a folding razor with two extra blades.

"I can see why you like this place so much. It's like the Garden of Eden. I don't suppose there's anything in that water that will want to take a bite out of me."

"Not a thing. The dangerous items are found mainly in the mangrove ponds."

McLeane began to strip off his clothes. "Janice, you've been around the pike a few times, like me. I assume you don't mind."

She smiled. "On the contrary, I've always wanted to see what a hero looks like without his armor on."

"Apart from a few more cuts and bruises, about the

187

same as anyone else."

"Somehow, I doubt it."

"We'll see. How deep is the water?"

"Five feet, no more."

McLeane took off all his clothes while Janice watched, then dove into the water, staying submerged a minute, then coming to the surface. "It's warm," he said.

Her voice came not from the bank, but from behind him. She was in the water, too. "It's volcanically heated. Good for the sorts of aches and pains that heroes get."

He spun to look at her. She was naked, too, and her long blond hair hung beautifully over her neck and shoulders. "Your soap, sir," she said, and handed him a bar.

"Thank you, Corporal," he said with a twinkle in his eye.

McLeane soaped himself from head to toe, then found the bar taken away from him. "Here ... I'll get your back." She got a good deal more than that, as her fingers ran down his spine, over his buttocks and down the backs of his thighs. Finally, she washed herself, last of all her long, thick hair.

She was about to toss the soap onto the bank when he took it from her. With one arm encircling her just below the breasts, he soaped her back, behind, and thighs, as she had done for him. Then he tossed the soap onto the bank.

"Are we even now?" he asked.

She turned saucy, putting on a phony cockney accent. "Sure, mate. You saved my life, and I saved yours. You washed my arse, and I washed yours. I'm supposin' that makes us even."

"The hell it does," McLeane said, grasping her and pulling her against him. Her large, round breasts were flattened against the muscles of his chest.

"Are all heroes so rough with their women?"

"Only when they find their women in the jungle, where roughness is expected."

Janice sighed, relaxed her muscles, and let him wrap her in his arms. They kissed, long and deeply, while the warm spring waters whirled around them. They felt each other out, and explored each others' bodies.

At last they were on the soft moss of the bank, lying side by side, staring up at what few stars could be seen through the canopy of rain forest vegetation. She was counting on her fingers. He watched for a moment, then resumed looking at the stars.

"Making your own notches?" he asked after a time.

Her reply was immediate. "No, Mack. I'm just being safe. It's been awhile, you know. What day did you say today is?"

"The 29th, and it was you who said it."

"So it was," she replied with a smile. "I guess that means we're safe."

"It's good to be safe," he replied, rather philosophically.

"Make love to me," she said in a hoarse whisper.

He rolled toward her, and ran a hand up and down her body.

McLeane caressed her breasts, which had nipples larger than Margot's and ran his hands through her still-wet hair. She lay flat on her back, an object to be used, and he used her. McLeane parted her thighs and bent down to kiss and caress with his tongue the tender spot there. She gasped. Then he slipped a finger inside her—she was already wet for him—and another up her ass, and rubbed the two together inside her, making her cry out.

Janice reached down and took him between her hands. "It's been so long," she said, nearly in a gasp.

McLeane rolled between her welcoming thighs, and when he thrust inside her, Janice cried out loud enough to be heard halfway to Guadalcanal.

When McLeane and Janice got back to the base camp,

189

the Rangers were studiously pretending not to have the slightest idea what had transpired farther up the stream—all except Heinman, who was whittling away at a stick and whistling what sounded like a Sousa tune.

McLeane listened for a few bars, then snarled, "You've had it, Heinman. This time it's your ass for sure."

"Fair is fair, Major," Heinman replied.

Janice said, "I don't understand."

"The place I went to school has two marching songs. I busted Heinman's chops by making him sing one called 'Who Owns New York?'"

"I take it this is the other one. What's it called?"

"'Roar Lions Roar,'" McLeane said, blushing as the rest of his Ranger unit erupted in laughter.

"King of the bloody jungle," Heinman said, to make the point perfectly clear.

"Very funny, very funny," McLeane said.

Janice smiled, then stuck her hands on her hips and said, "If you *children* are finished, do you think you could come up with something to eat? I've had nothing but rice for months."

Twenty-two

Wilkins, true to his hunter's inclination, was up before dawn, and after half an hour's sojourn into the rain forest, he emerged with four gray ducks. He had them plucked, cleaned, and roasting by the time the rest of the unit was waking up. Now that their ill-kept secret was out, McLeane had seen little point in sleeping alone, and so Janice had been nestled under his arm for the entire night. It felt good to have someone warm and soft to sleep with after so many weary hours and harrowing escapes.

The smell of coffee and roast duck awoke all the Rangers nearly at once. McLeane yawned, gave Janice a little squeeze, and said, "Wilkins, have you been prowlin' the bayou again?"

"Yes, sir. I thought I'd whip us up a decent meal for a change."

Janice agreed. "Your standard-issue rations leave a great deal to be desired. Come on, king of the bloody jungle, let's wash up before breakfast."

They went back up the stream to the pond for another plunge. This time, McLeane had daylight on his side and explored the bottom during several dives. He found an assortment of water plants, a small turtle, and a school of tiny fish that scooted away whenever he came near. When he came to the surface, Janice was already on the bank, drying herself off. "As I told you, the animals here are reasonably benign. There are a few species of poisonous snakes, but seeing one is quite rare. All that changes the closer we get to the river.''

''Yeah, crocodiles and all that sort of stuff.''

He joined her on the bank, embracing her before she had the chance to get dressed. He pressed his body against hers, and kissed her.

''What if any of the others happen along?'' she asked.

''I'll shoot the first one that rears his ugly head. Besides, being caught in the act didn't seem to bother you last night.''

''I was randy as hell last night.''

''So that's all I mean to you, huh? Just another handsome face.''

''I was going to say 'just another pretty cock,' but I'm too much a lady.'' She laughed. Janice pulled away from McLeane and said, ''Get dressed. We have a long day's walk ahead of us.''

Agreeing reluctantly, he began drying himself off. ''How do we get back to the trail? The same way we came?''

''No. It's too dangerous to go through the swamp in the daytime; the crocs are active. Besides, I know a shorter way.''

''Which way is that?''

''The way I always used—straight down this stream. It never gets more than two inches deep, it skirts the swamp to the west, and enters the Tauvi about three miles downstream from where we turned off last night.''

''And that means it has to cross the trail.''

''Right you are.''

She pulled on her shorts and slipped into her shirt, knotting it below her breasts. ''What a terrible waste of scenery,'' he said.

''Hey, if you want all world to see it . . .''

''I was just kidding.''

She wrapped her arms around his neck and they kissed again. "I could get to like you, McLeane," she said.

"Yeah, and the same goes the other way around. But we *do* have a war to fight."

"I suppose we do at that. I don't suppose that when it's over, or if you ever get some time off, I could have you for a week in my flat in Sydney?"

"I think we might discuss it," McLeane said, "when the war's over or I get some time off."

By the time Janice and McLeane rejoined the Rangers, their breakfast was laid out and ready: roast duck and C-rations on tin plates. "If you don't like it, I think you can find your way back to the Japanese," McLeane said.

"It looks terrific," she said quickly.

The stream wound a good deal; but as Janice had assured them, it never was more than two inches deep, and there were no crocodiles. One occasionally could be heard bellowing off in the distance, but nothing more dangerous than goanna and gecko lizards could be seen. Geckos were everywhere, it seemed, on rocks, tree trunks and branches. Their independently moving eyes were unsettling at first, but after a while became amusing.

"I once knew a buck sergeant that could see in two directions at once," Wilkins said.

"Yeah," Contardo said, "up his ass and up *your* ass."

"Gentlemen, we have a lady present," McLeane said. "You will please confine your obscenities to the usual four-letter words and not attempt to be creative."

"I don't mind." Janice laughed. "I've heard worse in Sydney pubs."

Wilkins said, "Hey, Miss Blythe, how far have we got to go before we get to the trail?"

"About a mile."

"I wonder what we'll find there," McLeane wondered out loud.

"Just more snakes and bugs," Contardo said.

"It could be worse," McLeane said. "We could find the Brooklyn Dodgers."

"Hey," Contardo said.

"On second thought, they're probably still hiding from their fans for losing the pennant this year."

"What would a 'pennant' be?" Janice asked.

"The league title," McLeane explained.

"I will not lose my temper," Contardo said to himself, clenching his teeth. "I will not."

"You don't have to. It's your ball team that loses things," Heinman said.

Contardo growled and turned on Heinman, swinging a wild and angry fist in his direction. Without seeming to break stride, Heinman side-stepped the punch and gave Contardo a sharp blow to the stomach, dropping him to his knees in the water.

McLeane said, "Don't step on him, Janice. You'll get grease on your sandals."

Contardo caught his breath, regained his footing, and caught up with the rest. Now bringing up the rear, he called out, "That's twice you sucker-punched me, Heinman."

"Wrong. The first time—at the beach party—I believe I sucker-footed you. Really, Major, you ought to have a right-hand man who can keep his temper."

"Yeah, I'll have to work on that."

"I think we can put up with the poor man—as long as the Japs don't hear about the Brooklyn Dodgers," Janice said.

The Rangers were nearing the intersection with the Tauvi River. Mangroves and nipa palms were growing in numbers, as was the sour smell that accompanied mangrove swamps. The bellowing of bull crocodiles grew nearer as well.

"How far?" McLeane asked Janice, his voice lowering.

194

"A few hundred yards," she said, her face taking on a quizzical expression at his quieter tones.

"O.K., everybody shut up. I'm going up in front. Heinman, watch over Corporal Blythe, would you?"

"Mack?" she asked. No answer. He had moved to the front of the line.

"He just wants to see if there's anything up there we might not like," Heinman explained. "The major is reputed to be the best there is at detecting subterfuge in the wild."

"What did he say?" Wilkins asked.

"He said that Major McLeane is the best at tracking," Janice replied.

"Hell, I don't mean to take nuthin' away from the major or nuthin', but m'daddy—"

"Shut up, Wilkins," McLeane said, and moved on well ahead of them until he was out of their sight.

McLeane double-paced until he was within a couple of hundred feet of where the trail should be. Then he readied his Winchester and walked at a slower pace and in a crouch, ready for anything. Fifty feet from the trail he stopped entirely, and waited for a full minute to listen. He heard nothing, and proceeded.

The trail was buried by the stream for its entire width— a whole five feet. McLeane stooped to examine both banks, concentrating on the southern. What he saw distressed him. When the rest of the Rangers caught up, he motioned to them to get low and keep quiet. Wilkins was the first by his side, but the others soon gathered around.

"Whatcha got, Major?" Wilkins asked.

"A number of men. At least four or five, and it could be as many as ten. You can see their prints in the mud after they walked through the stream."

Wilkins ran his fingertips lightly over the prints. "No more than eight, Major. And I would say they passed by a couple of hours before dawn."

"Moving how fast, judging by the space between the prints?"

"Normal fast walk considering the terrain, I should say," Heinman chipped in.

"So they're between four and six hours ahead of us. Let's assume they, too, stopped to eat and are four hours ahead," McLeane said.

"A normal Jap patrol? Those *are* Jap boot prints."

"Not on this trail," Janice said. "At least, never before."

"Then they're the remnants of the crew of that enemy river boat we blew to hell, after us and hot for vengeance," McLeane said. "We have to catch up with them before they catch up with O'Connor from behind."

"There's not much chance of that," Heinman said, "unless, of course, O'Connor had to stop for some reason."

"O.K.," McLeane said, "so we have to go after them. Double pace."

"Funny," Contardo said, "us chasin' them for a change."

"Yeah. Real funny. I just hope there's only eight of the bastards. Frankly, I don't know if I'm ready to take on another twenty or thirty guys."

"Do we have a choice?" Heinman asked.

McLeane shook his head. "Well, at least we're all rested and, thanks to Daniel Boone here, well-fed. I think we can catch them by nightfall."

"Major," Heinman said, "I think we had better catch them a good deal before that. Otherwise, we might lose them . . ."

"And O'Connor and those in the boats . . ."

"Forever."

Grimly, McLeane, followed closely and directed by Janice, headed down the trail at a slow jog.

* * *

196

At noon they stopped to rest. All morning the Rangers had been jogging two miles, walking another, then repeating the performance. Finally, Janice had had it and flopped along the riverbank, her blond hair resting on and squashing a patch of moss.

"Maybe you guys are accustomed to this," she said, "but I'm not. You forget I just spent a lot of time in a POW camp, and while I'm not totally helpless, I'm not ready to try out for the Olympics yet."

"O.K.," McLeane said, "we rest. But half an hour, no more." He sat next to her and rubbed a slight cramp out of his right calf.

The other Rangers found spots to their own liking upon which to sit or lie down. Finally, McLeane stretched out beside Janice.

"I wonder why I only get cramps in my right calf," he mused. "Never my left."

"I wonder if we're going to get out of this alive," she replied.

"Of course we are. I lead a charmed life. Weren't you told?"

"After we first met—on opposite sides of the wall at the prison camp—Colonel Biggins told me of some of your exploits. Weren't you part of that business on Vella la Vella?"

"Lady, I *was* that business on Vella la Vella."

"Your modesty is touching."

He laughed. "Actually, I just did a little recon work prior to the invasion. Anyone could have done it."

"Sure. Anyone could have taken photos of the entire enemy installation, including the airstrip they had built, killed the company commander and half his senior staff, blown up six Zeros and a Betty bomber, then stolen another Zero and made his escape."

"I *was* shot down over the Slot by an army P-38."

"Christ, Mack, nobody's perfect."

"Yeah, but it's embarrassing to get shot down by your own side. If only I could have gotten that goddamned Jap radio tuned to the navy frequency."

"And what about your recon work at Segi Airfield on New Georgia?" she asked. "Could *anyone* have done that?"

"Well, the Japs *had* to be gotten off the place. They had a workable airstrip and were playing hell with our invasion of Guadalcanal. I just did what anyone would have done."

"Sure. Anyway, it's nice to know I'm in capable hands."

"You have some pretty capable hands yourself," McLeane said.

"Be quiet. We have acquired quite a reputation among your men already."

"So what? They know better than to say anything— except among themselves, and who cares about that?"

"Major?" Wilkins said.

"What?"

"I been havin' a look-see at some of these Jap boot marks, and they seem pretty fresh."

"How far ahead do you make them?"

"No more than two hours, sir."

McLeane reluctantly got to his feet and joined Wilkins, a bit farther down the trail. He, too, inspected the boot prints.

"But they must have stopped to eat. We didn't see any evidence of a fire, and they sure didn't go into the swamp like we did to build one."

"They could have lived on rations and tossed the tins into the river."

McLeane sighed. "I guess that's what they did. Janice, how far are we from the lagoon?"

"Ten, maybe twelve miles," she replied, sitting up.

"Can we make it by sundown?"

"Not a chance. From five miles on, the trail gets a lot more complex, then disappears entirely. We'll have to make the last five miles by picking our way through the swamp."

"That means we have five or six miles between the Japs and the end of the trail," McLeane said.

"Or less," Heinman added. "They could have reached the end and turned back . . . which means . . ."

"They could be within a mile or two of us, and headed in our direction."

Almost as he said it, there was a flurry of noise culminating in shouted orders, in Japanese. The Rangers dove for their weapons, and a shot rang out. Heinman was thrown back onto the trail, a bullet wound in his shoulder. Seven Japanese soldiers, three of them with bandaged wounds, stood over them with weapons raised.

The one who stepped to the forefront wore the uniform of a lieutenant. Smiling vengefully, he aimed a Nambu 8-mm automatic pistol at Janice's head.

"You! I remember you from the prison camp!"

"Oh, shit," Janice replied.

"Heinman . . . you O.K. to translate?" McLeane asked.

"Yes, sir," he replied, and did so. The Japanese lieutenant seemed somewhat perplexed at the translation of the word "shit," but kept his resolve.

McLeane stood. "I am the leader here. William McLeane, United States Marine Corps."

"And your rank?"

"Major."

Quite properly, the Japanese lieutenant saluted. "Your weapons, Major, if you please."

McLeane handed over his rifle and ammo belt, including his .45. He neglected to mention the razor-sharp throwing knife kept in his right boot.

"Your name is familiar, Major. And over the past several days you have caused us a great deal of trouble. But it is you who are in trouble now."

"The thought has occurred to me," McLeane said, without understating his position.

Twenty-three

The Rangers' weapons were piled in a heap in the center of the trail. The Rangers themselves, less McLeane, were seated in a circle twenty feet down the trail, guarded by two Japanese soldiers with semiautomatic 6.5-mm Type 44 carbines. For some reason, Janice was separated from the rest. She was allowed to sit against a nipa trunk along the riverbank, her chin resting disconsolately on her drawn-up knees.

McLeane was the only one of them on his feet, and he was pressed against the trunk of another palm, the Japanese lieutenant's bayonet against his neck. Heinman's shoulder had been given a cursory bandage, and although in pain he was still able to translate from Japanese to English for McLeane.

"I suppose you must know that our munitions dump at Kara was totally destroyed," the enemy soldier said.

"That was the general idea," McLeane replied.

"And *that* means that the long-awaited invasion of Bougainville is not far off."

"Is *that* what it means?" McLeane said, forcing a smile.

"What other possible explanation could there be for your action?"

"We came here to rescue the prisoners, and decided to have a little fun while we were here."

The point of the bayonet pressed deeper into the flesh

of McLeane's throat.

"Your *fun* has cost us dearly. Let me be frank with you, Major. Until now I have been frustrated in my efforts to capture you, and the prisoners have gotten away. I need to bring *something* home to my commander. . . ."

"Or he'll have your head."

"The date, time, and location of the Allied invasion will do perfectly," the lieutenant said.

"Go climb a tree."

The blade was pressed even more tightly against McLeane's neck. "Look," he said, "even if an invasion is on, what makes you think they would trust the information to me? I'm only a major, and on a mission behind enemy lines. The possibility of capture is always there, as you have shown. I know of no invasion, other than some rumors about an attack on Rabaul."

"That has been expected for even longer than the invasion of Bougainville," the Japanese said irritably.

"From here on in, buster, all you get outta me is name, rank, and serial number. You may have heard of the Geneva Convention?"

"We are a very long way from Geneva," the lieutenant said. But he sighed and relaxed the pressure on McLeane's neck. That was a fatal mistake. The instant he relaxed, McLeane swept the rifle aside and gave the man a sharp right jab to the side of the head.

The lieutenant recoiled, then lunged at McLeane with his bayonet. McLeane ducked, and the point of the bayonet was firmly implanted in the soft bark of the katari tree. McLeane came back up, his throwing knife in his hand, and he buried it firmly in the lieutenant's gut. One of the two Japanese guarding the other Rangers whirled toward McLeane. Heinman's legs moved faster than anyone thought possible. He flattened that man with a scissors takedown, then rolled and brought a knife-hand attack straight to the man's throat, crushing his Adam's apple and leaving him to strangle to death.

McLeane's knife flew through the air into the stomach of the other guard. He dropped to his knees, then rolled to his side, quite dead.

The four remaining Japanese soldiers rushed up from where they were resting down the path, but by then both McLeane and Contardo had acquired Japanese rifles. The first two were dropped immediately; the third reached frantically for a grenade, but Heinman caught him with another scissors takedown, one that flipped him into the Tauvi. The grenade went off underwater, blowing the Jap apart and creating a fine stream of blood for the crocodiles to follow. They did.

The last enemy soldier broke and ran. Wilkins snatched up a rifle and, firing from the hip with one hand, blew the top of the man's head off.

Janice looked up in amazement. The fight was over in less than half a minute.

"Do you chaps do this all the time?" she asked.

"We try to get it over with before breakfast," McLeane said, retrieving his knife and wiping off the blood off on his latest victim's pants. "Let's chuck all of these bastards into the river. I want to get rid of the evidence, and those crocs look like they haven't had a good meal in months."

Janice looked at the carnage in the river, then looked away. "And I thought my people had a talent for creating havoc," she said.

The Rangers—without Heinman, whose shoulder hurt too much to allow him to do much in the way of lifting— threw the remaining bodies into the water, where they were welcomed indeed.

When that was done and they had retrieved their gear, the Rangers regrouped for the final trek downriver to Tauvi Lagoon and the short flight to safety. "I think we've seen the last of them Japs," Wilkins said.

"I hope so," McLeane said. "I sure hope so. Anyway,

Janice, it's up to you now. You'll have to be our guide, since we're running out of trail."

She smiled and gave him a friendly sock on the shoulder. "Leave it to me. Of course, given the time of day and the distance we have to go, we may have to camp out another night."

"Not another night in this blasted jungle," Heinman lamented.

As they worked their way downstream, the path grew narrower, and the tall areca palms and tree ferns gave way to the short, dense vegetation of yet another mangrove swamp. At last the path disappeared entirely, and Janice took the lead, drawing from the memory of her years of working and living in south Bougainville.

She led them inland to get away from the crocodiles, since the undergrowth along the river had grown so thick that it had become entirely possible to mistake the ridged back of one of the giant lizards for a fallen and rotting log. The price of this safety was steep. The Rangers had to hack their own path through a dense wall of ferns, wild plantain, karu, wild ginger nakia, and the inevitable temuli, a small and ever-present short weed, the yellow sap of which was used as a stain by the natives.

Several small streams were crossed, all of them wending their way through the soft, volcanic soil to the Tauvi River. By daylight's end the Rangers had made their way to within five miles of Tauvi Lagoon, where their adventure had begun.

"How long do you think it will take to make it to the lagoon?" McLeane asked.

"Considering five more miles of this undergrowth, five hours at the least," Janice said.

"We'll have to spend the night then. I don't suppose you have a convenient campsite."

"As a matter of fact . . . no. But let's walk up one of

these streams and see what we find. Eventually there will be dry ground and a wide, mossy bank. There always is."

"No pond this time?"

"We might get lucky," she said with a smile.

They walked up a narrow, meandering stream. Its rocky bottom was lined with ferns that now and then touched one another across the water. Within three-quarters of a mile Janice led them to a broad, flat, moss-covered bank that lined the north side of the stream. Heinman flopped on the soft moss, rubbing his wounded shoulder.

"I'll change that bandage in a little while," Janice said.

"I'll take care of the bum, miss," Contardo said.

"We'll need a cookfire. I don't know about you guys, but I'm all out of Sterno. And Wilkins, if you still feel up to it . . ."

"I'll take a little hike and see what I can scare up, Major."

McLeane sat on the bank, stripped off his shirt, boots, and socks, and lay back, dangling his feet in the cool stream water. "There's nothing that's going to swim up and bite my feet off, is there?" he asked.

"Not that I've ever seen," Janice replied. "But you never know." She took off her sandals and joined him.

"God, I'm tired of walking," he said. "When we get back to Guadalcanal, I'm gonna stay in bed for a week."

"Mmmm. I may join you."

McLeane suddenly thought of Margot. "That may present some problems."

"Why?"

"Because . . . because marine cots are only made for one."

"So we can sleep on the floor. It has to be an improvement over this."

"We'll worry about that when we get to safety," McLeane said, assured he would think of something when the time came.

"And after I sleep for a week," he went on, "I'm gonna requisition a wheelchair to get around in."

"Some hero," she said, patting him fondly on the thigh.

"Look, lady, in the past week I have blown up one munitions dump, freed a couple dozen POWs, been shot at a few hundred times, and walked through a hundred miles of jungle. I think I'm entitled to be just a little bit tired."

Off in the distance, there was the sound of three quick shots.

"What's that?" Janice asked, startled.

"Dinner," McLeane said. He yawned and added, "Wake me when it's ready."

"You can't go to sleep now," she protested as he closed his eyes and began to snore.

It was nearly eleven in the evening before the Rangers had the gray ducks cleaned, cooked, and eaten. Heinman's wound had been properly dressed, but he was weak and fell asleep before he had his meal half-finished. Most of the others were soon out on their feet, too, and found soft patches of moss on which to sleep for the night.

McLeane was washing in the stream when Janice came up and wrapped her arms around him from behind. "Hi, sailor," she said. "How are you feeling?"

"My feet feel better now."

"What about the rest of you?"

"Pretty good, all things considered."

He faced her, and they kissed. "You don't mind if I find out for myself, do you?"

"This isn't a very private place to do it," he said.

"While you were asleep I did some scouting. Follow me."

They walked up the stream a hundred feet or so until

they reached another soft, moss-covered bank like the first, only a good deal smaller and ringed with wild white orchids.

"We ought to go into the florist business when the war's over. We can open a little shop in Sydney."

"You can't see it in the dark, but on the other side of the stream is another trail. I'll bet it leads south all the way to the lagoon."

"You're a genius."

She climbed onto the bank, slipped out of her clothes, and lay down. McLeane did the same, pausing only to pluck an orchid and slip it into her hair.

He cupped one of her breasts between both his hands, teasing the nipple with the tip of his tongue until it was hard and she was writhing with pleasure.

He brought his hands between her thighs. She was already wet. McLeane started to roll over on top of her, but Janice stopped him. "No . . . I want to be on top." She straddled him, breathless, and helped him into her. "I want to do the work tonight."

Settling back, McLeane held her by the hips as she worked up and down on him, gasping with pleasure and whipping her hair around until all he could remember was a vision of her exquisite body against the night sky and the soft motion of her body on his.

Twenty-four

McLeane felt something wrong; there was a flickering in the darkness. At first, with his eyes partly open, he thought it was the dawn, or the reflection of the day's earliest rays off the mist-wet leaves of the palms. Then he opened his eyes and saw, quite clearly, the glow of native torches coming up the newly found trail from the south. He jumped to his feet, pulled on his pants, and took out his .45. Janice, startled from her sleep, "What the matter?"

"You've been caught with your knickers down again."

"Damn," she said, and scrambled into her clothes.

The torches stopped a score of yards away when the natives carrying them heard the English voices.

"What the fuck is *this?*" McLeane said.

"I hope to bloody hell it's the Tauvi."

"Can you ask them? I don't know more than five or six of their words."

"I know more than that. Let me try." Janice called out *"Tiga fina?"*

"What's that mean?" McLeane asked.

"Where have you come from?"

The answer was, "Tauvi village." It was spoken very cautiously.

"Tell them who we are."

"We are friends of the great Chief Lalafa," Janice said.

The torches moved nearer, until each group could see the other across the stream. There were six or seven Tauvi warriors. McLeane thought he recognized two of them. "McLeane," one said.

McLeane smiled. "Go get Heinman,"

Heinman appeared within a minute, bleary-eyed but steady on his feet and with his dander up. "It's four o'clock in the bloody morning," he groused.

"Heinman, some Tauvi are here. I want to know why. They are not known for going this far inland except on extraordinary occasions."

Heinman asked them what they were doing that far inland at four in the morning. The answer made McLeane's spine turn chill: "Chief Lalafa, many of our people, and all of your people are taken by the Japanese."

"How?" McLeane asked, astonished.

"The Japanese came by boat . . . found the lagoon . . . Biggins, O'Connor, Corrigan, and the POWs are prisoners. These few Tauvi escaped."

"How big a boat?" How many Japanese?"

Heinman exchanged words with the Tauvi, and replied, "as long as three war canoes . . ."

"A Jap PT boat," McLeane said.

"And about twenty soldiers."

"Where are the prisoners being kept?" McLeane asked.

"In a huddle at the eastern side of the lagoon."

"And the Catalina? Is it guarded?"

"They think so, Major," Heinman replied.

"We'd better get cracking, then. I want to be back at the lagoon before the sun rises. I want to take out the Japs guarding the Catalina."

"You don't mean to escape leaving our guys behind, do you?" Contardo asked.

"For Christ's sake, Contardo, I want the 20-mm Brownings aboard her, not the plane itself. And I want to take them before seven in the morning."

"What happens at seven?" Janice asked.

"Today *is* November 1, isn't it?"

"Yes. Why can't you remember the date?"

"I don't know. But I can tell you that starting at seven this morning—three hours from now—the Japs will have a whole lot more to think about than our guys."

"The invasion," Heinman said.

"Yeah, and the bastards in the lagoon may just decide to wipe out our guys when they get called to defend Empress Augusta Bay."

"Mary, mother of God," Contardo said, and ran off to get his equipment.

One of the Tauvi spoke up again, and Heinman translated. "Chief Lalafa told the enemy that we—that means us—were coming down the river by canoe like O'Connor. The Japs are looking for us in that direction."

"Well, we'll just have to surprise them, won't we?" McLeane asked.

The new trail led the Rangers to the shoreline about a mile west of Tauvi Lagoon. The native warriors had decided to follow them back to the shore, secure in the knowledge that McLeane was their best bet to see their people freed from Japanese hands.

Moving at a fast pace, they made the coast by five in the morning, an hour and fourteen minutes before dawn. By peeking out from behind the many coconut palms that lined the beach, McLeane could see a Japanese Type 15 PT boat at anchor a half-mile offshore. A small motor launch was beached near the far side of the entrance to the lagoon.

McLeane consulted his watch. "In about forty-five minutes the task force will open fire on the beaches near Cape Torokina. If the task force hasn't been detected already, that will be the time the Japs sound the alert to send reinforcements to Empress Augusta Bay including, I hope, that PT boat."

"We ain't got too much time," Contardo said.

"We ain't indeed."

Heinman asked if McLeane had a plan. He was rewarded with a shake of the head. "I hadn't figured on this. The Japs never found the lagoon before."

"I imagine that after we blew their munitions dump and headed south, they figured that the Tauvi River was navigable after all and probably terminated somewhere in this vicinity."

"Yeah."

"May I suggest a plan?"

"I'm open to anything at this point."

"If our native friends could create a diversion—perhaps by eliminating some of the enemy soldiers they say are watching the river—I think our friends entirely capable of sneaking up from the south on Japanese soldiers who have their guns trained north."

"O.K., but that PT boat carries a five-incher and God knows what else. I think we have to keep its crew occupied as well."

"How do you plan to do *that?*"

"Contardo and I will snatch the plane. We'll swim out to her and overwhelm the guards. There can't be more than two aboard. I'll take her out of the lagoon, and Contardo can use one or both of the Brownings to keep the crew of that boat below deck."

"Gee, Major, I didn't know you could fly a plane," Wilkins said.

"I'm no ace or anything, but I can fly that bird."

"Once the Tauvi attack the Japs guarding the river,

the attention of the Japs guarding Biggins, O'Connor, and the POWs will be drawn north," Heinman said.

"Giving the rest of you a chance to catch them with their pants down."

"*That* will be a welcome change," Janice commented idly.

"It just may work," Heinman said.

"Only one way to find out," McLeane responded, and they started east.

Heinman having explained the plan to the Tauvi, McLean took the lead, and the Rangers picked their way toward the lagoon, running from tree to tree. The western side of the lagoon was thickly forested and not much used by the Tauvi, but given all that had happened to them lately, the Japanese might be expected to be looking in *all* directions. Indeed they were. A hundred yards away McLeane's suspicions were confirmed. Two Japanese sailors were stationed in the middle of a newly cut clearing on the west bank of the lagoon. One was reasonably alert; the other seemed to be nearly asleep.

McLeane said, "Wilkins?"

"Yeah, chief?"

"Two fast head shots, with the silencer on, if you don't mind."

"Comin' right up."

Wilkins affixed the silencer to the muzzle of his Winchester and adjusted the night-vision equipment. For the first time, McLeane saw the man fire from the shoulder, using a tree trunk as a brace. But the two guards dropped silently to the ground.

"Nice work."

"Shoot, if they was lined up right I could have saved us a bullet."

"I'm coming to believe it. O.K., let's move out. Heinman, tell the Tauvi to get moving. Then you and Janice find a place to hide and stay there."

"Major, I—"

"No arguments. I want Janice protected, and I'm counting on you and your flying feet to do it."

"I'm quite capable of protecting myself," she said. "Give me your .45."

"May I remind you that my flying feet did rather a good job on a number of the enemy in recent days," Heinman said.

McLeane frowned, but relented, handing the girl his handgun and two fresh clips. He led them to the clearing where the bodies of the two enemy soldiers Wilkins had so recently sent to their rewards were lying.

Using his night-vision equipment, McLeane scanned the surroundings. He could see four Japanese soldiers walking sentry duty over a huddled group of several dozen persons whom he assumed to be the people he had to rescue. There was no sign of life aboard the Catalina, although the twin canopies had been left wide open. There seemed to be no guards on the far side of the lagoon. Apparently, the enemy CO deemed the four sentries, and whoever might be aboard the PBY, guard enough. McLeane could see at least six enemy soldiers near the northern terminus of the lagoon. The Tauvi were even then moving up behind them.

In a loud whisper, McLeane said, "O.K., Contardo and I will take the plane. We'll all go in the water together, taking weapons only. I have a feeling that when I fire up the engines on the Catalina, at least two of those four sentries will be drawn in this direction. Contardo will get them with the portside Browning. The others I leave to you."

"We'll do the job, Major," Heinman said. Janice and Wilkins nodded in agreement.

"Janice . . . what about crocodiles?"

"They should still be dormant. The sun's not up yet."

"Should? Well, I guess *should* will have to do."

McLeane took off his boots, unshouldered his pack, and placed his throwing knife between his teeth. He slipped into the cool waters of Tauvi Lagoon with the others.

Swimming silently, the Rangers made their way to the open canopies at the stern of the Catalina. McLeane whispered, "Heinman ... say something in Japanese ... like 'Hey stupid, wake up.' You know what I mean."

"I can think of something," Heinman replied.

McLeane knocked on the fuselage of the seaplane three times, and Heinman said something appropriately colloquial in Japanese. In a minute, a bleary-eyed enemy sailor stuck his head out of the canopy and said, "What do you want, you idiot?"

McLeane plunged the knife up through his throat and mouth and into his brain; then he yanked the man out of the plane and into the water. He tossed the knife into the plane and pulled himself in after it. From the other side of the fuselage, Contardo followed. Off to the north, there was the sound of screaming.

"The Tauvi," McLeane said.

The rest of the Rangers swam toward the east bank, while Contardo manned the portside Browning, which pointed east.

There was a second guard in the plane. Like the first, he had been asleep. As he scrambled about in search of his rifle, McLeane hit him with a left jab that sent him reeling. Then McLeane straightened the man up and laid him flat with the roundhouse right that General Thompson had mentioned to Margot.

"Those four sentries who was watchin' our guys have taken a real interest in what's goin' on up by the river," Contardo said.

"I'm gonna fire up the engines," McLeane replied. "Pick off any of 'em that you can."

Climbing into the cockpit of the Catalina, McLeane slipped into the pilot's seat. He had a clear view out the mouth of the lagoon, the enemy having cleared away the several native canoes left there to block it. McLeane saw a light go on aboard the PT boat offshore. He turned on the ignition, and the two twelve-hundred horsepower Pratt & Whitney Wasp engines roared into life, waking everyone and everything within two miles.

Two of the Japanese sentries ran pell-mell toward the lagoon, only to be cut down by a burst from Contardo's Browning. The Rangers clambered ashore while the other two sentries looked around in confusion. Six sleeping companions searched for their weapons as the Rangers, led by Heinman, took up positions behind palm trees.

McLeane pushed the throttles forward, and the Catalina moved slowly, then more rapidly, out of the lagoon. More lights went on aboard the Jap PT boat. McLeane put on his headset and switched the control to internal intercom, praying that Contardo had done the same. He had.

"Contardo . . . I'm gonna be about ten feet in the air when we cross the bow of that PT boat. The five-incher is your first priority. After that, personnel. After that, shoot at anything you think we might induce to blow up."

"Like maybe one of those torpedoes on deck?"

"I had that in mind. Once we're in the air, I'll bank and sweep low along the shoreline. Use the starboard Browning for anything that looks Japanese."

"Gotcha, boss. No problem."

Although dawn had not yet broken over Bougainville, the predawn light made sight reasonably clear. The deck of the PT boat was aswarm with enemy sailors when McLeane shoved the throttles as far forward as they would go and pulled back on the wheel.

"Come on, baby, up, up," he said to himself.

"You talkin' to the plane or your dick?" Contardo asked.

McLeane growled into the mouthpiece, and the silence that greeted his growl told him the message had been received.

The PBY crossed the bow of the PT boat just as the boat's crew was scrambling to mobilize the anti-aircraft weaponry and the large five-inch artillery piece. Contardo fired point-blank at the five-incher, cutting its crew in half and sending the barrel of the gun itself spinning far to starboard.

"Nice work for a kid from Brooklyn," McLeane said.

"Do we gotta start that up again?" Contardo asked.

McLeane now had the plane a hundred feet above the crystal-clear waters of the Solomon Sea and began to bank to port. As he did so, Contardo continued to rake the decks of the PT boat with 20-mm fire. Crewmen dove for cover as shell after shell careened off the decks and the small superstructure.

"Switch to the starboard gun. I want that motor launch of theirs out of action."

"Right."

McLeane completed his turn and came in low and slow, knowing that no arms the Japanese had on shore could harm the plane. Contardo cranked up the starboard Browning and opened up on the thirty foot boat as the Catalina ran low along the shoreline.

"Did you get it?" McLeane asked.

"A piece of it, anyway."

"O.K., back to the port gun. I want that five-incher out of service for good. Without the five-incher and the motor launch, that PT boat can't do anything to our guys on shore."

McLeane dropped down to wave-top level and made another pass on the PT boat. Two enemy crewmen were

215

trying to get the five-incher back into service, and four more were at work on the smaller anti-aircraft guns.

"The five-incher first."

"Sure thing, Major."

This time Contardo's use of the Browning was much more effective. He shot up the replacement crew; then in the short space of a second or two poured several dozen rounds into the feeding mechanism which brought shells from the magazine below decks to the five-incher mounted on the deck above. There was a flash of fire, then a brilliant explosion that relieved the boat of her bow section.

"Got her!" Contardo shouted triumphantly.

"Nice work. Let's get out of range of their AAs now and let the sons of bitches sink. I only hope that sharks like yellow meat."

"You wanna make one more run down the beach?"

"Yeah, get on the starboard gun and finish off that motor launch. Then we'll land and pull back into the lagoon," McLeane said. He banked to port again, and Contardo switched to the starboard gun.

As they dropped down to wave-top level, Contardo saw three Japanese sailors run out onto the beach in the direction of the launch. He killed one and pinned down the other two; then he set the launch ablaze with half a dozen well-placed shots to the gas tank.

"That about does it, unless you want to waste ammunition on doing what the sharks can do for free."

"Nah, they'd only take the cost of the ammo outta our daily rations. We'd be eatin' Spam for the rest of the war."

McLeane circled preparatory to landing, while Contardo secured the Brownings, taking off his headset to do so. It was then that McLeane felt once again the tip of a Japanese dagger pressed against his throat.

It was held by the man he had knocked out with the haymaker. The Jap was behind him, saying angry, incomprehensible things that sounded only like death to McLeane.

Twenty-five

The Japanese PT boat had broken up, and both parts were burning. A similar but much smaller fire burned where the motor launch had been beached. McLeane said, "Hey, maybe we can talk about this."

The reply was another shout in Japanese. This one sounded more like a command.

"You want to fly the plane? Is that it? I don't have a license to give lessons, but what the hell."

And he let go of the controls.

The Catalina went into a sharp starboard bank, roaring out of control. The Jap, screaming in anger, lost his footing, and the blade of the knife fell away from McLeane's throat.

McLeane got him by the shirt front and slammed the man's head, first into the port bulkhead, then into the starboard. The knife skittered from the Jap's fingers and onto the floor.

Then there was a loud blast, and the Jap's head was turned into sushi. His body slumped to the floor, but blood and brains were spattered about the inside of the cockpit. Contardo holstered his automatic and joined McLeane, who had regained control of the airplane. Contardo stepped over the fallen enemy body and helped himself to the copilot's seat. There was a bullet hole in the copilot's side of the windscreen.

"Thanks," McLeane said. "But Corrigan is never gonna forgive you for that hole."

"Who gives a shit what Australians think?"

"Thanks just the same."

"Hey, what are partners for?"

McLeane put the Catalina back into the water on the same approach pattern used by Corrigan in the first place. As they neared the shore, McLeane and Contardo saw Wilkins and O'Connor, smiling and waving triumphantly, walk out onto the beach. Biggins, Janice, Corrigan, Heinman, and a few dozen POWs and Tauvi weren't far behind. Already, several Tauvi warriors had station themselves on the beach, ready to greet the few Japanese survivors who were swimming ashore from the sunken PT boat.

"It looks like the good guys won for a change," Contardo said.

"Yeah." McLeane switched the aircraft's radio to the special Ranger frequency.

He pressed the button on the mike several times to test it, then spoke into the instrument. "Redbird, this is Lone Ranger, do you copy?"

There was nothing but static. McLeane repeated his message.

"Wake up, Margot, goddamnit."

"You got her accustomed to staying in bed," Contardo said.

"Enough."

"What are you going to tell her when you come home with Janice? That she's just something you found in the woods?"

"I will think of something ... when we get home."

"Redbird, this is Lone Ranger, do you copy."

The static grew louder; and then came the frantic reply—a voice McLeane hadn't realized how much he had missed.

"Lone Ranger, this is Redbird. Mack . . . are you O.K.?"

"Obviously. Tell Archie that we have done our duty and will soon be on our way home. You might also mention that we have a few extra passengers."

"Who?"

"A few dozen limey POWs and one Aussie coastwatcher. You never know what you're going to stumble over in the Solomons."

"I'm so glad you're O.K.," Margot replied.

"This must be love," Contardo said idly.

"Let's keep it short, Margot. I don't want to give the Japs a signal long enough for them to triangulate on us. See you in a few hours. Lone Ranger out."

"Redbird over and out."

"See you in a few hours?" Contardo asked.

"Yeah, I want to get the hell out of here before anything else goes wrong. I suppose the wisest thing to do would be to sit out the rest of the day right in the lagoon, but the Japs would miss that PT boat before long and this time I doubt they'd have too much trouble figuring out who was behind its loss."

"I'll buy that. Let's get the hell outta here."

McLeane brought the PBY into the lagoon, turned it around, and shut down her engines. Before long, the seaplane was moored and Corrigan's old roll-up dock in place. McLeane and Contardo went ashore, pausing only long enough to carry the dead Jap to the stern exit and toss him into the water.

"The crocodiles have never had it so good since we got here," McLeane said.

"You ain't kiddin'."

Heinman and Biggins were the first to greet them.

"All accomplished without loss of life, Major," Heinman said proudly. "Though one of Colonel Biggins's men took a superficial wound."

"That was the most spectacular display I have ever seen, Major. You richly deserve your reputation," Biggins said.

"Thank you, sir."

"*How* did you get that PT boat?"

"Actually, Contardo did it. He scored a few hits on the magazine for her five-incher."

"I got lucky," Contardo said, scuffling his feet in embarrassment.

"Nonsense, Corporal. Luck is made, not found. Good job." And he pumped Contardo's hand.

Corrigan came up and gave McLeane a suspicious glance.

"If you fucked up my plane . . ."

"I just borrowed her for a while, Corrigan. She's in perfect shape."

"I'll be the judge of that." He went across the bridge to the stern canopy.

"I think a little discreet distance is in order," McLeane said, urging the others away from the lagoon.

"I give him thirty seconds," Contardo said.

"You're an optimist, like all Dodger fans. I make it fifteen seconds."

"What *are* you talking about?" Biggins asked.

The British colonel's question was soon answered. Corrigan's face, beet-red with rage, reappeared in the canopy.

"You're a dead man, McLeane!" he roared.

"Come on, Corrigan, it's not that bad. A little work with a rag and soap will clean up the mess."

"And will it also clean up the bullet hole in the windscreen?"

"We *are* in a war, Corrigan, or hasn't the news reached Australia yet? Bullet holes are an occupational hazard of war."

"This hole was made from the inside!"

"What *did* go on in there?" Biggins asked.

"A Japanese sailor, whom I didn't have time to send to his ancestors but merely rendered unconscious, woke up and tried to relieve me of my head, using a knife. Fortunately, Contardo relieved him of *his* head first. Unfortunately . . ."

"I used my .45," Contardo said.

"It made quite a mess."

"Yes. A rather considerable mess," Contardo said, doing a poor but funny imitation of Heinman's accent.

"And left a hole in the copilot's side of the windshield," McLeane concluded.

"That would explain the unusual flying maneuvers you made prior to landing, I suppose."

McLeane nodded. "It kept us busy for a few seconds, and the plane had to fly herself."

Corrigan growled, but disappeared back into the fuselage.

"Doesn't it count for anything that we saved your life?" McLeane shouted.

He got no answer, except from Janice who embraced him. "It counts with me."

"And with all of us. We're deeply indebted to you, Major," Biggins said.

The other POWs had gathered around, as had a number of the Tauvi. McLeane embraced Chief Lalafa, and, through Heinman, said, "I wish to thank you and your people for your valiant help. And I wish to disclose a secret."

McLeane consulted his watch. It was nearly quarter to six in the morning, and dawn was beginning to break. "At this very moment fifteen of our warships are firing on the Japanese at Cape Torokina. Within an hour, several thousand American warriors will have landed. I guarantee that you will have no further worries with the Japanese. Soon they will be gone forever from your

221

island, and you and your people will be able to live once again in peace."

The chief seemed to have tears in his eyes, but fought them back. Embracing McLeane, he declared him to be a valiant warrior. McLeane and Heinman thanked him for the compliment.

Contardo asked, "What now, boss?"

"See if Corrigan has calmed down. Then get everyone aboard who should be aboard. We'll take off in fifteen or twenty minutes."

"Why so long, since the plane is O.K.?"

"Because," McLeane said grandly, "I am going for a swim."

He broke and ran for the beach, shedding clothes as he ran. As the POWs and the Tauvi cheered and Janice turned her back, McLeane stripped naked and plunged into the sea.

The PBY, carrying a heavy load of passengers, took nearly a mile to get out of the water. Through the patched windscreen, McLeane and Corrigan could see a bit of the stern of the PT boat sticking a few feet out of the water. The Australian had calmed down when he'd realized that his aircraft wasn't really damaged, and Contardo had worked with rags and soap to clean up the mess he had made.

Colonel Biggins was hunched down between the two seats. "I thought we'd never get off that bloody island."

"I had the same thoughts myself on occasion," McLeane admitted.

"Was it a rough slog down along the river?"

"Rough enough. We ran into an enemy unit and had to spend some time ridding the world of them."

"Was that when Heinman was wounded?"

"Yes, sir."

"We had it easy until we barged out of the river into

222

the lagoon like children going to Sunday school and found the place infested with Japanese."

At this point Corrigan entered the conversation. "The bastards came ashore during the night, took the natives as prisoners, then threatened to blow up my plane if I didn't surrender."

"Don't tell me you gave up without a fight?" McLeane said with a smile.

"Hey, I had to save my plane so I could evacuate you blokes, didn't I? I knew you'd turn up sooner or later."

"Very thoughtful of you, Corrigan."

The PBY was climbing rapidly and heading on a general south-southeast course.

"How'd you like to take it this time, Major? You want to go out the same way we came in?" Corrigan asked.

"We have problems no matter which way we go." McLeane sighed.

"How so?" Biggins asked.

"There will be a lot of enemy air activity no matter which course we take. We can't go east of the Shortland Islands."

Corrigan said, "For one thing, that's way out of our way. We're using a lot of fuel with this much weight aboard."

"For another, the Second Marine Parachute Battalion is staging a diversionary raid on Choiseul. The Japs will no doubt be flying heavy traffic to Choiseul from their Ballale Airfield on the Shortlands."

"I'd just as soon not run into *that*," Corrigan said.

"Another complicating factor lies to the other side of the Shortlands," McLeane said. "The Third New Zealand Division has been assigned to take the Treasury Islands. They'll be coming in by boat from Guadalcanal right about now. So the Japs will have to counterattack by air there as well as worry about Choiseul and Bougainville. But the two diversionary raids should make it easier for the main force attacking Cape Torokina in Empress Augusta Bay."

"How many men are you sending in, Major?" Biggins asked.

"I'm not sure of the exact figure, but I think around seventy-five hundred men from seven LCTs and LCIs, supported by twelve destroyers."

"And what of the opposition?"

"The last best guess was no more than a few hundred. But they're well dug in."

"And what of our air cover?"

"Marine fighter squadrons operating out of airstrips on Vella la Vella, Munda, and New Georgia."

Biggins seemed astonished. "I thought those islands were in enemy hands."

"They were, until the past few months. You've not been reading the papers, Colonel."

"I suppose I *have* been rather out of circulation."

"So what do you want to do, McLeane? It's decision time," Corrigan said.

"We'll have to by-pass the Treasury Islands to the west," McLeane said.

"Christ, that's farther out of the way than going around the Shortlands. We'll never make Guadalcanal carrying all this weight."

"But we *will* be flying over our convoy route from Guadalcanal to Bougainville."

"They'll probably shoot us down," Corrigan grumbled.

Biggans laughed. "I think the American Navy can recognize a Catalina when they see one."

"And we'll have the advantage of marine air cover from Vella la Vella to protect us."

"That's all fine and well, but we still won't have the petrol to make Guadalcanal," Corrigan grumbled.

"Then we'll refuel at Vella la Vella. Or, better yet, at the naval base at Barakoma, on the far side of Vella la Vella."

"I hope you know what you're doing, McLeane."

"Shut up, Corrigan, and turn to the west. Two more minutes and we'll be over Shortland Island, and I don't think any of us wants *that*. Shortland is the most heavily fortified enemy garrison this side of Rabaul."

Corrigan nodded, and put the PBY into a smooth bank to starboard.

"Take us to ten thousand and look for clouds to hide in," McLeane ordered.

"Why?" Biggins asked.

"I have to assume that the Japs will be attacking our convoy west of the Treasury Islands, and I assume them capable of recognizing a Catalina as well."

"You're right, of course."

"Colonel, do you have any good air gunners among your men? I'd like our two Brownings manned just in case we run into something we don't like."

"Do we have any good air gunners? My God, man, this is the Royal Air Force you're talking to."

"If you don't mind . . ."

Biggins called out, "Hawkins and Bentley, front and center."

Within seconds, two British airmen appeared in the entrance to the cockpit. "Yes, sir?" one said.

"Man the Brownings in the stern. We might run into enemy opposition, and there's no sense taking chances."

"Right you are, sir." They went off to do as they were told.

McLeane closed his eyes and leaned back in his seat. "Now, all we need is a nice, smooth ride home."

Twenty-six

The Catalina, having given Treasury Island a wide berth to the west, spotted no traffic, either air- or waterborne. Corrigan then made a sharp turn to port, and he set a course east-southeast for the southern coast of Vella la Vella and the naval base at Barakoma. The Catalina had reached ten thousand feet and was cruising at one hundred thirty miles per hour to conserve fuel.

McLeane looked around and saw nothing but blue sky. "My kingdom for some clouds," he said. "I thought this was the rainy season."

Janice had replaced Biggins at McLeane's side. "Actually, we're due to enter the monsoon season any time now."

"Then give me some nice, thick cumulus clouds."

"I understand it's raining up north. I had a peek at the horizon, and it looks fairly dark."

"Probably over the invasion zone," McLeane said glumly.

She gave him a friendly poke. "Cheer up. It's a beautiful day, and we're on our way home. Nothing can go wrong now."

"Care to put any money on that?"

"The Japs took every penny I had. Sorry, Mack."

"I've got a surface target about ten miles ahead of us," Corrigan said. "No, make that four targets."

McLeane trained his binoculars on the horizon.

"Four warships, two medium-sized, two smaller."

"I don't see any air cover," Corrigan said.

McLeane sharpened the focus on his binoculars.

"I'm no expert on navy ship types, but I think I see a transport, a destroyer-transport, and two destroyers."

"Are they ours?" Janice asked.

"You want to radio the blokes and tell them we're on their side? I'd hate to see their AA men get edgy."

"Me, too, but I don't want to call attention to ourselves. Take her up to fifteen thousand feet. That's out of range of any antiaircraft guns they have."

Corrigan pulled back on the wheel and pushed the throttles forward. The Catalina began its climb to a higher altitude, and safety.

Biggins noticed the change in engine speed and felt the climb. He came forward into the pilot's compartment.

"Anything doing, Major?" he asked.

"Four Allied warships on the horizon, sir. We're getting well above them, just in case the bastards can't tell us from a Jap bomber."

"Good idea."

In a few minutes Corrigan announced, "Fifteen thousand feet," and leveled off.

It took another minute or two for the Catalina to be over the small convoy. McLeane kept a watch with his binoculars.

"Yeah, I was right. Two destroyers, a destroyer-transport, and a transport. Uh-oh."

"What's the matter?" Biggins asked.

"And I got six Zekes, twelve o'clock low."

Biggins leaned forward to have a look, and so did Corrigan. "What's a Zeke?" Janice asked.

"Yank lingo for Japanese fighter plane," Corrigan said.

"Do you think those ships see them?" Biggins asked.

"I doubt it. The Zekes are planning to come down at

them out of the sun," McLeane said. "Damn it, I'll have to use the radio."

He picked up the mike and switched the radio to the navy frequency being used for the Bougainville operation. "Navy convoy, this is marine Rangers 1040 en route to Vella la Vella in a PBY, do you copy?"

The answer was quick in coming. "This is the destroyer *Sayville,* Rangers. We saw you coming. What's your problem?"

"The problem is yours, *Sayville.* Do you see those six Zekes about to come down on you out of the sun?"

"Stand by, Rangers."

There was a minute of very pregnant silence, then the reply, "Negative, Rangers. Can you give us an altitude on them?"

"About seven thousand feet," Corrigan said.

"Angels seven, *Sayville,*" McLeane radioed.

"Roger on that angels seven, Rangers. Stand by."

McLeane said, "We've got to get into this."

Corrigan's face turned red even before he got his mouth open. "Are you out of your bloody mind? Haven't you had enough for one mission, McLeane?"

"Yes, but . . ."

"But you won't rest until you get me killed. I knew it from the start. Has it occurred to you that this ain't no Spitfire?"

"We have two 20-mm guns. We have the advantage of surprise. We'd be coming down on *them* out of the sun. We have the chance to break up their formation before they attack and maybe take out a couple of them."

"*And* there are several thousand sailors down there who are about to be ambushed," Biggins said.

"McLeane . . ." Corrigan pleaded.

"Do it."

"Oh, fuck," Corrigan said. But he pushed the wheel forward, and the Catalina started diving down on the unsuspecting enemy fighters. "I'll notify our guns," Biggins said.

McLeane got back on the radio. "*Sayville*, this is Rangers 1040. We have two 20-mm's and will try to break up the enemy formation before they get to you. Please tell your guns that we're friendly."

"Insane, but friendly," Corrigan said.

"This is *Sayville*, Rangers. Thanks for the help and good luck."

"Rangers out."

"Out of their bloody minds," Corrigan groused.

"Shut up, Corrigan and do as you're told."

McLeane put on the headset and switched from radio to internal communications. "Hello, guns?"

"Yes, sir."

"We're going to wreak a little havoc on that Jap fighter squadron. We'll come down at them from six o'clock high, out of the sun, and level off right over their goddamned heads, right atop the middle of their formation. Raise as much hell as you can, then we'll turn sharply to starboard and reverse course, with the hope of getting as much distance as possible between them and us before they catch on to what's happened and who did it."

The tail gunners acknowledged their orders.

Corrigan was scornful. "They're flying six abreast and we have half a minute to reach them. What with our increased descent speed we should be able to keep up with the sons-of-bitches, but only for ten or twenty seconds. Once we level off they'll pull way ahead. You forget they can fly in the order of one hundred and fifty miles an hour faster than this bird."

"All we need is ten or twenty seconds," McLeane said. "Our gunners will shoot up the nearest Zekes, hopefully knocking down at least two of them. That will throw the rest into disarray and the destroyers will be better able to cope with them."

"And supposing one of those Jap planes decides to come after us?"

"Bank to starboard and dive like hell. We'll be in the cover of the destroyers' flak for a while, and that will give us time to get well away."

"You've got everything planned, haven't you?"

"Actually, I'm making it up as I go along."

"I thought as much."

"We can't just let them shoot up that convoy, Corrigan."

"I know it. Hold on, McLeane; we're gonna pull some heavy G-forces when I pull back on the wheel."

"I know how these things work, Corrigan. What would you say . . . twenty seconds before we're over them?"

"Fifteen."

McLeane thumbed the microphone. "Guns, fire at will. Best possible targets. You won't have more than ten or twenty seconds."

"We can do a lot of damage in that time, Major," one gunner replied.

"Do it. Then get ready for a crash dive and turn to starboard."

"Right you are, sir."

McLeane turned his head back into the cargo/passenger compartment and shouted, "Everybody grab something to hold onto."

The Japanese fighters were preparing to peel off for their diving attack on the convoy when Corrigan came in out of the sun and flew straight at them from above.

The Catalina's guns opened up five or ten seconds before Corrigan pulled back on the wheel and leveled the Catalina fifty yards above the enemy squadron. He was flying at over two hundred and fifty mph, the Zeros at about three hundred. The Brownings maintained fire for as long as possible, picking out the wing leaders as their targets.

Two Zeros began to belch smoke from their engines and a third had its tail section blown entirely off. That fighter spiraled down toward the sea as the enemy formation, confused, and disrupted, broke apart in the disarray McLeane had predicted.

McLeane shouted, "Now, Corrigan! Bank to starboard and head for the deck!"

Corrigan did as he was told, pushing the throttles all the way forward and praying silently that his beloved flying machine would hold together.

"Good shooting, guns," McLeane said.

The gunners were too busy holding on to reply.

Two of the remaining three enemy fighters dove on the convoy. The third went after the Catalina. When Corrigan neared wave-top level he pulled back on the wheel. Luckily, the wings stayed stuck to the plane, although those aboard were slammed down into their seats.

Corrigan leveled off little more than a hundred yards above the water. "I hope you're happy now, McLeane. She held together."

A message came over the radio. "Rangers 1040, this is the destroyer *Sayville*. Nice job. But you have a Zeke on your tail."

"I knew it," Corrigan said, speaking more to his plane than to any mere mortal. "The man has meant to have me killed all along."

McLeane spoke into the intercom. "Guns, we have a follower. Can you get him?"

"We'll have a bash, Major."

The stern gunners extended their Brownings out of the canopies so they could fire to the rear. The Zeke was persistent and good. Though the twin Brownings fired all-out, the Zeke also had two 20-mm guns, and the advantage of greater speed and maneuverability. There was an explosion, and fire flashed from the Catalina's port engine.

"Goddamn it, McLeane. We've lost an engine."

"Head for the convoy."

Corrigan shut down the port engine and cut off the fuel supply to it.

McLeane was on the radio. "*Sayville,* this is Rangers 1040. Can you pick off this bum? He just shot off our port engine. We'll fly between you and the two transports."

"We'll try, Rangers."

"Corrigan . . ."

"I heard what you said," the Australian replied, and made for the convoy.

"Try some evasive maneuvers."

"I know how to fly, goddamn it. But I told you this wasn't a fighter plane. It's a goddamned flying boat and transport. Coming to port of the *Sayville* now."

The guns on the destroyer opened up on the Zeke that was chasing McLeane's Rangers. Caught in a triple crossfire—the Catalina's Brownings, the guns of the *Sayville,* and those of the destroyer-transport *Bayport,* the Mitsubishi Mark I Zeke soon was set afire and plunged into the sea, blowing up on impact.

Corrigan struggled with the controls.

"We're out of danger now," McLeane said.

"Bloody hell we are."

There was a radio message from the *Sayville* confirming that their antiaircraft fire had shot down the two remaining planes. "Are you O.K., Rangers?" the destroyer's radio operator asked.

"We're trying to figure that out at the moment," McLeane replied.

"Do you want us to notify Air-Sea Rescue?"

"Negative. Our radio is functional, and we're not that

far from Vella la Vella."

"Very well, Rangers. I hope we get the chance to repay the favor someday."

"You already have. Rangers out."

" 'You already have.' Bullshit, McLeane, we're going down."

"Come on, Corrigan, it's only fifty miles or so to Vella la Vella and you still have one engine left."

"Yeah, well if you know so much about flying, take a look at the temperature and oil pressure gauges for the starboard engine."

McLeane did so, then frowned at what he saw.

"That's right, mate, that Zeke got a piece of the starboard engine too. We're going down."

"How long can you keep her in the air?"

Corrigan checked his instruments, then rechecked them. "I can keep this thing up a couple of minutes, worth maybe ten miles. But if the temperature keeps going up and the oil pressure keeps going down . . ."

"We could lose the engine anytime. Well, at least we're on the convoy route to the naval base at Vella la Vella and it's a calm sea. The radio still works. We can call for Air-Sea Rescue or a tow."

"A tow! Isn't that wonderful? The great McLeane returns from his glorious mission under tow."

"Hey, I didn't ask that reporter from *Life* to put my picture in the magazine. I came here to fight, not make headlines. I don't care how we get home, as long as we get there."

"Terrific."

"Catalinas have been towed into port before."

"Mine hasn't," Corrigan said sharply.

"So it's *your* ego that's being bruised. Admit it, Corrigan. You're afraid of being towed in because people might blame it on you."

"Ah . . ." Corrigan scowled.

"Admit it."

"If you've nothing better to do, McLeane, why don't you tell our passengers that we may be taking a slight ocean voyage before too long?"

"I'll do it," Janice said, and went into the passenger-cargo compartment.

"Is there *no* chance of making it to the island?" McLeane asked.

"Look at the gauges, mate."

The gauges offered grim news. "Pressure dropping fast on oil," McLeane admitted. "Temperature getting critical."

"You have a choice. We try to get a few more miles out of her and risk losing the right engine entirely, or put her down now and hope the engine can be patched."

McLeane buried his face in his hands.

"Playin' ostrich won't help."

McLeane looked up. "I was thinking. O.K., Corrigan, let's save the engine. Put her down."

"Dumping fuel first," Corrigan said, turning the valve that did it. "No sense in floating around in a sea of petrol."

Within a minute, fuel was down to a bare minimum.

"At least we've got a calm sea," McLeane said.

Corrigan lowered the plane until it was skimming the mirrorlike surface of the Solomon Sea; then he eased it into a perfect landing and quickly shut off the right engine.

McLeane brought the microphone to his lips. "Barakoma tower, this is marine Rangers 1040 calling with a Mayday. Do you copy?"

"Roger, Rangers 1040. Please give location and problem."

"We are in a PBY Catalina in the water about forty-five miles west-northwest of you. One engine is out. The other had to be shut off. The hull is intact. We are a unit of six men and are carrying twenty-seven POWs liberated from an enemy camp on Bougainville."

"Stand by, Rangers."

"Since I've now got nothing better to do, perhaps I'll go make certain that the hull *is* intact," Corrigan said, leaving the cockpit.

The five minutes that McLeane stood by seemed more like an hour.

"Rangers 1040, this is Barakoma tower."

"Rangers 1040, Barakoma."

"We are dispatching a PT boat to get you. Expect arrival of PT-452 at about 0900 hours. Sorry we can't offer air cover at the moment. Are you armed?"

"Yeah, we're armed. I suppose we can take care of ourselves."

"Anything else, Rangers?"

"Yeah, please radio General Thompson's HQ on Guadalcanal and apprise them of our situation. Tell them we'll be a bit late but not to let the beer get warm."

"Will do, Rangers. Barakoma out."

"Rangers over and out."

Janice rested her hand on McLeane's shoulder. "Help is coming, I hear."

"Yeah, in an hour and a half."

"Impatience is a curse, Mack."

He smiled and rested his hand on hers.

In a short while, Corrigan came back, and retook the pilot's seat. "The hull seems to be intact. At least you didn't get *that* shot up for me."

"We can expect a PT boat to tow us in."

"When?"

"About an hour and a half."

"Sensational. Let's hope the Japs don't get here first."

"I think they have enough on their minds by now,"

McLeane replied.

"They had enough planes to take on that convoy you got us shot up over. And that wasn't so far behind us, if I may remind you."

"Corrigan, you're an incurable pessimist on top of being a pain in the ass. You still have that fishing pole?"

"Yeah, that was one thing the goddamned Japs let me keep. It's in the cargo hold."

"What sort of tackle do you have?"

"Nothing for bait. I got her rigged with a three-ounce jig."

"Do you mind?"

"Have I ever had a say in what goes on around here?" he asked with a shrug.

"You're not going to go *fishing?*" Janice asked.

"What else is there to do?"

Twenty-seven

Right in front of the windshield, the Catalina had a flat surface that served as a roof for the bow cargo and mooring equipment. It was also an excellent place to rest in the sun or from which to dangle a fishline over the side. While Janice lay back in the morning sun, McLeane used the borrowed fishing pole, letting Corrigan's three-ounce jig with the yellow feathers attached to it drop about a hundred feet beneath the surface of the sea.

"You don't really expect to catch anything, do you?" she asked.

"Well, I come from bass country and have never been much at deep-sea fishing, but you never know. I've always been lucky."

"True. Not every man runs into a beautiful woman in the middle of the jungle."

"Not to mention a modest one."

"Would you have me lie to you?"

"No, I'd have you lie beside me."

She was quiet for a moment, then said, "Mack, do you have a girl friend?"

He thought for a moment. "No," he said.

"Not even someone you see?"

"I have a friend on Guadalcanal whom I've ... I guess you can say 'dated' ... a few times. But whether

237

I'm entitled to call her my girl friend . . ."

"Will you marry her?"

"I don't know. We haven't known each other long."

"Will you marry *anyone?*"

"I don't plan to think about it until the war's over. I can't keep running off on missions from which I might not return if I have a family to think about, can I?"

"No," Janice said with a sigh. "I guess that's the sensible approach to take."

"Why are you suddenly so interested in my future?" he asked.

"Because . . . because maybe I want to be a part of it."

He reached down and kissed her, but said, "Janice . . . we've known each other for a week."

"I happen to believe in love at first sight."

"And I don't mean to get involved until the war's over," he insisted. "I'm not exactly in what you would call a low-risk profession . . . even for a soldier."

She sighed. "What *will* you do when the war's over?"

"When the war is over," he said, a little exasperated, "I mean to . . . I don't know what I mean to do."

"Will you go back to the States?"

"Probably."

"And what will you do for a living?"

"I haven't the faintest idea. I live from day to day. At the moment, my job is killing the enemy. When I get laid off from that job, I'll find another."

"I believe we spoke of opening a florist shop in Sydney," she said.

"We said a lot of things."

"And meant none of them, right?"

He set down the fishing pole and cradled her in his arms. "Janice, what can I give you? I mean, what can I promise you, right now, when I don't know if I'll be alive in a year?"

She fought back tears, then nodded reluctantly. They kissed passionately, and she said, "you can give me you ... at least for a little while."

"Yes, I can do that. But I hope you don't mean here and now."

She laughed away the tears. "No, I don't mean here and now. Maybe when we get to Vella la Vella or Guadalcanal."

"You have a deal, Janice Blythe."

"And when the war's over, you'll ring me up, and we'll see what happens?"

"*That* is an absolute promise."

"Then there *is* a possibility for us. I can live on possibilities."

McLeane's borrowed fishing rod suddenly jumped to life, and McLeane had to lunge for it to keep the thing from going over the side.

"I've got one!"

Line peeled off so fast the normal click of the reel had become a hum.

"I've got goddamned Moby Dick on there!"

Janice sat up excitedly by McLeane's side.

McLeane yanked back hard on the rod. He was using fifty-pound test line, his need to catch fresh food greater than his urge to practice sportsmanship. Anything short of Moby Dick would be caught. Still, the rod bent nearly double and the line played out another hundred feet before McLeane stopped the fish's run and began to reel him in. Corrigan, taking notice of the struggle, had stopped fiddling with the cockpit controls as he had been doing for nearly an hour. Opening the windscreen, he stuck out his head.

"Don't tell me a Yank from bleedin' Nebraska — wherever that is—has actually caught a blue-water fish?"

"I don't have him yet," McLeane said, reeling in as fast as he could, for the fish had reversed course and was headed not for the deep, but for the surface. If McLeane let the line go slack, the hook might fall free. Bass fishing was not quite so different after all.

Within twenty seconds, a large bonito broke the surface eighty or ninety feet from the plane. McLeane heard some cheering from the few curious passengers who had noticed the battle.

"That's a nice one, mate," Corrigan said. "I'll bet a fiver you lose him."

"You're on."

The fat, mackerellike fish thrashed about on the surface as McLeane hauled him in. When he got the fish to the side of the plane, Corrigan said, "Don't get your hands near his mouth, McLeane, or you'll be eating with your elbows. I know more than one man whose hands have been diminished by those beasts."

"Mack?" Janice asked, curiously distracted.

"I'll grab the leader. I don't suppose you have a net?"

"No, but I have a good cosh. You get the fish on the deck, and I'll beat his brains in."

"Good enough."

"Mack?" Janice said again.

He paid her no attention. He was busy pulling the bonito up onto the foredeck of the seaplane, while trying to keep all his fingers at the same time. In a moment, Corrigan appeared in the bow hatch with a small billyclub and gave the fish a good whack on the side of the head. It stopped struggling, and McLeane stood, proudly hefting his catch.

"Fifteen pounds," McLeane said.

"Looks more like twenty to me," Corrigan said, showing pride in his CO for the first time. Funny, McLeane thought; after all they'd been through it took catching a good-sized fish to make the stubborn Aussie proud of him, or at least to show it.

"Mack?" Janice said again.

"What?" he replied irritably.

"I'm not sure, but I think I see about a dozen planes coming in our direction."

Both men looked in the direction Janice was pointing, that of Treasury Island.

"Bloody hell! I knew you'd be the death of me," Corrigan said, disappearing into the innards of the plane. McLeane tossed fish, line, and tackle into the bow hatch after him.

There were indeed about a dozen planes on the eastern horizon, flying at about five thousand feet and straight at them. Corrigan's face reappeared, this time in the opened windscreen.

"The goddamned Japs have got us. We're dead for sure this time!"

"Give me my binoculars," McLeane said, sitting back down and leaning against the windscreen without taking his eyes from the approaching squadron.

Corrigan handed him the binoculars through the opened window.

"If I can get the starboard engine going, we might be able to get into the air. At least we'll have a chance."

"Wait a minute."

As McLeane focused his binoculars, a smile crossed his lips. "Corsairs," he said.

"What?" Corrigan asked.

"Corsairs. F4U-1 Corsairs. A marine fighter squadron. I'd recognize those inverted gullwings anytime. They're ours, Corrigan, probably returning from a strafing run on Treasury Island."

"Are you sure?"

"Trust me."

"Oh, right away."

McLeane handed back the binoculars and asked for the radio headset. "Switch me onto the marine air frequency."

In less than two minutes, he heard the call no one could refuse. "Downed Catalina, this is VMF-214, do you guys need any help?"

Corrigan let out a sigh that McLeane would later claim could be heard all the way to Guadalcanal.

"VMF-214, this is marine Rangers 1040. Good to see you, Black Sheep. We are intact and expecting a tow to Vella la Vella in twenty minutes or half an hour."

"There's still some Zekes in the area. I think a couple of us can stick around awhile until your tow comes."

"I won't turn that offer down, Black Sheep."

McLeane heard the squadron commander order two of his men to circle at five thousand feet and fly cover for McLeane's Rangers until the PT boat arrived.

McLeane radioed, "We won't be going back to Guadalcanal for a day or two—until the engines are fixed. Is the beer cold on Vella la Vella?"

"Damned straight it is, Rangers, and we're buying."

"The hell you are."

"Peters and Jenkins will fly cover for you. The rest of us are going home. What do you say to eight o'clock at our base? Anyone on the island can tell you where to find us."

"I've been to the island before," McLeane said. In fact, it was his reconnaissance information that had helped make it possible for Allied forces to take the island. "I think I can find my way around. Just pop open a bottle, and I'll follow the scent."

"You got it, Rangers. Black Sheep out."

"Rangers over and out."

Through the window, McLeane handed the headset back to Corrigan, then pulled Janice to him. "Do you think beer goes with bonito?" he asked.

The beach on Vella la Vella was wider and whiter than that on Bougainville, where the sand often was dusky gray. McLeane and Janice, their bellies full and feeling at ease for the first time in quite a while, sat back to back near the high-water mark. A slight surf lapped against the beach, and the party between the Black Sheep and McLeane's Rangers raged on half a mile away.

"It isn't quite home," Janice said, "but it's the best I've seen in a long, long time."

"Same here."

"I wonder how work is coming on the plane?"

"The way those engineers were going at it, I think we can be under way by the morning."

"I've never been to Guadalcanal; did you know that? I came to Bougainville straight from Darwin via New Guinea and New Britain."

"It's not very different, except the natives have lighter skin and we've introduced more of the amenities of civilization."

"Such as a hot shower?"

"Can't you get that here?"

"No."

"The sea is warm."

"No way. I'm tired of being caught with no clothes on."

"Go ahead. I'll keep a watch out."

"I'll wait for Guadalcanal, if it's all the same to you."

"A shame. I had gotten to enjoy watching you run around starkers."

"And I've enjoyed running through the jungle with you, William McLeane."

They were silent for a time; then he said, "Will you go home to Australia now?"

"For a time, yes."

"And then?"

"Back to work. There are a lot more coastlines to watch."

He said, "I wish I could go to Australia with you."

"Maybe you can. Didn't you fellows ever get time off?"

"Rarely. However, I'll see what I can work out once we get back to Guadalcanal."

She said, dreamily, "You'd love my flat. It has a gorgeous view of the harbor, and there's a terrace with a little cookout stove."

"Does it have a bed?"

"Big enough for two, yes it does."

"Soft?"

"Goosedown. One can get lost in it for a week."

"Then I'll definitely have a word with General Thompson about some time off."

They twisted their heads and, with some difficulty, kissed.

"You're something very special," she said.

"You too."

They were interrupted by a solitary figure walking down the beach toward them. It was Colonel Biggins, in a new uniform and shaved properly for the first time since McLeane had met him. He looks a bit like Montgomery, McLeane thought, with all the fuzz removed.

McLeane got to his feet, and so did Janice.

"I'm afraid it's bedtime. As much as I'd like to leave you two to your own devices, the powers that be want us in our bunks and ready to fly to Guadalcanal for debriefing at first light."

"Where will we stay?" McLeane asked.

"You and your men will stay with the Black Sheep. Corporal Blythe will stay at the nurses' quarters."

She walked off, kicking idly at a clump of sand. Biggins lowered his voice conspiratorially. "Don't be disconsolate, Major," he said. "Every man jack in my unit has made a pass at her, but you're the only one she's taken a liking to."

"I guess I'm just lucky, as I've so often been accused of being."

"Nonsense, Major. If anything, it takes more skill to be good with women than to be good at war."

McLeane smiled. "Let's go to bed, Colonel. We can't let the powers that be down, can we? Not after coming so far and fighting so hard to get here."

Twenty-eight

Tango Lagoon looked as good as the Riviera to the Rangers. The Catalina slipped smoothly to her berth, despite a port engine that ran erratically all the way down the Slot from Vella la Vella to Guadalcanal. There were two more launches on the west bank, and the beach-front undergrowth had encroached upon the Rangers' tents.

"Once you're done with fixing the port engine you can get to work on the weeds," McLeane said.

Corrigan growled. "I'll fix no engine. I want a new one or I'm not flying you any place ever again."

"That may take some doing."

"I have the utmost faith in you, lad."

"Yeah. I can feel it in my bones."

"I'd rather have you feel the bowline in your fingers. And while you're up front tossing the mooring line ashore, get your goddamned fish off my plane."

McLeane went into the bow cargo compartment and shortly emerged from the bow hatch, a coil of three-quarter-inch line in his hand. He tossed it to the marine private who had been assigned the job of handling ground-support duties for the Rangers. McLeane meant to speak to him about letting the weeds grow wild. He had only pestered Corrigan with the matter to get him worked up. McLeane was beginning to like provoking the easily irritated pilot.

The fuselage slid alongside the discarded tires used as fenders at the end of the dock, and the seaplane was secured. Corrigan shut off the engines, and the propellers slowed to a halt.

"That left engine is a real fuckin' mess, McLeane. You'd better get off your ass and buy me a new one."

"I'll work on it," McLeane said, taking his fish and leading the way out of the plane. Janice followed him, then Biggins, the rest of the Rangers, and the POWs. Typically, Corrigan stayed aboard to fuss with the plane that at times seemed to mean more to him than life itself.

A small group of well-wishers waited on the shore. Margot was there, as well as General Thompson, Major Flagg, and a passel of aides. Margot, dressed to the hilt, had had her hair done for the occasion. McLeane winced when he saw her eyeball Janice, who strutted down the dock like Cleopatra entering Rome.

McLeane saluted General Thompson, then shook his hand and received a hearty clap on the back. "Good work, Mack! I knew you'd pull this one off. You've got your unit—permanently—and I'll see if I can't dig up something for you guys to live in that's better than these tents."

"I think we need a twelve hundred-hp Pratt & Whitney more than new quarters, sir."

"Oh yeah, I heard about that. I think we can pry something out of the navy in exchange for that little assist you gave that supply convoy. I'll get on it right away."

"Thanks, General."

McLeane introduced Janice and Biggins, and the rest of the POWs hedged around them. Thompson said, "We'll need you all for debriefing right away. Colonel, you and your men—and woman—first. We need to know everything you can recall about enemy strength near Kara Airfield. I'm afraid we'll take up the better part of your day."

"We'll do anything you like, General. Just show us the way."

"My HQ is just inland. Mack ... you and your men can relax today, but I'll need you all first thing tomorrow. That's a nice fish, by the way."

"Yeah, I'll show you my technique someday."

"Get yourself a good rest first."

"Oh, you can count on that."

As the group of POWs moved off in the trail of General Thompson, McLeane felt a slight tug at his back pocket. He reached behind to feel a piece of paper, and the slight brush of a woman's hand. He didn't turn to see what was happening. He knew.

McLeane said, "Heinman, off you go to get that piece of Japanese lead taken out of your shoulder."

Heinman objected. "I can assure you, Major, that I'm quite healed, and furthermore—"

"Bullshit. Contardo, take this bum to the hospital."

"Will do, boss. Come on, Adolph, time to go see the doctor."

Heinman continuing to object, was hauled off. To the rest of the Rangers, McLeane said, "The day is yours, gentlemen. Feel free to hunt, fish, drink, sleep, or whatever you feel like."

They drifted off.

Margot was staring out to sea, her arms crossed. McLeane wrapped his arms around her from behind and kissed her on the back of the neck.

She said nothing. He kissed her again, and still there was no response.

"Hey," he said, spinning her around to face him. "Redbird, what's the matter?"

"For one thing, you could get rid of that fish!" she snapped.

248

"Oh, sorry," he said, tossing the bonito onto the sand. He wiped his hand on his pants.

"What's the matter?"

"Who was *that?"*

"Who was what?"

"That woman!"

"Woman . . . oh, Corporal Blythe? She's the Australian coastwatcher I told you about on the radio."

"You didn't say on the radio that the Australian coastwatcher was a woman, and not a bad-looking one at that."

"It didn't seem important at the time. I had twenty-six other POWs to look after. She was hardly the only thing on my mind."

Margot appeared slightly convinced. Her stern expression relaxed.

"There was nothing . . . special . . . about her?"

"Sure there was. She was the only woman. How often do you run into a woman in the middle of the jungle? Then again, you never know what an Aussie will do. Take Corrigan for example."

"Mack, I . . ."

"Come on into my tent. I want to get these boots off."

He took her hand and literally dragged her behind him. He sat on the edge of his bed—with her beside him—and unlaced his boots. Freed from them and his socks, he wiggled his toes happily and leaned back until his head touched the bed.

She turned to look down at him.

"That woman—"

"Margot, jealousy is beneath your dignity."

She sighed, and lay beside him.

"You're right. I'm sorry. I guess I was so glad to see you back, when that woman showed up, I lost my head."

"Forget it. How have you been?"

"Tired. I haven't slept a wink since you left on the mission."

McLeane got up, closed the front flap of his tent, and zipped it up. "There's no time like the present," he said. "I'm tired, too."

"Not too tired, I hope," she said, smiling for the first time.

"No. When you're here, I'm never too tired." And both began to strip off their clothes.

"I like you with a beard," Margot said, scratching at the quarter-inch stubble on McLeane's face.

"Do you?"

"Yeah, I think you ought to grow a great big Santa Claus beard that hangs to your knees."

"If anything is gonna grow so that it hangs to my knees, it ain't gonna be a beard."

She gave him a playful slap. "What you have now is fine with me."

The first rays of dawn crept through the cracks in the tent.

"I believe we've been here close to a day and a half," he said.

"Make that a day. But a full day. Boy, was it ever a full day."

"Spending a week in the jungle can whet your appetite for lots of things."

"Then you have to do it more often. But next time take me."

"I don't think a week or more in the rain forest would suit you," McLeane said.

"Try me."

"At anything but that, yes."

She frowned. "Time to get out of bed, slugger. The general wants to see you in an hour."

Reluctantly, and not without his share of aches and

pains, McLeane hauled himself to the showers.

General Thompson was poring over a conference table full of maps when McLeane walked in.

"Did you get a good rest?" he asked.

"Definitely. Most of the time, anyway."

When the general smiled, McLeane asked, "How goes the invasion?"

"Well, the first boats to hit the beach carried elements of the Second Battalion, Third Marines, which grounded at 0726."

"Four minutes before H-hour," McLeane said.

"We strive for perfection and sometimes err on the side of zealousness. By 0730 the 'landing successful' parachutes were flying everywhere."

"That sounds like success to me."

"There *was* some trouble with the 75-mm gun on Cape Torokina, but we took it out. Actually, one man did it, at the loss of his life. I understand he's going to get the Medal of Honor posthumously."

"How many defenders were found?"

"About three hundred, and all well dug in. Apparently, your earlier reconnaissance caused the enemy to beef up the garrison somewhat. There's not many of them left, and we've got two solid beachheads extending several hundred yards inshore. Intelligence says there's a Jap naval task force steaming from Rabaul, and we've got one steaming equally fast to meet them. I think we can anticipate a small naval confrontation in Empress Augusta Bay within the next few days."

"Are you worried about the outcome?"

"Admiral Merrill has four light cruisers and eight destroyers at his disposal. I wouldn't worry. And thanks in part to your disruption of their two main land supply routes, the enemy has had to try to supply their defenders by coastal barges. Our destroyers have made short work of most them."

"Leave no bridge unburned, I always say," McLeane said.

"I thank God that you had the foresight to do just that."

"Really, I just wanted that enemy river boat off our asses. It's relatively simple to turn a bridge into a dam."

General Thompson left the conference table and sat behind his desk. He offered McLeane a cigar and lit one for himself; McLeane declined.

"Sit down, Mack. I'll need your complete report now, and I want to hear everything that you did on that island myself."

"Everything?"

"O.K., so I noticed her, as has every man on Guadalcanal."

"Where is Janice?"

"Flown home for R&R. She left an hour ago. Too bad she didn't have time to say good-by, but the plane for Sydney was leaving."

"She said good-by, in her fashion."

"You can leave her out of your report, at least the more personal aspects. I'd hate to submit a report of *all* your activities to Comsopac."

"Why? Doesn't Big Doug like women?"

"I'm sure he does. However ... look, Mack, let me send for the steno, and you can dictate your report. I know how you hate typewriters."

Four hours and six cups of coffee later, the stenographer was dismissed. McLeane had finished his report.

General Thompson poured two glasses of Scotch on the rocks, and walked to the window. McLeane joined him. Beneath them, a confusion of supplies, foot-soldiers, and armored vehicles was moving toward the loading docks on the various lagoons.

"We'll have the Solomons mopped up by the end of the year," Thompson said.

"Where then? Rabaul?"

"No. Doug wants to by-pass and isolate Rabaul like we did with some of the smaller islands in the Solomons. To be sure, we'll play some hell with Rabaul, and you may have a hand in it."

"Whatever you say."

"As for what comes next, Comsopac hasn't decided yet, and I'm in no position to speculate. But the Imperial Japanese lines are growing smaller by the day, and whatever move we make will be in the general direction of their main islands."

"A tall order," McLeane said.

Thompson took a hefty sip of Scotch. "Mack ... ?"

"Yes, sir?"

"Were you really the second-string quarterback at the '34 Rose Bowl game?"

"Well, second or third. Records weren't kept all that precisely. All I know is I never got into the game."

"But it must have been a thrill being there."

"That it was."

Thompson drained his glass. "Well, you've done a whale of a job, as always, and you have your unit. What now? You're due for some R&R of your own. A week or two, as I recall."

"Ten days, sir."

"Where would you like to take it? Do you want to go back to the States?"

"I think I'll go stateside next time. Now, I have another thought."

He reached into his back pocket, took out a crumpled piece of paper, and read from it. " 'Seventeen Chichester Lane, #4, Sydney, Australia.' I have the phone number if you need me for anything."

Thompson smiled conspiratorially. "I can't imagine

what's waiting for you there," he said.

"I'll bet you can't." McLeane smiled.

THE SURVIVALIST SERIES
by Jerry Ahern